Aspen's Ascent

Catherine Boyd

Copyright 2016 by Catherine Boyd

Chapter 1

Reality burst upon him with a blunt force. Unfamiliar sounds and sensations bombarded him from every angle. A steady, soft hissing noise came from somewhere near him. He opened his eyes, but only a soft gray color permeated his vision. He slowly moved them from side to side, trying to take in his surroundings, but the gray was unrelenting. Twitching his right index finger, he felt a moderate pressure. Something seemed to be clamped to his finger, and while he could move it, doing so required great effort. Where was he?

Who was he?

He tried to take a deep, cleansing breath in an effort to clear his head, but something was in his throat and he was unable to breathe. Suddenly terror-stricken, he tried to scream but nothing came out. He felt trapped, as if he were drowning. Was he dying? He tried to thrash, but he was so weak he was unsure if he was actually moving or only imagining the movement in his head. In his mind, his body was crawling toward a nebulous surface, but it was fruitless, like trying to swim upward through sand or combined wheat. The harder he swung his arms the farther away the surface seemed.

Alarms started screaming around him. He tried harder to thrash, to flail his arms, but nothing was happening. He began screaming for help, silently, in his head.

He heard a cacophony of sounds seeming to come from everywhere at once. Footsteps, calls for help, and then a warm hand on his arm. Comforting. Soothing. He calmed a little, but he was still disoriented, frightened. Feelings washed through him that were now completely new, and that was part of his terror. He seemed to have no memory of anything. He just "was."

The alarms and bells were silenced as he heard a voice calling out:

"You're awake! Oh my gosh, you're awake! Someone call Dr. Camlin, quick. Tell him Room 302 is awake; his eyes are open and he's moving his fingers!" The hand moved from his arm to his own hand and grasped it tightly.

"You're OK, don't try to breathe. You're on a vent, a machine that's breathing for you, so just try to relax. I'm normally telling patients to take slow, deep breaths, but in your case that's the wrong advice altogether. I know it's hard, but I'm here and the doctor is on his way. You're OK, but you need to relax as much as you can. I understand that seems impossible to do right now, but try. Try hard."

He thought he could hear a smile in her voice. There was more than one person in the room. He couldn't tell how many, but he heard several different voices conversing among themselves. How many were there? His mouth opened as he tried to speak.

"No, no, you can't talk while you're on that vent so don't even try. Just realize that you are in good hands. You're going to be fine but it's going to take a while. When the doctor gets here we'll see about getting that tube out of your throat, and then you can take those deep breaths and talk to us. But for now, why don't you just close your eyes and try your best to stay calm."

He felt her starting to withdraw her hand and he gathered all of his strength to retain her hand in his. *Don't go! Don't leave me!* He felt his head moving from side to side. He wanted to tell her not to leave him, that he was terrified, but he couldn't utter a sound. The tube? He didn't want to be alone. His eyes darted vacantly from side to side in his fear.

"Maura, 10mg of Valium IV, quick! He's losing it!" She squeezed his hand tighter. "Calm down, calm down. We're giving you a little something to help you relax. Give us just a minute and you're going to feel a lot better. Hang in there for me."

That voice was his anchor. The IV medication was in and he was almost instantly nearly sedated and back into the void, to the nothingness. It was safer there. He nearly smiled as his hand relaxed its grip on hers. *Yes, let me just stay in here where it's quiet. Let me . . .*

He woke later to a hand once more on his arm and a man's voice rousing him.

"Mr. Windchase, welcome back! I'm Doctor Camlin. You're in a rehab center in Billings, Montana, and you're on a ventilator. That's why you can't talk and you can't breathe on your own, but don't worry about a thing, you're going to be just fine." The hand was removed but the voice continued. "Can you open your eyes for me? Open your eyes, Mr. Windchase. That's it. Now try to focus on my face. Can you see me?"

He tried, he really did. His eyes were open, but only an all-consuming flat grayness met his vision. He was unable to focus and his stare was fixed.

"Mr. Windchase," the doctor continued, "look at me." Doctor Camlin lowered his face to within inches of Aspen's in an effort to make eye contact with his patient.

But Aspen Windchase saw only that gray veil. Why couldn't he focus? Why couldn't he see the doctor's face? Why . . . The terror was back, more consuming than before. He started trying to thrash about again. He wanted to get out of this . . . this . . . whatever vault he seemed to be locked in, he wanted out! He heard the doctor call out the sedation order.

"Maura—another 10 of Valium, STAT!" With that, he heard the doctor's footsteps as he left the room.

They were talking about him in the hall. The door had been left open and even though they were talking softly, he could still hear everything they said very plainly. Sedation was ordered every hour as needed. Good. He liked that stuff they gave him in his IV. Call his sister right away. He had a sister? He didn't remember having a sister. Begin weaning him off the vent as soon as he was stable. Continue to monitor vital signs. Advance diet as tolerated once off the vent. Physical therapy consult. Ophthalmologist consult. Nutrition consult. It was all too much for him to assimilate. He was tired, so very tired. He started to drift off to sleep again.

He was calmer the next morning, the Valium having done its work throughout the night. People kept coming in and out regularly every few minutes, but then he was sleeping a lot, and he couldn't see anything, so who knew how often they were actually in his room? Every five minutes? Every half hour? He couldn't see the clock. He supposed there was one, but he couldn't find it. When he opened his eyes there was only that sepulchral gray. It was less disturbing to keep his eyes closed. But he was so very tired! Tired to his very marrow, and he didn't understand this. Where was he again? They had told him but he couldn't remember. He did remember about the tube in his throat, however. He hated it. He wanted it gone. Someone had said they would be taking it out; he was sure he had heard them say that. He felt almost as if his body was in some sort of a vice, rendering him immovable. He couldn't even take a conscious breath on his own. In his brain, the silent screams *Let me out!* echoed nearly nonstop. But there was nothing he could do but lie there and wait. Wait for what?

Dr. Camlin came in to see him midmorning. He was cheery but impersonal, and obviously in a hurry.

"OK, Mr. Windchase, we're going to start weaning you off that breathing machine this morning. Be aware that it might take a while before you can totally breathe on your own. You will probably have a few minutes off, and then some time back on it. The periods without it will gradually increase, however, and you should be fully breathing on your own within a few days. Some people take longer to wean off the vent, but you're young and basically healthy, so it shouldn't be too much of a problem for you. Blink your eyes for me if you understand what I'm saying, please."

He blinked his eyes twice. He understood.

"I'm also ordering physical therapy. You've been having therapy the whole time you have been here, but this go-round it's going to be work for you. Before we just kept you limber and prevented contractures and bedsores. Now we want you to get your strength back as soon as possible. Oh, and you have a tube sewn into your stomach since you haven't been able to eat for some time. As soon as you can breathe well on your own, you can start feeding yourself some real food again, so be thinking of foods you like to eat. You're awake and it's time to get you home again!" He smiled, but he noticed that the patient's eyes remained closed. Unseeing. He wondered if there was a vision problem they weren't aware of. The patient was acting as if he couldn't see. Was it just a normal atrophy condition from being comatose for so many months, or was there a real problem that was not going to resolve in short order? He wrote the ophthalmologist consult order for ASAP. He frowned. It was going to be hard enough for this young man to get his life back after being in a coma for so many months, but if his vision was also impaired, well . . . they would just have to wait and see.

"I'll see you again tomorrow morning, Mr. Windchase, and I'll be expecting a big change in your condition. Your life is about to get very busy once more."

He heard staccato footsteps leaving the room. Two sets of footsteps; there must have been a nurse in the room with the doctor. Why hadn't she said anything? He guessed it didn't matter. He was sleepy again. Some more Valium would be nice, but, well, he guessed he could sleep for now without it. He wasn't quite so terrified today, but he felt acutely imprisoned. He wanted out!

That afternoon the ventilator weaning process began. The doctor had been right: it wasn't going to be as easy as just pulling the tube. The respiratory staff worked with him several times over the next few hours. Minutes off the vent, then back on when his muscles screamed silently in his chest and he began fighting for air. He had thought it would be so easy! He kept his eyes closed at all times. He didn't want to see that flat misty gray color that greeted him when he opened them. The darkness behind those closed lids was somehow more tolerable than the unending gray.

Around four-thirty that afternoon, new footsteps came racing into his room. He heard them nearly running down the hall as the person approached.

Suddenly his hand was grabbed and clenched tightly between both of someone's hands.

"Pen, you're awake! Thank you God, you are finally awake! I never gave up, Pen. Never. Not for a minute. I just knew you would come around one of these days, but I have to admit I never dreamed it would take you this long. But who cares how long it took? You're back and that's all that matters."

He tried to place the voice. It was a woman, and she obviously knew him. He opened his eyes but only for a couple of seconds. It was no use to try to see who it was. There was only gray. He moved his head slightly from side to side, and then attempted to slowly remove his hand from her grasp. The nurses were familiar to him; this woman was not. She made him uncomfortable for some reason.

The staff had warned Raven that her brother was still on the vent and would be unable to speak. They had filled her in completely regarding what they knew of his condition, and cautioned her not to expect too much right now. He was awake and would know she was there, but he was still unable to communicate in any meaningful way. She would have to wait a week or so before he would be able to talk to her, so maybe she would want to wait a while before making her second visit. It was nearly a two-hour drive one way for her to come to Billings from Bozeman.

"It's OK, Pen, don't try to talk. I know you can't as long as that tube's in your throat. But I'm here, Pen, and I'll be back. It might be a week or two because I know you're going to be awfully busy with all the rehab they'll be putting you through, but I WILL come back, don't worry."

She was coming back? He really didn't want her to come back. He had no idea who she was.

"Pen, you may not remember, but Gus and I got married a few months ago. You were right about him all along."

She had called him "Pen." The staff had all been calling him "Aspen." For some reason he liked "Pen" a lot better. "Aspen" sounded dumb.

His sister continued: "He's a wonderful, good man. It took me a while to see that, but I am glad you hired him at the stable. He has definitely changed my life in so many ways. He wanted to come with me today to see you, but he was just too busy at the stable. He'll come with me next time. And there's something else, Pen." She leaned over closer and whispered into his ear, "I've become a Christian, Pen. I understand, finally, what you were trying to tell me all those years, what our parents believed and why. I am finally a believer. Isn't that just the most amazing thing? Me, the girl who hated church and God, is now a Christian. See, you were right, miracles really do happen; I'm living proof of that, and obviously, so are you!"

A believer? A Christian? What was she talking about? Their parents? So this was the sister the staff had told him about? The sister he had no memory of? The sister he felt nothing for. And who was Gus? He had apparently known Gus before . . . well, he sure didn't have any idea who he was now. He hoped neither of them came back to see him. Everything around him was unfamiliar, frightening. It was all too much. He didn't want to meet any new people, not now. He wanted to at least be able to see them, not just hear them. He wondered when that would happen, when he would be able to see again. When he got rid of that tube in his throat he could ask. The woman was chattering again. He wished she would leave him in peace.

"Oh, the nurse just walked in and gave me the high sign. Guess she thinks you've had enough of me for now, so I suppose I should be heading home." She leaned over and gave him a light kiss on his cheek.

The kiss was repulsive to him. He couldn't help it.

"Bye, Pen. I'll be back as soon as they tell me you can talk. If you need me to bring you anything just let them know and they'll pass it on to me. See you in a couple of weeks, if not sooner! Bye!"

He heard her footsteps leave the room. Then light laughter. She was happy to have seen him. Foolish woman. She had no idea she was a complete stranger to him, and an unwelcome one at that.

"Hi Mr. Windchase, my name is Allie and I'm the new CNA. I'm here to give you your bath."

If he could have choked at those words, he certainly would have. A woman was going to give him a bath? Were they serious? No way. Absolutely no way! He could stink for a few days until he was up and around and able to do that for himself.

"I know there were a couple of other CNAs that were your regular people, but I have a lot of experience and I'm sure we'll get along fine. You'll still see Nancy every few days, but it will be mainly me from now on. Cliff got transferred to another floor."

Cliff? Nancy? He had no memory of either of them. They must have been doing his personal care while he was "away."

"So, let's get started, shall we? You just rest easy and let me do all the work. You'll feel much better in no time. Clean sheets and a clean gown and you'll feel like a new man, I promise."

He wanted to protest, oh how he wanted to protest, but there was nothing he could do. He was a prisoner, still, in this weak and basically unresponsive body.

Allie was good, and heaven help him, she smelled very nice. Maybe some of his senses weren't working so well, but others definitely were. She had a pleasant voice, not too high pitched. Easy. Comfortable. Her hands were skilled and she seemed to work effortlessly, keeping up a constant monologue that for some reason was not boring or impersonal. Informative? And she was right. When she had finished he really did feel a lot better and more relaxed. Allie was one person he didn't want leaving his room. It would be OK if she stayed for hours. It surprised him that she had that effect on him and it pleased him also. At least not everyone was repulsive to him. He hoped she came back soon.

Allie came back twice a day from then on to do his personal care. As he started gaining strength she encouraged him to do more and more on his own, and he was happy to oblige her. He pushed himself until he shook with exhaustion, both with Allie and with the physical and respiratory therapists that now filled his waking hours. They were all relentless and demanding. He didn't care. He wanted out of that bed and off that vent!

In five days they were able to remove the vent completely and he was finally able to breathe totally on his own. It was such a relief! He was able to talk again, although it was difficult and his voice was very raspy and nearly unintelligible at times. It was so much work for his atrophied muscles that he only tried to speak when he absolutely had to. He heard there was a consult for speech therapy ordered. Fine.

He was also able to recognize his caregivers by their voices and their scents. It surprised him that he could differentiate different body odors. Surprisingly, no one asked him about his vision or his memory. They all just assumed, what? Or were they leaving it all for therapists and specialists to deal with so they wouldn't have to? If they suspected he had no memory or vision, they kept it to themselves.

The feeding tube was removed from his stomach and they began advancing his diet. With the help of two CNAs he was able to sit up in a chair for short periods of time. He began asking everyone who entered his room various questions, and was getting frustrated with the lack of answers. His most important question: when would his vision finally return? And just what had happened to him that he ended up in a coma? All he got for answers were "the ophthalmologist will be in soon and he can give you all the answers about your vision, and apparently you were kicked by a horse causing you to go into a coma." That's all he knew but he wanted more answers. He thought about asking Raven (was that her name?) those questions when she called, which was nearly every day, but somehow he just didn't get around to it. He would wait for the eye doctor that was supposed to be coming.

The ophthalmologist came soon after the vent was permanently removed and he could talk once more. Doctor Hogenson spent very little time with him, however. It didn't take long to determine that Aspen Windchase was very nearly totally blind. That persistent gray color was the only thing that gave the doctor hope. Color, any color, was a hopeful sign. The optic nerves had obviously suffered a lot of trauma in the accident. While severely damaged or bruised nerves had a remote possibility of regeneration, severed nerves would never be restored. It was sad. Aspen Windchase was such a young, handsome man with his whole life ahead of him. He would heal physically, but mentally?

"Well, doc? What's the verdict? When do I get my vision back?"

"I want to go over all these tests to be sure I have everything right. I'll be back tomorrow and we'll talk about the results." There was time enough to deliver the bad news tomorrow. Let Aspen have one more day without the knowledge that he would probably never see again. Yes, tomorrow was soon enough for that news. He exited the room slowly, happy that the patient was unable to see the expression of profound sadness on his face.

Chapter 2

The next morning Dr. Hogenson was back in Aspen Windchase's room. Pen was seated comfortably in a chair, clean-shaven, a smile on his face, obviously expecting good news, hoping to get on with his life again soon.

While Pen was concerned about his constant gray "companion," it really never dawned on him that blindness was a possibility. As he had begun to regain his strength and blood once more coursed through him carrying vitality to all of his being, blindness was not an option. It was nowhere in the equation, as far as he was concerned. He was sure the doctor was going to give him a timetable for his sight to return. That was fine. He could wait a week or two, even three if he had to.

"Mr. Windchase?"

"Doctor. Have a seat. I think there's another chair in here somewhere."

"Yes, there is." He pulled the extra chair up closer to Pen and leaned forward, narrowing the distance between them. "How are you doing, Mr. Windchase?"

"Please, Doc, call me Pen. That's what everyone else has been calling me. Guess that's what I generally go by. Sounds better than 'Aspen' anyway, don't you think? Can you imagine what the kids must have called me in school? Horrible name. Can't imagine why anyone would give their kid a name like that."

"OK, Pen it is. And you are . . . ?"

"Doing OK, Doc. Just let me know how soon this lousy gray is going away so I can get out of this place. I know they aren't going to let me out until I can at least see where I'm going, even if everything else is looking good. So, when? A week? Two? I can wait, just give me an idea, would you?"

Dr. Hogenson cleared his throat and began, as kindly as he could. "Mr. Windchase . . ."

"Pen, remember?"

"Sorry. Pen, I ran some tests yesterday, but I wanted to be absolutely sure before I talked to you about your vision problem. Well, today, I'm relatively sure about what's going on." He sighed softly, and then continued.

"Pen, I heard the cause of you ending up in a coma was an injury caused by a horse's kick to your head. That blow seems to have severely bruised or injured your optic chiasma. I don't believe your optic nerves have been severed, which is good news in the grand scheme of things, but . . ."

"But what? Spit it out, Doc, in layman's terms. When do I see again?"

"I'm sorry Pen, but I'm pretty sure your condition is permanent. There's no other way to say it, I'm afraid."

The blood drained instantly from Pen's face. Ashen and suddenly very, very cold to his very core, Pen blinked his sightless eyes and shook his head in the negative.

"No, Doc, don't be telling me that. It isn't true! It simply cannot be true!"

"Pen . . ."

"Doc, are you trying to tell me I'm permanently blind? That I'm never going to see again? No way, Doc, no way on God's green earth! There must be some sort of surgery or something? Tell me I have options, please."

"I will say this, although I certainly don't want to give you any false hopes. I am positive the optic nerves are still intact, which means that there is a possibility, a very remote possibility you must understand, that you may regain at least partial sight at some point in the distant future."

Pen grabbed at this as a starving dog grabs a bone. "OK, you're telling me there's a good chance I'll see again, just not right away, right?"

"No, Pen. I'm not saying that at all. I'm saying there is a very, very remote possibility that you may at some point regain at least partial sight in maybe one eye."

"That's what I said—why are you being so negative about it?" He smiled at the doctor.

"Pen, you aren't listening to me. You are blind. That's the reality, and you will probably remain blind for the rest of your life."

"But you just said . . ."

"I said that, yes, in fact there is some small hope. But Pen, you can't wait around for that to possibly happen. The odds are not in your favor. No matter what, you are blind and you're going to be blind for years to come. I'm sorry, but those are the facts."

"What are my odds, doc? 50/50? 70/30? Give me something to hang on to here, will you?"

"Pen, the odds of you ever regaining your sight are about one in a thousand, and then only after several years, if at all."

"Get out, Doc." Pen said the words softly, his head down. "Get out."

"Pen, I . . ."

Pen's head jerked up, and if his eyes would focus, they would have been drilling laser holes in Dr. Hogenson. "Did you not hear me? I said GET OUT!" He started to come up out of his chair, reaching out for the doctor. He felt he might actually strangle the man if he caught him.

The doctor rose quickly and nearly ran from the room. At the doorway he turned back.

"Pen, I know it's hard, but we're here to help you. With training and help, you'll be able to function quite well. I . . ."

"OUT!!"

The doctor closed the door firmly behind him, and then sagged against it. His job was not an easy one.

Pen sank back into the recliner that was his chair when he was up and out of bed. His head rested against the back of the chair, and his arms fell limply at his sides. It couldn't be. It simply could not be happening. Blind? No. But when he opened his eyes once more only the grayness met his gaze. He started mumbling as reality finally started to sink in. Random words tumbled out of his mouth with increasing volume. It wasn't long before words learned as a child on the Blood Indian Reserve in Canada erupted from him. Nasty words, Indian words, vicious words.. Words tumbled out over themselves dredged from somewhere in that vacuum that was his mind. His fists began pounding the arms of the chair.

Doctor Hogenson had warned the nurses at the station after he left Pen's room, so they were prepared when they started hearing the escalating verbiage from Pen's room.

Maura walked swiftly down the hall to his room, syringe in hand.

"Pen, it's Maura. I've got some of that Valium you like so much." She approached him cautiously, having experienced the gamut of behaviors with patients like him over the years. Violence was not out of the ordinary.

"I don't think I . . ."

"Yeah, Pen, I think you do. Just this once, perhaps. Give me your arm and I'll be quick."

Like a child, Pen held his arm out for Maura to administer the injection. He did like his Valium, and yes, he probably did need some right now. But the effects would only last so long, and then what? Then what? What was he going to do? Where was he going to go?

"Pen, Doctor Hogenson is talking with your sister now, explaining everything, and I'm sure she'll be down to see you later today, or at least tomorrow. She'll help you through this. You aren't alone, no matter how you feel right now. It's all going to be OK. Believe me."

"Sure. Easy for you to say, isn't it! You're not the one who is living in a gray world, are you? You can see where you're going when you put one foot in front of the other. You can cook your own food, feed yourself. Look in the mirror and see if there's food in your teeth. It's not going to be OK, Maura, it's never going to be OK."

She sat in the vacant chair as the Valium began to work its magic on her patient. Pocketing the used syringe, she reached out with both hands and took both of Pen's big hands in her own, clasping them firmly, warmly.

"No, I'm not blind so I really don't know how you feel. But I can imagine. You aren't the first blind patient I've had and you won't be the last. Your life isn't over by any means. People learn to live with blindness every day. Family, friends, schools, guide dogs—there are tons of resources available for you. Your sister will . . ."

"I don't want to see her. Tell her not to come."

"Why don't you want to see her, for heaven's sake? She's your sister, Pen. She's your twin! Who else would you go home with? You have no other family that I know of."

"I don't know her. Don't you people understand? I've not only lost my sight, I've also lost my memory! The only people I know are you and the rest of the staff here. She's a stranger to me. Even if I knew her, I can't do that to her."

"But she will want to take care of you. She loves you, I know."

"You aren't listening, Maura. I don't love her. I have no memory of her or anyone else, for that matter. The only people I recognize are here, in this, this 'place.' None of you seem to 'get it!' I have no memory and I have no sight! I am nothing more than a walking, talking vegetable—and a poor one at that. I can barely talk and I can't walk at all without someone guiding me. What earthly good am I? I should have just died. I shouldn't be here at all. That's the long and short of it." He buried his head in his hands. "You should have just let me die. We all would have been better off and you know it." A single tear found its way out from under a clenched eyelid.

"I could argue with you from now to doomsday, but I know nothing I say at this point will change your mind. All I can do at the moment is promise to come back with more Valium in a few hours to help keep your nerves settled for the time being. OK?"

Yesterday he had been willing to fight. He would have refused the Valium and soldiered on, willing to fight for every bit of progress he could wrestle from this weak body. But now? Today? What was the use of fighting for anything? Nothing was going to change. The Valium sounded like just the ticket. He would take all he could get now. He could lose himself in sleep. Maybe he'd get lucky and someone would accidentally give him a little too much. He could only hope.

His sister, Raven, came the next day. She brought her husband, Gus, with her. Pen was not happy to "see" either of them. He tried his best to be at least polite, but it was hard. He really just wanted to be alone with more Valium, and maybe Allie. Yes, Allie in the room with him would be good. She never seemed to care one way or the other whether he talked or remembered anything or was blind. He liked Allie more every time he saw her.

"Hi Pen! I told you I'd be back, and I brought Gus with me this time. It's a little hard to get away from the stable 'cause we really are awfully busy right now or we would have been down here more often. Sorry about that."

Pen snorted inwardly. Yeah, his sister loved him all right. But the two of them were too busy with horses to come regularly to visit him. He was right to mistrust them. Both of them.

"Pen, hi. It's Gus. I heard from the nurse about all you're going through. I'm sorry for all of that, I really am. And I know you probably don't even remember me, do you?"

"No, can't say that I do. This is the first time I've ever met you. Sorry. You sound like a nice person, I'll give you that." He turned his unseeing head to the side, away from his guests.

"It's OK. I'm pretty sure it will all come back to you eventually. It's just gonna take some time. Have patience. You WILL remember me, I'll make sure of it. Shouldn't be too hard, though, since I'm a pretty unforgettable character!" If Pen only remembered, Gus was actually the most forgettable man on the planet. Oh well, it made a pretty good joke.

Raven broke into the conversation. "Pen, how much do you remember of the accident? Anything at all?"

"I told you, I don't remember anything. And I don't remember you either. You say you're my sister but anyone could tell me that and I wouldn't know the difference. So no, I sure don't remember any accident."

Raven carried on as if she hadn't heard him. "Well, we have a training stable outside of Bozeman, Chase the Wind Stable. You were always pretty good with horses," she smiled, forgetting for the moment that her brother couldn't see her, "but I was better. I did most of the finish training and you did the basics for the most part."

So, she was arrogant too. Raven wasn't making any points with her brother.

"Anyway, you were working a colt with the 'W,' and apparently when you went to take the ropes off, the horse kicked you in the head. That's where Gus found you. We're guessing at everything since you were alone at the time."

"We really thought you were going to die," Gus interjected.

Pen's head snapped around, his eyes open and gazing in their direction, unfocused. "I wish I had." It was uttered softly, but sincerely.

"Oh, Pen, you don't really mean that! We're going to be taking you home with us, hopefully next week sometime, and it's all going to be good. We'll be there to take care of you, and you'll be doing fine in no time. I love you. You may not remember me, but trust me on this one—we were close. We're twins, and we grew up through some hard times, which only made us closer. We're sure not splitting up now. We'll get through this with time and God's help; it will all work out, you'll see. You just have to get out of here and it will all start to come together."

"No."

"What do you mean 'no'?"

"Just what I said. No. I won't be going home with you."

"Pen, of course you're coming home with us! Where else would you go? You and I, we're all the family we've got, so don't talk nonsense. You're coming home with us to the stable."

Gus sat silently, observing the interchange between the twins. Something was really off with Pen; he could see it. Something besides no memory or sight. Pen meant exactly what he was saying. He had absolutely no intention of leaving this facility with them in a few days, a week, or ever.

Aspen started to pound his fist in the arm of the chair, but changed his mind at the last second. "I'm not going to say it again. I'm not going anywhere with you, so get that out of your head. You can leave now. I'm tired and I think I need a nap."

Gus, ever the observer, read the confusion and hurt on his wife's face. Taking Raven's hand, he rose to leave, pulling Raven up with him. "Sure, Pen. I can see you're tired. I bet they keep you pretty busy with all the therapy and stuff they're putting you through. We'll come back in a few days, OK? Let us know if you need us to bring you anything."

"Do me a favor, will you, Gus?"

"Sure, anything. Just ask. What do you need me to do?"

"Don't come back."

"What?" The color faded from Raven's beautiful face. "What do you mean, 'don't come back?' Why wouldn't we come back?"

"I don't want to see you again. Not now and maybe not ever. I don't know yet."

"Well, brother dear, if you think you're going to keep me away, you've got another thing coming. I will most definitely be back!"

Pen was getting angry now. He might be impaired but he was still a person, a man. He would have his own way about a few things! "I will tell the staff not to let you back here if you come again, so you will only waste time and gas. Don't bother. If I ever want to see you I can get your phone number easily enough. So, don't come back. Good-by." He turned his face away from them.

Gus and Raven, both stricken, quietly left Aspen Windchase alone, as he requested. They would not be back until they were invited.

Chapter 3

After his sister and her husband had left the room, Pen sat quietly in his chair, pondering, going over their visit. Why had he been so rude to them? What was it about his sister that annoyed him so badly? He hadn't really given her a chance, he realized that, but if he was honest with himself, he didn't want to. He saw that he was intentionally erecting a thick wall between himself and his twin. Why? *Honesty, honesty, honesty, Pen! Why are you doing this?*

Introspection. Not fun. Could it be that because he had no memory of her he was shutting her out on purpose rather than choosing to get to know her? What was he afraid of? That she was, in reality, his best friend before . . . ? That he had truly loved her before his accident and, knowing how much care and attention he was going to need, there was no way he was going to inflict himself on her? It was better to have her stay away. There was no good reason for him to ruin her life just because, well, because he "was." He shouldn't be. He truly felt he should have died, and if there was a way for him to accomplish that feat today, he surely would do so. But he couldn't. He was so weak he could still barely get around, and, being sightless, he couldn't find anything to take his life with. He was well and truly trapped, as much so as he had been while lying there in that coma. The coma was far better than this; this, now, was like dying a very slow death. In that coma he didn't exist. Or . . . ? Wait, he had what seemed like a quick flash of a memory of some sort. What? Voices. He had a faint recollection of some voices. But whose? He had no idea. Nurses? Doctors? Raven? Maybe if he concentrated really hard he might be able to recall some conversations. But not now. It was too hard and he had other things to think about, like where he was going to go from here.

Just what exactly was he going to do? He had no money, he somehow was pretty sure of that, and even if he did, by now Raven would have total control of it. She could use his funds as a weapon to force him to come back to Bozeman with her and Gus. Gus, he seemed like a really nice guy. He felt a little bad about being rude to the man. So here he was, his thoughts having gone full circle, with nothing solved. Where was he going to go when he left here? He knew they would be kicking him out soon. When they thought he had had as much therapy as they could give him here, he would have to leave. How? How on God's green earth could he leave this room? It had become his only safe place. *Nowhere to go and no one to go with! God, just let me die!*

God? Where had that come from? He didn't know, but God was one Person he actually did seem to remember; well, at least he remembered that there was a God, and somehow that was important. But that was all he grasped at the moment. Relationship? He had no idea. But somehow in a nebulous sort of way, he understood that God had been very real to him. He wished that God was real to him now. But He wasn't. He was there, He existed, but so did that recliner he was sitting in. He sighed deeply. It did feel awfully good to be able to fill his lungs with deep, cleansing breaths of air. No more tube in his throat.

And it was pleasurable, he guessed that might be the right word, pleasurable, to be able to taste food in his mouth. Simple things, breathing and eating; they felt so very good! *Careful, Pen, you're finding a few good things in this miserable existence of yours. You won't want to die if you are finding stuff that brings you some sort of joy or contentment.* He wanted to end his life, not enjoy some little aspects of it. Eating and breathing were basic for life, but there was so very much more, and he would never enjoy those other parts. He was a prisoner in his body. He would never be self-sufficient, he would never . . . he would never have a wife or a family. He was unlovable. No woman would ever want a man that could barely feed himself without help. He didn't even know what he looked like? He couldn't see himself in a mirror, like most people did without thinking. Was he ugly? Repulsive physically? Handsome? Tall? Short? He had no idea.

He sank back deeper into the recliner. Valium. He could really use some more Valium. His hand fumbled around the arm of the chair until he found the call button. He pressed it and waited for his favorite form of release to be delivered. He smiled, waiting.

Maura was there in minutes. "Mr. Windchase? What can I do for you?"

"Call me Pen, please. And Valium. Can I have some more yet?"

"I think so. Let me check the med chart but I'm pretty sure it's been long enough. Do you really think you need some, though? Maybe you should start trying to get along without it?"

"No, not today. I need it before I go nuts in here. Please."

"OK. I'll be right back."

She returned in just a few minutes but this time the Valium was a pill. "No more IV goodies for you, my friend. Pills from now on. It's time to let those veins of yours heal up. It will take a little longer for the Valium to kick in, but it will work just the same. Hold your hand out."

Aspen held his hand out, palm up, like a child waiting for a piece of candy. The good little boy. How he hated this!

Maura carefully placed the tablet in his palm, and then handed him a glass of water as soon as he put it into his mouth. "About twenty minutes. It takes about that long to hit your system, so just be patient."

"Thanks." He leaned back with his eyes closed, waiting for the desired effect.

"Pen?"

"Yes?"

"I heard you decided not to go home with your sister, is that right?"

"Yup, you got it right."

"Then just what do you plan on doing? Any plans?"

"Nope. No plans. Any suggestions?"

"Well, since you refuse to go home with your sister, and you're going to need some specialized training for your new, 'reality,' wherever you end up staying, we're going to have to find some place for you to go. I'll talk to the discharge planner here and see about getting you into the Montana School for the Deaf and Blind here in Billings. That's a day care facility, however, and you're going to need a place for off-school hours."

Pen groaned inwardly. His life was sounding worse and worse. School for the deaf and blind? He was going to have to start his life all over like a, a, well, like a stupid baby. But he wasn't a baby! He was a full-grown man!

Maura turned to leave. "I'll be sure our discharge planner makes it in here today, Pen. She'll take care of everything, so don't worry." Her footsteps treaded softly out of the room.

He called out to her, "Close the door behind you, will you?"

She did.

When he heard the latch click into place he knew he was alone in his darkness and the tears, so foreign to one-quarter Crow Indian Aspen Windchase throughout his life, warmly meandered unchecked, marring his handsome face.

In the break room Maura, Allie, and several other staff members were sitting around the worn rectangular table sipping coffee and soft drinks. The topic of conversation was the newly awakened coma patient down the hall. They were all compassionate people who actually really cared about their patients, and Aspen Windchase had become someone very special to all of them, and especially to Maura and Allie who had spent the most time with him. He was so young—only thirty years old, and so very handsome! It was such a shame. Tall, young, handsome, and blind. Tragic. Just tragic.

"If he won't go home with his sister, where's he going to go from here? "

"I have no idea. Laura, the discharge planner, should be in with him right now. We'll have to check with her and see what she can come up with, but I'm pretty sure there aren't many options for him."

"Yeah, I was looking through his chart and someone else has been paying his bills every month, not his sister. A Mr. Martin, I think it said. I wonder if he'll keep paying his living expenses when he leaves here?"

"But again, where on earth can he go? The Rescue Mission? That's about the only option for him as far as I can see. Anybody else have any ideas?"

The comments and questions passed around the group as they speculated about Pen's immediate future, but no solid, workable solutions were forthcoming.

About ten minutes later Laura Winston, the discharge planner, entered the break room and took a seat with the rest of the staff on break. Her face wore a bleak look.

"Well, Laura, what did you come up with for Mr. Windchase? You're not exactly wearing a happy face, so we're assuming the outcome wasn't great?" Maura asked the question on everyone's mind.

"No, it's not great. He still absolutely refuses to go with anyone who knows him, his sister and her husband being first on the list. They suggested his pastor in Bozeman who apparently was most agreeable, but he is refusing him also. I called the pastor and had the two of them talk while I was there, but Pen is simply adamant about his position. He is a lost soul right now, I'm afraid."

Allie pinned Laura down. "So, where is he going next week when he's discharged?" She leaned toward Laura, her concern evident on her face.

"There seems to be nowhere else but the Mission for now. We have to work out regular transportation to and from the school for him, but they agreed to let him sleep at the Mission at least for the time being, until we can come up with something better." Laura turned her face away from the group.

"The Mission! That's the best you could come up with? You've got to be kidding! Come on, there must be someplace else he can go!" Maura was incensed. She had become more emotionally involved with Aspen Windchase than any other patient she could remember in her career, and she was appalled at this turn of events. He didn't deserve this!

Allie sat quietly, apparently deep in thought. She was obviously in distress over this turn of events also, but voiced no comments.

They conversed among themselves for a few minutes longer, but then their break was over and as a group they exited the break room, Aspen Windchase still weighing heavily on their minds.

Pen hadn't moved from his chair. That Laura person had been nice enough, but she had been pretty frank about his situation. He had no money. He didn't remember anyone so he had no friends. He was blind and had no place to go. There remained his sister and his pastor, but there was no way he was going to dump his miserable self on either of them. How could he do that? He couldn't. The depression had settled so heavily over him that in truth, he really didn't care where he went. What did it matter? He would be nothing but useless baggage wherever he ended up. He could just live on the streets. Maybe . . . maybe out there he could take one of those "long walks in the traffic" and end all of this. There had to be some way to kill himself; he promised himself he would find it if it killed him. He actually chuckled at his own joke, but the grimace that was supposed to be a smile faded quickly.

That planner lady had finally come up with the local Rescue Mission. She had sounded reluctant to place him there, but he didn't care. What did it matter to him where he slept? On the street? In a box? On a cot at the Mission? It was all the same to him. He wouldn't be around for long anyway if he had anything to say about it. He was getting out of this place next Wednesday. He would just keep asking for the Valium as often as they would let him have it until then, and hoped they would give him a supply to take with him when he left. If they didn't he wasn't sure what he would do. He was starting to rely pretty heavily on those little pills; they really helped to settle his mind. In fact, he could sure use one right about now. His hand found the ever-present call button and he pressed it forcefully. Relief would be here soon, and at that thought, he actually did smile slightly.

The next ten days were filled with all sorts of therapies in a concerted attempt to rehab Pen as much as possible before he was discharged to the Mission. Physical therapy, occupational therapy, psychotherapy, speech therapy—any program that included the word "therapy" had Aspen Windchase on the client list. His days were filled with these activities and he was exhausted most of the time, but he never forgot to request his "happy pills" and pain pills at the regularly scheduled permitted times. Tylox and Valium were his new best friends. While depression exploded within him, the pills enabled him to conceal his true feelings. He was well aware that his plans to self-destruct would be more easily carried out in a less-regulated environment. The Mission should give him the relaxed space to do what he wanted. There would be few, if any, people watching him closely. Once there, he would blend in with a crowd of what he considered "losers"; the perfect place for him. There was way too much supervision at this rehab facility where he now resided.

The discharge date finally arrived. One by one the staff came to wish him well, promising to keep in touch. Pen smiled and was polite, thanking them for their concern, all the while well aware that he would never hear from any of them again. He was a number in this place, and that was all. Oh, they might feel a little more personal toward him, but that was only for the time period that he was physically there. Once he walked (or in his case, was led) out the front doors he knew he would be forgotten. Another poor soul would be sleeping in his old bed. That was fine. He didn't want to be remembered. The void was waiting for him.

Allie and Maura, however, were different. They came to say goodbye separately, each wanting to wish him well privately. Allie was first.

"Pen, it's me, Allie."

"I know, I knew it was you before you said anything."

"How? How did you know it was me?" She really didn't understand.

Pen wasn't about to confess that her unique scent always somehow preceded her. Some things he would keep to himself. "Oh, I just knew. Guess it's your footsteps. Anyway, thanks for coming. I'm going to miss your pretty face, you know!"

Allie blushed. "Thanks, but you haven't a clue how I really look and we both know it. But that's fine, I'll take the compliment anyway."

Pen smiled, a genuine smile. Allie always gave his spirits a lift just by entering his room.

Allie coughed in her nervousness. "Well, I just want you to know that I'm really going to miss giving you those baths!"

"I'll bet you will!"

"No, seriously, I'm going to miss you, Mr. Windchase. I've gotten kind of fond of you since I got to know you on a more personal basis, shall we say? And I like you. I really do."

"Enough, Allie. You really don't know me well enough to know whether you actually like me or not. I'm not such a nice guy right now. My fuse is a little short at the moment I'm afraid, and frankly I don't see that fuse lengthening any time soon. So while I appreciate the gesture you're trying to make, you can skip it. Thanks for all your help while I've been here, but I don't expect any more from you,"

"Well, I'm serious. I'm going to miss you. And I plan to come to the Mission to visit you, so be watching for me, OK?" She grimaced as she realized her poor choice of words.

"It's OK. You don't have to come. And there's no reason to say things you don't really mean. No regrets and no promises, Allie. You've been a good friend and I appreciate all you've done for me. But when I leave here, I'm gone. Truly gone and out of your life. And it's all OK."

"Pen, I'm serious. I really do like you and I really am going to be visiting you. So don't be surprised when I show up. I'd tell you when I'll be there, but the next schedule hasn't been posted yet so I don't know what days I have off for the next few weeks. But I WILL be there, I promise."

"Sure, Allie."

"Hey, Cowboy, you're too handsome for me to let you get away. I'm planning on keeping you, if I can!" As she spoke those words, which had come out of her mouth totally unplanned, she realized that they were true. Pen WAS handsome, and she really did want to keep him. Even blind, he was a better catch than her current boyfriend. Wheels began spinning in her head, and she was suddenly thankful that this man couldn't see the expressions on her face as they warred against each other.

"Pen?"

"Yeah?"

"Can I give you a hug goodbye?"

If he was surprised at this he didn't show it. Actually, a hug would be kind of nice. "Sure. Come and get it!"

Allie took the few steps needed to close the distance between them as Aspen rose from his chair, his arms outstretched. She settled herself against his chest, embracing him tightly.

"Remember me, Pen. I'll be coming to see you!" She gently disengaged from the embrace, turned, and left the room.

Pen had thought he was used to the empty feeling he carried with him most of the time now, but he was wrong. When Allie left he actually sucked in his breath at the pain he felt with her departure. People had been touching him constantly, everywhere, ever since he woke up, but hugs had been few and far between. He knew now that there was a vast difference in the types of human contact; touch was good and necessary, but hugs were life-giving. He missed her. He missed Allie a lot. Confusion set in. Life, or rather death, wasn't looking quite as simple as it had a few hours ago. He sank back into the recliner, lost in thought.

A knock on the door woke him from his reverie.

"Yes? Come in."

Maura entered shyly, carefully. She had seen Allie leave and waited a bit before coming to say her personal farewell to her favorite patient.

"It's me, Maura. Your favorite pill lady."

Pen smiled broadly. He liked Maura. She was different from Allie and he liked them both, but in different ways. Allie was, well, she was sexy. Maura was just "good people." Warm. Genuine. Always on his side without needing to say so.

"I know you've been deluged with 'goodbyes' all morning so I wanted to wait until the rest of them were gone. I see I just missed Allie."

"Yes." That's all he volunteered.

She pulled up a side chair and sat in front of him, leaning inward. He felt her nearness and inhaled her clean, fresh scent.

"Well, I don't really know what to say here. I don't know how to tell you just how much I'm going to miss you. You're more than a patient to me; I hope you know that."

It occurred to him that what she said was true. He felt it; he really was much more than a patient to Maura. He would miss her probably as much as he would miss Allie.

"I do know that, Maura, and I thank you for it. I'm going to miss your smiling face and those wonderful pills you always bring with you. By the way, will I get a supply to take with me this afternoon?" He carefully hid his anxiety over this matter. He didn't want to leave without a good supply of those magic pills!

"Yes, we'll be sending some with you and I'm sure the doctor will write you a prescription so you won't run out. At least for a while, anyway."

"Good. I don't know if I can make it without them. My nerves, they start to rule me, you know?"

"You're going to be OK, Pen; you do know that, don't you? Your blindness and memory loss are not the end of the world for you. You may not get your sight back; that's actually a very real possibility. But it is also a possibility that you will eventually regain as least some vision. It's going to take a lot of patience on your part, so you need to hang in there."

"Yeah, right." He turned his head away in disgust.

Maura reached over and took one of Pen's hands in both of hers. "But Pen, I am convinced that you will get your memory back. All of it. Somehow, deep inside, I know that's going to happen for you. All of that 'stuff' in your head that makes you who you are isn't gone—it's still in there. You can't call it up at will right now, but that will change. Again, it's just going to take some time."

Her words were comforting to him. "Do you really think so or are you just saying that to try to put me in a good mood or something?"

"No, I'm not trying to snow you here. I really mean everything I'm saying to you. You are going to be OK. I'm a Christian and I feel all that I'm telling you deep inside of me. God has not forgotten you and you will get through this whole thing. Just don't give up!"

He turned his sightless gaze upon her face. If only he could believe her! If only! When Maura spoke to him his desire to die faded a little. Somehow she inspired hope in him. But not quite enough.

Suddenly he was overcome with emotion. He couldn't describe it, but he rose to his feet, taking Maura with him. He didn't ask permission, in fact he said nothing, but pulled Maura tightly to himself, wrapping his arms around her as if she were a life jacket and she was the only thing keeping him afloat. His head found hers and he rested his cheek against her hair.

"Thank you, Maura. Thank you for always being here for me, and for being, well, for being you." He found he didn't want to let her go. She was, he realized, his best friend.

After Maura left, Pen sat for a while in a languid state, trying not to think too much. Maura and Allie. Two women he decided he loved, but in different ways and for different reasons. Perhaps "love" was too strong a word for his feelings, but in his world where he knew no one outside of the facility walls, they were the most special to him. He would miss them.

At two-thirty a young man from the Billings Montana Rescue Mission came to pick him up and escort him to the facility. A generous supply of his favorite pills and a script for many refills went with him. His sister had been advised as to where he was going, but he still refused to see her or even talk to her. Laura told him that Raven had cried over the phone when she was told where her brother was going. He didn't care. As long as he had his pills he didn't much care about anything or anyone. He was very much alone and he preferred it that way. It would make it easier to permanently leave.

Chapter 4

His life settled into a routine at the Mission. He slept on a cot in a dormitory with about fifty other men from all walks of life. Drug addicts, alcoholics, Indians off the Reservation, homeless people, people from everywhere and of every size, shape, and color. Of course he couldn't see any of them, but he knew just by listening to the conversations. Someone always escorted him to the bathroom, meals, the shower, and back to his cot. Sometimes a staff member and sometimes just whoever was around. He couldn't keep his pills on his person as there was too great a risk that they would be stolen, but the staff was really good about handing them out whenever he asked.

Within two days he was enrolled at the Montana School for the Deaf and Blind where he spent his days learning to use a cane and perform daily hygiene tasks on his own. He still didn't seem to get enough time to himself to end his life. There was too much of a chance of an interruption, and when he planned his death, the last thing he wanted was to be rescued at the last minute. His sister called every few days, but he always refused to speak to her.

Two weeks went by and Pen was learning independence in spite of himself. The staff was well trained at both facilities, and there was little free time. When he was allowed to rest, he always took his pills first. He slept very well.

When he returned from school on Tuesday of the third week at the Rescue Mission, he was escorted to a small private room just for visitors where he was told someone was waiting to see him. His first thought was that his sister had come even though she had been warned not to. But it wasn't Raven; it was Allie.

"Oh, Pen! I've missed you so much!"

He barely had time to register who it was before she flew into him, wrapping her arms around his torso. She kissed his cheek and as he turned his head, still stunned, she kissed him full on his mouth.

He might have been stunned, but he was definitely a man, and he kissed her right back soundly. Allie was here! And she felt and smelled so very good!

He hadn't realized how emotionally starved in many ways he was. He hugged her tighter and tighter, so happy to see her.

"You actually came! I really didn't think I would ever see you again, Allie. But you came! Thank you."

"Silly, I told you I would come to visit you. You didn't believe me, did you! You should learn to listen more carefully, mister." She snuggled against him, enjoying his obvious pleasure at seeing her again.

"How long can you stay? Just a few minutes, I suppose?" He was already missing her again.

"Actually, yes, not very long. But I have a proposition for you. Are you willing to listen?"

"Well, sure, go ahead, but I can't imagine I could have anything you would want. I'm broke and blind, and forgetful doesn't quite describe my situation. Pretty darn useless all around, remember?"

"Not to me. Look, I've been thinking. I want you to come home with me."

The color drained from his face. What on earth was she saying?

"What? You want me to go home with you? Are you nuts or something? Why on earth would I do that? I'm nothing but trouble and a burden, and you have to work. You don't have time for a lump like me and you know it."

"Not true. You're not a burden. I've thought it all over and I really think it's the best thing for both of us. You like me, I know you do, and I obviously like you, so what's the problem?"

"Allie, I . . ."

"Look, Pen. I know you need to continue at the School for the Blind, and I've got that covered. You can take a cab to and from the school. You're pretty good with a cane now; I saw you walk in here, so you'll be fine with the school thing. You'll be company for me, you know?"

"And just what all are my 'responsibilities' to you?" Cached in that statement was his very real concern that she wanted him to sleep with her. Did she want a 'boy toy' or something? While he had to admit he didn't remember anything about sex, he was sure he wasn't into anything casual like that! No, he wasn't going to be a kept man, no matter how much he liked her! No way!

Allie saw the look on his face.

"Let me reassure you, Pen, this is all about you, not me. Well, I really like you and would love having you around, but I live alone. I would feel safer with a man in the house. And you don't belong in this place, Pen. You belong in a home where someone cares about you. Not here. Come home with me, please?"

"Allie, you're a CNA and I know you don't make that much. I'm broke. I can't even pay for my groceries. You haven't thought this through enough. The fact is you can't afford me."

"I didn't want to confess this to you because I'm sure it will hurt your pride, but I looked through your chart and contacted that Tom Martin person who has been paying your hospital bills all this time. I told him what I wanted to do and flat out asked him to pay me to do it. He actually said he would! Said I was a heck of a lot cheaper than that rehab hospital place you'd been in. So we made a deal. I get paid to take care of you and you keep me company and give me protection. Sounds like a 'win-win' to me. So how about it? Oh—and you won't have to be asking anyone for your pills. You'll be able to get to them whenever you want them. I figure you're a grownup. You can handle your own medication, I think."

Her offer was a heaven-sent gift to him.

"I don't need to think. How soon can we leave?"

"Right now. You don't have much to pack, so I'll have someone gather your stuff up and I'll take you home with me. No sense in waiting, is there?"

"I could hug you again, Allie. I don't know how to thank you for this, but thank you anyway. I'll try not to be in your way too much, really. I know I'll mess up, but I'll do my best."

She laughed at his earnestness. This was going to be fun, in more ways than one; she knew it.

"Let's get out of here then!" She took his hand in hers and walked out to the front desk. They waited only minutes before a man came back with a small duffel bag containing his few belongings. Still holding hands, Allie walked him out to her car and drove him home to her apartment.

Pen allowed himself to be escorted safely to his new environment. Hating every step that necessitated someone's assistance, he nonetheless went along, grateful to escape yet another seemingly confining facility.

There were only three steps up to the front door of Allie's apartment, negotiated fairly easily thanks to his recent days spent at the Blind and Deaf School. He hated attending that school, hated being officially grouped with the "handicapped," but he had to admit they had certainly made it easier for him to navigate, even in the short time he had been attending. His cane was fast becoming his best friend, and he had learned to depend on its solidness. It seemed to be one thing in his new life that he could depend on. In fact it had been the only thing. Perhaps Allie could also be depended upon. He had never dreamed, even for a moment, that she would actually come to visit him, let alone take him home with her. He couldn't fathom yet why she had done that, but so far it was more than OK with him.

She helped him to an easy chair in the living room and left him to take his things to her room. It was only a one-bedroom apartment, a fact she had neglected to tell her new roommate. It was still a whole lot better than the Rescue Mission. Allie was not highly paid, but she was careful with her money. The apartment, while small, was nicely furnished, clean, and neat.

Coming back into the living room, she took a seat across from Pen on the love seat.

"Well, I've taken your things back to the bedroom. I'll show you that room and the bathroom whenever you're ready."

"Thanks, Allie. I still can't believe you're doing this for me. Heck, I didn't think I'd ever see you again after I left that rehab center."

Allie chuckled softly. "Don't give me too much credit, Pen. I am getting paid for this, remember? It's going to be good for both of us, so just relax."

"I am pretty tired. School is exhausting for me. It's like they're trying to cram a lifetime of learning into a couple of days. Physically and mentally, they really work you over at that place. But I have to admit they have taught me a lot in the short time I've been going. And the staff is pretty good. They treat me like a regular person, not a pathetic blind waste. It's good for my ego even if I know I actually really am a 'pathetic, blind, waste.'"

"But that's where you're wrong, Pen. I don't see you as pathetic. Actually, you're what I call a 'hunk'!"

"Yeah, right."

"Oh, I know, you can't see what you look like, but trust me, Pen, you are one good-looking guy. And I get to keep you all to myself. Golly, how lucky can a girl get?"

"About the time I spill coffee on the floor or mess up the bathroom you won't feel so lucky. And Allie, it's going to happen, I promise. Not because I want to make extra work for you, but I'm just so clumsy. I can't help it. I'm too new at this blind thing. Sorry."

"It's OK, I can handle it. Just remember that it really is going to get better. You have to give it time. And hey, what else pressing do you have to do right now?"

"Well, you're right about that. All I have right now is time." He snorted. "Hey, can I get a pain pill and a Valium? I haven't had either of them in a long time, and I could sure use a little help. What do you say?"

"Sure thing. Actually, why don't I take you to the bathroom and show you where they're kept. That way you can help yourself whenever you need them. How does that sound?"

"Sounds great to me; lead the way, fearless leader." He got to his feet and held out his arm for her to take, intending to leave his cane next to the chair.

"No, bring the cane. You need to learn how to navigate this castle without me since you're going be here on your own most of the time. Follow my voice, but use the cane. It's probably more dependable than I am." She laughed at her joke.

He did use the cane, and successfully too. She escorted him to the bathroom, pointing out the bedroom on the way. In the bathroom he found the drawer where his medications were kept and was able to distinguish them by their shapes and sounds when he shook the bottles. He fumbled around and found the plastic glass she had put out for him next to the sink, and helped himself to his favorite "candy."

"Good job, Pen. You managed that without a hitch. You're going to do very well here."

He heard the smile in her voice, and smiled back at her. "I seem to have a pretty good teacher. Thanks."

"Why don't you go rest while I get supper going. Do you want to lie on the bed or back in the chair?"

"The chair is fine for now. If I lie down I may not get up for dinner and that would be a waste of your cooking skills. Ready to lead me back?"

"Nope. You had all the help you're going to get until we head for the kitchen. Take yourself back." She turned and left him to find his own way to the living room.

Settled once more in the easy chair, it wasn't long before the pills kicked in and he was pleasantly oblivious to most of his surroundings. Valium and Tylox. His new best friends.

Pen had not in any way given up on his plan to end his life. It was nice of Allie to let him move in with her, but he wasn't kidding himself. He was an invalid. His future was pretty much nonexistent, and if there was no real future, why should he stick around? As soon as he had enough pills stashed away, he would end his sorry life.

Allie fixed an easy meal of sandwiches and a hearty soup. Pen was able to feed himself with only one spill when he knocked over his water glass, which was a great relief for him. Allie didn't seem to get upset and it was, after all, only water. He cursed himself inwardly when it happened. Useless. A blind man is just useless and a burden. He was glad he hadn't gone home with his sister. Her pity would have been more than he could bear.

It was time to go to bed, and exhausted, Pen finally asked her where his room was.

"Well, sorry to tell you this, but this is only a one-bedroom apartment. Translation, there's only one bed. We're going to have to share. I didn't really think you'd mind, though. You don't, do you?" It was obvious it had never occurred to her that he would mind that sleeping arrangement. What man would turn something like that down?

Pen's face went ashen. "What?"

"Well, it's not like either of us is married or anything, so it's no big deal. It sure isn't to me, and it shouldn't be to you either. Unless of course you find me in some way, well, you know what I'm trying to say. Don't worry, I won't ask you to do anything you don't want to do, so it will be fine. Come on, I'll lead the way."

He liked Allie. He really did. He liked her voice and he liked how she smelled. He liked how she had felt when they had hugged, and he wouldn't be a man if he hadn't thought about more than a hug. Certain parts of his anatomy had responded robustly with that hug. But he certainly wasn't in love with her, and something inside of him just screamed "no!" at the idea of what she was suggesting.

"No."

"No, what?"

"No, I won't share a bed with you. Sorry."

"Pen, there's no need to be prudish about this. I don't sleep around if that's what you're worried about. I'm not a virgin by any means, but I am selective. I do have a boyfriend at the present time, but . . ."

"What? You have a boyfriend? Right now? Does he know about me?"

"Well, not yet, but I've been meaning to break up with him anyway. Our relationship isn't going anywhere and it's time to move on. I'll cut him out of my life tomorrow. How does that sound?"

"Well don't do it for me! I never would have come with you if I knew you were involved with someone. If I was him I'd be ready to slit my throat if I found out you had moved me in with you. You don't do that to a man, you know? It's just not right."

39

"I told you, I'm going to break up with him anyway. I simply haven't gotten around to it yet. Tomorrow evening it will be all over. Trust me, it's all going to be fine. Now, come with me."

"No, I'll sleep in here. Just bring me a blanket and a pillow, OK?"

"Pen, I don't even have a couch for you to sleep on. You'll have to sleep on the floor in here. I can't do that to you! Just sleep with me. I promise to leave you completely alone."

Pen's face was rigid. He was not going to compromise. If he had known this is what she had in mind he would never have come home with her. Never.

"Bring me the blanket and pillow. I'll change in the bathroom and sleep on the floor in here."

Frowning, she did as he asked. The confusion on her face betrayed the fact that she did not in any way understand his reaction to her offer. No man had ever turned her down before.

He changed into pajama bottoms in the bathroom and then settled himself on the living room floor. Allie said little else as she went to her room and softly closed her bedroom door behind her.

The floor was not all that uncomfortable for him, which he found surprising. Why didn't the floor bother him? A flash of memory, a fleeting picture, almost a snapshot of a bedroll and a grassy field burst with radiant color in his brain. Had he slept outside before? Had he been a camper? He must have.

It was his first real memory of any kind. First he had recalled slightly the voices and now this. He was curious. He was very curious. Perhaps before he killed himself he might have to ask his sister if she knew anything about this memory flash of camping out.

Then he thought about Allie and her presumption that he would be sleeping with her during his stay in her apartment. Foolish woman. It wasn't that he wouldn't like to partake of what she was offering, but there were several reasons why he wouldn't. In the first place, she obviously hadn't thought of the fact that some things simply wouldn't work when a person takes that much Valium and Tylox. No way, no how. That old "the spirit is willing but the flesh is weak" thing. He might have the inclination, but definitely not the wherewithal at the moment, thanks to his best friends. And if there was a choice, the pills were going to win, hands down.

Not only that, but he also had to admit once he got past the macho man idea of what she was suggesting, it just didn't seem right to him. He felt he should be in love with a woman before he made love to her. He didn't know exactly why he felt that way, but the feeling was so strong he knew better than to attempt to go against it. God would . . . had God been that important before his accident? Another thing to ask his sister, or maybe his pastor, that Benson person who had called him one day at the rehab center.

Why did he even want to know these answers? If he was planning to check out of this world in a few days or weeks, what difference did any of it make? He didn't know. Perhaps it was just something about being a human being. Before he left he actually did want to know who he was and where he came from. The answers might be comforting—but then again they might not. Perhaps those answers might reinforce his feelings that he was useless and had always been useless. Would the world miss him if he were no longer in it? It might make it even easier to leave, harder to stay. A sudden thought occurred to him—he obviously hadn't been married since no wife ever came to visit him, and his sister seemed to have full power of attorney. But had there been a girlfriend? Had he been engaged or anything? Was there a woman he had been in love with? He was the right age; most men his age were married already and had a family. Had he been about to get married and she left when he became, well, like he was now? Useless baggage. He always returned to the useless, unwanted, unlovable baggage theme that had become his mantra.

He had left the pills on the end table near his head along with a cup of water just in case he felt he needed some more during the night. He didn't need to wait and see; sitting up he took a double dose of the Valium, then lay back down to await the blessed effects. He was sound asleep within minutes.

The next morning Allie seemed in good spirits, and was cheerful, humming to herself as she fixed him a bowl of cereal, toast, and coffee for breakfast. He would get more food at the school later, so she didn't worry too much about cooking a lot for him.

She had called into work saying she would be late today in order to get the taxi routine set up for Pen. He would have to be able to navigate his way from the apartment to the taxi before she could leave him alone while she was working.

It all went smoothly, however. Pen was smart; he learned fast and remembered what he learned. The steps were handled without difficulty with his trusty white cane, and the sound of the taxi's engine guided him easily to the vehicle. At the school the taxi driver had instructions to escort him to the school's front door, which he did, and Pen got along fine. Partial independence was coming much faster than he had thought it would. Allie had arranged for the taxi service to come regularly at the specified time, both at the apartment to take him to school and at the school to transport him safely home at the end of the school day. He continued to take his pills with regularity, but began reducing the time between doses. Pen was becoming addicted.

Chapter 5

Allie was true to her word. On Friday she had a date with her boyfriend, Curt. They had been dating for only a couple of months, but Curt was a little too possessive and demanding for Allie. She was used to her independence and had begun to resent Curt's increasing boldness and restrictions. She had liked him well enough in the beginning, but lately she had been feeling more and more trapped in the relationship. It was time to break it off, and having Pen at her house gave her a very good excuse, since there was no way Curt would ever stand for that situation, no matter how innocent. No man in his right mind would, for that matter. But something told her not to mention Pen to Curt, so she didn't. She only told him she had changed her mind and wanted to end their relationship.

What Allie wasn't expecting, however, was Curt's response when she told him she wanted out.

He drew back his hand as if to slap her, and then caught himself. Sighing deeply, he grabbed her forearms with his steely grip.

"Curt! Stop! You're hurting me!"

"Allie, you can't leave. I won't let you, you hear me? We have a good thing going here and you're not telling me it's over. Not happening, you understand?" His grip tightened, if that were possible.

Tears sprang to Allie's eyes, but she held her ground. "I'm sorry, Curt, I really am, but I'm not going to change my mind. Let me go, please."

Curt very slowly released his grip.

Allie instantly began rubbing her arms, trying to soothe the pain he had inflicted.

"I'm leaving now. Don't bother to take me home; I'll find a cab. Good-bye Curt."

When she attempted to get out of his car, he grabbed her arms again, this time by her wrists. She struggled, but his grip was iron.

"Curt! Let me go! Now!"

He did. As soon as he released her, she was out of the car. Silent tears were her only farewell to Curt. She hoped never to see him again.

She arrived back at the apartment around eight-thirty, early for a Friday night date. Pen heard her key turn in the lock and knew it was her, since she had told him that they were the only ones with a key, which was actually a lie. Curt had a key also. She had forgotten to get it back from him when they broke up.

Tonight it was a blessing that Aspen couldn't see. Allie knew there were going to be bruises, and there were. Her wrists and forearms were covered with bruises where Curt had grabbed her. She was ashamed, but thankful that her new roommate would never know. She was aware that Pen was having a lot of trouble adapting to his new situation, and if he knew that her ex-boyfriend had hurt her in any way, she wasn't sure what he might do. Even though they weren't lovers, she liked Pen and she was pretty sure Pen liked her too. In time she was convinced she could persuade him to sleep with her. He might be blind, but Aspen Windchase was one of the most handsome men she had ever met in her life. And while he was still weak and his frame wasted from lack of use for the past months, in time he would be regaining his strength and when he did, he would be even more attractive. And he was nice. He was one of the most polite men she had ever been around. For now she was just happy to have him with her. While she had never thought about marriage before, now she found herself thinking about it a lot. She wanted to marry Aspen, blind or not; she didn't care. Did she love him? Was she in love with him? Well, if she was honest with herself, the answers to both questions were "no." But she sure did like him! And she knew she was never, ever going to find another man for herself like Aspen Windchase. It was too bad he was blind, but then if he wasn't, there was no chance at all for her. There had to be a way to make him fall in love with her since she had no intention of ever letting him leave. She was going to be so good to him he would never want to leave. All she needed was time.

Within a week Allie realized that Aspen was a drug addict. Being a CNA she knew the signs, since she had seen them often enough. Sadly for both of them, however, she decided not to try to wean him off his meds. Keeping him addicted meant keeping him with her. He was still functioning, going to school, eating, and carrying on conversations. He was learning to read in braille, which he seemed surprised that he was able to learn to do. He was a smart man, and if he realized he was an addict, it was something that was never mentioned, and he was able to hide his addiction well. But she began watching the pill counts. There was no way the doctor was going to be ordering more for him than the regular prescription doses, so she was going to have to find his Valium on her own. Allie, while basically a "nice" girl, knew the ropes, and in this case, it wasn't hard to find a way to get more.

She started by stealing them from work, a few here, a few there. It wasn't too hard in the beginning but before long before she realized she would have to find a regular supplier as the risk of being caught at work increased, and she couldn't afford the consequences of that scenario. Not only would she go to jail, she would lose Pen for good. Nope. A supplier was the answer. Allie knew a lot of people and it didn't take long to find someone willing to work with her on a regular basis. She wasn't after cocaine or anything, just Valium and Tylox, but she was going to need more money to cover the extra cost. She contacted Tom Martin and without having to give much of a reason, Tom agreed to send a larger monthly payment. It was still vastly less expensive than the rehab center had been, and he was happy to do it. Allie had no idea what relationship Mr. Martin and Pen had, but she was grateful he was more than willing to pay the expenses. Good old Tom Martin. If he knew what his money was really going for she suspected the funds would dry up immediately.

Pen seemed not to notice that his pill supply was increasingly abundant. She wondered if he had any idea that he had become an addict; she supposed he didn't. But if he did, given his situation he probably didn't care one way or the other. If she was in his place she would want that Valium also, and a lot of it.

Within a few weeks Allie discovered she had a different problem. She was pregnant.

Shocked, disillusioned, scared, pregnant. Never in her wildest dreams had she ever considered pregnancy a possibility. She had always taken precautions when she slept with someone. She had been careful with Curt, as usual, so how had this happened? She had been selective and careful. This just wasn't fair! What on earth was she going to do now? She couldn't afford a baby, and she didn't want one. Abortion? That was always a possibility, but she didn't really believe in that. It would have to be a last resort if she succumbed to that possibility.

Tell Curt and expect him to pay child support? Support of any kind? After his mild show of violence when she broke it off with him, she was adamant that he could no longer have any part in her life, and certainly not her child's. No way was she going to tell Curt he was going to be a father. Adoption? Perhaps. At least the baby would be born to a "clean" mother. Neither she nor Curt had ever used drugs or drank much. The baby would not be born an addict or anything so it shouldn't be too hard to find someone to adopt it.

A baby! Her parents lived in South Dakota. How on earth would she break the news to them? They might disown her for this. No, wait, maybe there was no reason to tell them, at least not yet. Maybe not ever. But if she were married . . .

If she told Pen, was there any chance he might marry her? She didn't know but it might be worth taking the chance. But what if he wouldn't? Then what? Allie was sick with the worry and uncertainty.

At least she was no more than a month along, so there was still time to make some decisions.

For the next few days Allie worked very hard at concealing her volatile emotions. She worked diligently, but her mind was spinning constantly with worry and confusion. She had to come up with a plan, and soon. It wasn't long before she did just that.

One evening, soon after she had formulated her plan, she cooked a very nice dinner of steaks done on the grill, baked potatoes, green salad, and a cherry pie she had baked especially for this occasion. She served wine with the meal.

Pen seemed to enjoy what she served, but halted at the proffered wine.

"What's wrong, Pen? Don't you like wine?"

"I'm not much of a drinker, Allie. I'll just skip the wine if it's all right with you."

"No, please, just this once, have a glass with me, OK?" So he did.

When it came time for bed, Pen took his regular prescribed dose of Valium plus two extra, along with two Tylox, and, coupled with the wine, he would sleep well, floor or not.

She waited a couple of hours before going to him, wanting to be sure he was well sedated. He roused with difficulty, and she despaired of ever getting him to her room, but somehow she managed as he stumbled and leaned heavily on her. In his stupor she was sure he would never knew the truth of how he came to be in her bed. When he found himself there in the morning, it shouldn't be too hard to convince Pen that her baby was in fact his. That would solve everything, she thought. His sense of responsibility would ensure their marriage, her parents would never know the baby was anyone's but Pen's, and neither would Pen. His sister would never know either. It was the perfect solution. Yes, it could work.

Finally, getting him settled on one side of her bed, she stood for a moment gazing down at this handsome, good man. Yes, she was doing the right thing. It was going to be OK. Aspen would make a wonderful father, and somehow she knew he would absolutely love her baby, regardless. Oh, he wasn't going to be happy about compromising his principles, but hey, he was a man, and men slept with women, didn't they? And there was no doubt that Pen was all man. Smiling, she bent to the task of removing Pen's pajama bottoms. He was a dead weight and sound asleep, and removing them was definitely not easily done. But she would have to be convincing in the morning for her plan to work, and if he awoke still wearing his pajama bottoms there was no way he would believe he had made love to her during the night.

She sighed, smiled, and removing her nightgown, she crawled under the covers, snuggling close to her man. He smelled so good! Was she falling in love with him? Did it even matter? She kissed him lightly on his forehead, inhaling his scent deeply as she did so. Resting her head on his bare chest, one arm draped across his waist, she drifted off to sleep, a slight smile on her face.

Chapter 6

Aspen was dreaming, a very nice dream. He was holding a cuddly, furry puppy, and a black-haired woman was there. He came awake slowly, trying hard to remember the dream. Was it real? Had the scenario really happened or was it just a meaningless, routine dream? It was Saturday and there was no school for him today. Allie had the day off, he remembered, so there was no reason for either of them to get up early. He started to drift off again when suddenly a great panic settled over him. He began to sweat profusely. What was . . . Allie was . . .

Allie was snoring softly, her head still on his bare chest, her arm draped across his waist. Allie. Here. In his bed. No, wait. This was her bed, not his. He slept on the floor, didn't he? What on earth was he doing in her bed? He couldn't remember going into her room. He tried, oh, how he tried, but he couldn't remember anything about it. How did he get in here? When did he come in here? How long had he been in her bed? And, heaven help him, what had he done?

Dear God in heaven, he hadn't, had he? But, she was here, with him, and it wasn't hard to tell she was naked under those covers. He was terrified, for many reasons. He wanted to bolt out of there, but he didn't even know how to get out of the room. He had never been in here before and he didn't know where the door was, for a start. And where was his cane? Without that he would blunder and stumble into every wall and piece of furniture. He would have to wake her up to get out of here. What on earth was he going to say to her? That he was sorry? That he didn't remember anything, even if it was the truth? How do you tell a woman you obviously just spent the night with that you didn't remember making love to her? That she was that forgettable? He couldn't be that cruel!

But wait . . . he made love to her? Was that possible? He had taken so many pills he couldn't believe he was capable of doing anything but sleeping. He was pretty sure he couldn't walk after taking them, so how on earth had he gotten to her room? And he was pretty positive he hadn't . . . but he was naked also. And if he was naked, and Allie was naked, then could he have possibly. . .

He actually groaned in his despair. He must have. He felt sick.

But the undeniable fact was that she felt good. Better than good. She felt wonderful, and even that was an understatement. He didn't remember ever sleeping with a woman, but then he didn't remember much of anything. So even if this wasn't actually the first time for him, it might as well have been. Everything in his world was new to him. He was starting over at the ripe old age of thirty. He gritted his teeth. He needed to move but oh, he didn't want to! This situation was right up there with a really good hug. But nature called and he needed to use the bathroom.

"Allie?" He stroked her back softly. "Allie, wake up."

"Hmmm?" She roused slightly, and then snuggled even tighter to him. She wasn't really awake yet, and didn't want to move.

"Allie, I need to use the bathroom so you need to move." He sighed deeply, embarrassed and ashamed. "And I don't know where it is so you're going to have to show me. I don't remember."

She slowly opened her eyes, remembering the events of the night before. She smiled as she remembered her deception, and yes, her utter delight at having Pen in her bed at last. While she was sorry that Pen was blind, this morning she had to admit she was thankful he was unable to read the lie she was sure her own eyes would reveal.

"I'll take you down the hall, just give me a minute." Withdrawing slowly, reluctant to move away from his solid warmth, she crept out of bed and came around to help him find his way. She almost stopped to put a robe on but quickly changed her mind. He couldn't see her anyway so what difference did it make whether she was covered or not?

When he was finished in the bathroom, he met her outside the door where she had waited for him.

"Where's my cane, Allie?"

"It's in my bedroom where you left it last night. Let's go back to my room. Neither of us has to be anywhere today so let's just go back to bed. I'm still sleepy."

"I think . . ."

"Oh, skip the arguments, Pen. We just spent the night together and you didn't seem to mind it too much, so let's talk about this later. I want to sleep some more. By the way, did you get a Valium while you were in there?"

"No, I actually forgot what with, well, you know."

"Hang on and I'll get it for you. Just wait here." She was back in seconds with a couple of pills and that plastic glass of water. "Here you go. Drink up."

When he was finished, she took the glass back to the sink, and then linking her arm in his, she walked him contentedly back to her room. He started to protest once more, but Allie simply maneuvered him up against the bed and pushed him down onto it.

"Put your feet up, mister, and I'll cover you up."

He did as she asked, but against his better judgment. What on earth had he gotten himself into? And how was he going to get himself out of it?

Allie crawled back into bed and snuggled right up against him once again, pulling the bedding up to cover them warmly.

"Pen, I thought you would never come to me. Thank you. It was wonderful. Better than I ever expected. Now let's go back to sleep. I never want to get out of this bed again."

He let her lie close to him once more. He hated to admit it, but it felt so good to have a woman next to him. Allie. She was so comforting in so many ways. But it bothered him that he couldn't remember anything about the past night. How could he make love to a woman and remember nothing at all about it? Was it possible? He had no idea. He didn't think so, but then the Valium was kicking in again and soon he didn't care one way or the other. He was warm, he had a naked woman next to him, and he was in a very blissful state. He would sleep some more and worry about things later.

Allie woke him a few hours later with a soft kiss on his mouth and three pills in her hand. Aspen would be spending the weekend sleeping.

They ate sandwiches when they were hungry, but never left the bed. Allie stayed naked, but Pen kept his pajama bottoms on. He was so drugged he forgot where he was or who was with him. The drug-induced euphoria and deep sleep kept him from his suicidal thoughts and desires—from any reality at all. He was in exactly the state he wanted to be in, if he couldn't check out yet. Leaving this world was still his goal, even if it was pushed to the background a little with Allie lying next to him.

Sunday morning rolled around and it was finally time for both of them to face some sort of reality. Allie cut the number of pills she brought him, but by just a couple. She knew they would need to do some talking, and it might as well be now as later while they had the free time to do it. Tomorrow it was back to school for him and to work for her.

She left him once more to take a shower.

He stayed in the bed with the very rumpled sheets, missing her. He missed her smell and her warmth, the feel of her next to him. Even though, being a gentleman, he had not touched her other than her arm. He thought it was the very best therapy in the world out of all the therapies he was involved with. He was still sad that he didn't remember having sex with her, but he was getting over it slowly. Perhaps one day he would be awake enough to do it again, and he would remember it that time. Wouldn't that be something? His guilt was beginning to recede. He wasn't sure if he was happy about that or not. Maybe in the end it didn't really matter.

She cooked a real breakfast this morning. Bacon, scrambled eggs, toast, hot, steaming coffee. They ate in silence for a few moments, and then Pen began.

"Allie, I'm sorry, but you must know I don't have any idea or memory of how I got to your room or what we . . . or I . . . well, what happened. I'm sorry about that, I really am. I guess I was just too tired."

"Pen, let's be honest here. It's the pills. You know that. You have to know that by now. But I understand why you want to keep taking them, I really do."

"But . . ."

"It's OK if you don't remember what happened. I do and that's enough." She proceeded to lay it on thick for him. "You were good, Cowboy. I wasn't a virgin, not that I sleep around a lot, but there have been others before you. But Pen, I have to tell you that you were the best. Unforgettable, actually. It was very special for me. Actually, you must know by now that I'm in love with you. You do know that, don't you?"

"You are?" No, he hadn't given her feelings about him even a fleeting thought. He knew he wasn't in love with her and that was as far as he went with their situation. But now? What was he going to do now?

"Allie, I have to be honest with you. I can't do anything about your feelings toward me, but I'm sorry. I like you, I really do. I like you a lot, actually. I'm sure I would never have . . . if I didn't like you. But honestly, I'm not in love with you. I'm sorry, but I'm just not. I don't think it's possible for me to love anyone right now, not at this stage of my life. Allie, I don't even know what you look like!"

"That's OK with me, Pen. You don't have to love me back. Just stay with me. Sleep with me. Be my friend and confidant. Just don't leave me. And who knows, maybe one of these days you will love me back. Let's give it some time. And as for what I look like, does it really matter? I'm obviously not a dog or I wouldn't have had any boyfriends, right?"

"But . . ."

"Pen, there's no need to be embarrassed with me. We're friends. We like being with each other, you're very, very good in bed, and that's enough for now, isn't it? We're doing OK, I think, so let's just let things be. There's time enough to dig deeper if we really want to later."

He wasn't happy about this, but she was right about most of it. They did get along well, she was taking excellent care of him, and he was more content than he had been since waking up from that coma. Maybe it was OK. He asked for another cup of coffee.

"There is one more thing, Allie. I have to ask this question."

"What?"

"You mentioned the pills. I know I'm taking way too many of them, but it's either that or go crazy in my head.

Please tell me you won't take them away from me. You won't, will you?"

"No, Pen, I won't take them away from you. I will keep you supplied with as many as you want for as long as you want them. When you're ready to stop, you let me know. Until then, I'll take care of it."

"Thank you. If you cut off my pills I will move out the next day, you do know that don't you? I can't—no, I won't be without them. I can't face the days without those pills and I don't want to even try. If I have to sleep on the streets, that's what I'll do. I'll get them however I can, with or without you."

"Don't worry, I told you I'll take good care of you." She smiled at him. "Want to go back to bed? You can take care of me in return. What do you say?"

"OK, lead the way. And thanks for breakfast."

They both knew he would be unable to take care of Allie in any way. He was an addict. He didn't care about anything as long as he could have his pills whenever he wanted them.

A few days later he stopped going to the school. He had Allie and she was taking excellent care of him. He was still planning to kill himself one of these days so he didn't need that stupid school anyway. He started staying in Allie's bed most of the day, every day. When he woke, he took more pills. Allie didn't seem to care as long as he slept in the same bed with her. She was adamant about that one thing. In the end that was certainly easy enough for him to do. It was a lot more comfortable than her living room floor and she still slept naked every night. What more could he possibly want? He had everything but his memory and his sight. Maybe next week he would make his final exit.

Chapter 7

It was after twelve o'clock on a Saturday night. Neither of them heard the deadbolt turn as Curt used the key Allie had forgotten to retrieve from him to enter Allie's apartment. He came in quietly, stealthily. He had missed Allie and even though it had been a few months since he had seen her, he couldn't believe she didn't miss him, at least a little. He had decided he liked her a lot more than he had first thought, and after she broke up with him he had a hard time accepting that breakup. He just had to reason with her and she would take him back, he knew it.

He closed the door softly behind him, turning the deadbolt for security. Taking his shoes off, he placed them neatly next to the door, remembering that Allie liked to keep her place neat.

Removing his jacket, he draped it over a chair in the kitchen, and then padded softly down the hall to Allie's room. The door was closed, and he turned the doorknob very slowly and quietly. He wanted to surprise his woman.

He entered the bedroom, and as his eyes became adjusted to the darkness, they dilated at the scene before him.

Allie was not alone in the bed! What the . . . ? Angrily he reached over and flipped the light switch. The room was flooded with light from the ceiling fixture and Allie was instantly awake.

She sat up in bed, not thinking, but only reacting.

"Curt!"

"Hi, Allie. Long time, no see." His anticipatory smile disintegrated into a sneer. "Looks like you didn't waste any time, or were you already seeing this guy when you broke up with me?"

Pen roused only slightly, too drugged to fully waken. He mumbled something unintelligible and turned over on his side.

Allie jumped out of bed and moved quickly over to Curt. Placing both hands on his chest she began to push him forcefully out of her room.

"What?" Curt tried to hold his ground.

"Look, we'll talk in the other room. Now move! I don't want to wake him up!"

"Oh no, Allie, girl. I think I want a piece of him. And maybe of you too."

"Out!" Grabbing her robe she walked swiftly out of the room, Curt following closely behind.

They sat in the living room, glowering at each other.

"What on earth do you mean barging into my home in the middle of the night, Curt? How could you! And how did you get in here, anyway?"

"With my key, stupid. How do you think? I'm not so low that I would actually break in or anything. I missed you, sure, but not bad enough that I would break and enter, for heaven's sake."

"Give me your key, and don't ever come back here again. I broke up with you, I have a new man in my life, and I don't want to see you ever again. Clear enough? And would you please lower your voice? I don't want to wake him up. Who knows what he'll do if he finds another man in my apartment!"

"OK, OK, I got it. I'm sorry. Look, I'm sorry if I hurt you when you left, and I'm sorry I came in here tonight. I miss you, you know? You're quite a girl, Allie. A good girl. One of the nicest I've ever dated, and I really did miss you. But don't worry, I won't bother you anymore. Guess I should have come around a little sooner, huh? I'm just late, aren't I?" He smiled ruefully.

"I'm sorry, too, Curt. Sorry it didn't work out with us, but hey, we had fun while it lasted. And thanks for being this much of a gentleman tonight. I appreciate it."

Curt rose to leave and went over to put his shoes on. He grabbed his jacket and then turned to Allie, who was escorting him.

"Can I have just one more hug for old time's sake?"

"Sure. One more hug."

Curt embraced her tightly, and then quickly drew back in shock.

"Allie, you're pregnant!" His voice boomed with the shock of his discovery and it carried all through the apartment. "It's mine, isn't it!"

"No, it's not yours. It's . . . his." She gestured toward the hallway and her bedroom.

"How far along are you?"

"About three months. But it's none of your concern, Curt. This baby has absolutely nothing to do with you, so you can leave with a clear conscience. Now go."

"Three months? But we were together three months ago, so how can you . . . ?"

"I'm sure. It's not yours."

Curt hesitated, but breathed a sigh of what appeared to be relief and turning away from her, he opened the door and slipped quietly into the night. He would not be back.

Pen was awake, or at least as awake as he could be given the number of pills he had taken. He had been dreaming about horses, Appaloosa horses to be precise. And that black-haired woman had been in the dream again also. But he thought he had heard people talking in the other room. Had he been dreaming or were there people down the hall? He couldn't be sure. It had seemed so real! How could he tell the difference?

He could have sworn he heard someone yelling out that Allie was pregnant. Real? Not real? And if it was real, was he . . . ?

Allie came softly back into the bedroom and noticed immediately that Pen was at least somewhat awake.

"Go back to sleep, Pen."

"But I thought I heard . . ."

"We'll talk in the morning. Sleep for now." She slipped her robe off and crawled into bed again, snuggling up to him as she always did.

In the morning Pen made a special effort to actually wake up. He didn't want to; he preferred the oblivion the pills gave him, but something was bothering him. He kept wondering how much of what he thought he had heard last night was real and how much was a dream. He had to know.

"Allie, about last night."

"How much did you hear, Pen? I'm sorry we woke you up."

"So I wasn't dreaming? There really was someone here last night?"

"Yes. Curt was here."

"Did he do anything? Did he hurt you? Why was he here? Did you actually let him in?"

"No, he let himself in. I forgot he still had a key. It's my fault, but he didn't stay long and then he left. Sorry about that."

"So does he know about me now?"

"Well, actually, he saw us in bed."

Pen groaned out loud. He was acutely embarrassed. "Oh, no!"

"It's OK, Pen. I had already broken up with him, remember? And he was actually a gentleman about the whole thing, which I'm thankful for. He left without any fuss and I remembered to take my key back so I'm sure he won't be returning in the future. All is well." She smiled, seeming to forget that he couldn't see her.

"Pen, how much did you hear last night?"

Pen looked away, the ever-present grayness enveloping his very being.

"Allie, are you pregnant?"

"You heard that?"

"Yup. I sure did. I wasn't sure if I was dreaming or not, but something tells me if Curt was actually here I really did hear him yell out that you were pregnant. I did, didn't I?" He was afraid to hear her answer.

"Yes, I'm pregnant, Pen. Isn't it wonderful? We're going to have a baby!"

Pen's face paled. "It's not my baby, Allie. You and I both know it's not mine, so don't say 'we're' having a baby. I suppose it's Curt's?"

"No, Pen, it's your baby. We must have made that baby the first night you came to my bed. I was so surprised! Shocked, really. I don't know how you made it down the hall and, well, with all the pills you were taking, I don't know how you did it, you know, made a baby and all."

"I didn't." Pen scowled, convinced it had not been possible for him to accomplish that feat.

"Oh, yes, Pen, you most certainly did. I was surprised when I felt you crawl under the covers with me, but I was really happy, too. You know how I feel about you. You must know that. I think I've made it pretty plain, haven't I? And Pen, I'm thrilled I'm going to have your baby. Absolutely thrilled." She reached across the table to take his hands in hers.

He pulled his hands away abruptly. "Well, I most definitely am NOT thrilled. Allie, I'm blind, remember? I can't be a father! And we're not married!"

"Well, that little item we can take care of right away, so that's nothing to worry about. We'll be all legal by the time the baby's here."

"How far along are you?"

"About three months."

"That baby is Curt's. I know it's not mine. I don't know what you're trying to do to me, but it's not right. Don't do this to me, Allie. Please don't."

"Look, Pen. Just because you're blind and have no memory of anything before your accident doesn't mean you get a free pass here. The fact is, you came to my bed and we made a baby together. You are going to be a father and I'm going to be a mother. We can get married or not, whatever your preference is, but we will stay together and we will be parents to this baby. End of story." She rose to her feet.

Pen heard her rise. "Where are you going now?"

"Why, to get you some more Valium, Pen. I think you probably need some more, don't you?"

He nodded. He did need some more. God help him, he needed a lot more.

The drug-induced fog settled over him, welcoming him into its compassionate embrace. Nothing mattered there. If he couldn't be dead he could at least rest in that precious fog he had come to love so much. It was all that mattered to him. He still wanted to end his life, oh, how he wanted to do that, but killing himself took courage and the drugs required none. The end result was very nearly the same, wasn't it? He knew nothing, he needed nothing, time was meaningless, and he was alone, at least until the pills started to wear off. But then Allie kept him supplied so he could always drift right back to his favorite place.

But this time it was different. Something was different, and he was having a hard time vacating reality. Baby. It was the baby. He asked Allie for more pills and she brought them; and this time she brought Tylox also. He drifted off, going to his favorite place.

Four hours later reality was setting in once more. Baby. Baby. Baby. No!

"Allie, come here, would you please?" He had to know for himself. He couldn't take anyone's word on this.

Allie came to his side of the bed.

"What do you need, love? More pills? Did you like the new ones I got for you?"

Pen reached out for her hand and she gave it to him.

"Put my other hand on your stomach. I need to feel the baby." He had never touched Allie that intimately that he knew of, and it disturbed him to think of touching her that way, but he had no choice. He had to know.

She did as he asked, and he immediately knew that she was indeed pregnant. There was no mistaking the hardness below her navel. He quickly withdrew his hand and turned onto his side away from her.

"You can go now."

"Pen . . . I . . ."

"Go. Leave me alone."

She left.

He curled up into the fetal position. If his life wasn't rotten enough, now there was this. He had made a woman he didn't love pregnant, or at least she swore that was the case and he had absolutely no way of disproving it. He should have killed himself months ago when he had the chance. If he hadn't been such a coward! If he hadn't decided the drugs were good enough for the rest of his life! But he had. He had chosen, consciously or not, to live. And now this. How much lower could he go? He pounded his pillow. What was he going to do? Even if he really wasn't the father, the fact was that he was living with Allie, and he was going to have to take some sort of responsibility, somehow. But how? He couldn't see his hand in front of his face, couldn't walk anywhere without a stupid cane, couldn't work, couldn't even remember who he was. He really, sincerely, vehemently wished he were dead. Anything was better than this reality that was now his.

Chapter 8

Raven was beside herself. It had been nearly two months since she had spoken to her twin. The last time she called the Rescue Mission she had been informed that Pen had left with a woman and had taken all his things with him. It didn't appear that he would be returning. She had then called the Montana School for the Deaf and Blind, which he continued to attend, and she was able to at least get updates on his progress and condition, since she had POA. But one day when she called she was told that he had quit attending the school; he hadn't been in for weeks.

Where on earth was her brother? Who was the woman he had left the mission with? Where had that woman taken him? How was she going to track him down? Gus had calmed her down repeatedly, assuring her that while Pen was in a bad way, he was still a strong man and not a stupid one either. And most of all, they could be assured that God was watching over him. Pen was a strong Christian, and whether he remembered that fact or not, God remembered. And they were praying constantly for him along with the church and Pastor Benson. They could be confident that nothing bad was going to happen.

But Raven had come to the end of her patience. She was frantic, and the panic within her was escalating daily. She simply had to find her brother, and soon. But where would she start? Perhaps as with most things, she needed to start at the beginning.

It was a Wednesday morning when Raven broke her plan to Gus as they ate breakfast.

"Gus, I can't take it anymore. I'm going nuts not knowing where Pen is, or how he is. We haven't heard anything in weeks, actually months now. I've decided I can't wait any longer. I'm heading to Billings today to look for him. I'll start at the rehab center and go from there. Any objections?"

"Only that you're not going down there by yourself, Raven. Let me get the horses fed and watered and I'll drive down with you. How does that sound? You don't mind a little company, do you?"

Raven smiled warmly at her husband. He was such a good man! "I'd like nothing better, Gus."

They headed for Billings about two hours later and arrived at the facility around noon. They started at the front desk, asking for any information about Aspen Windchase. They were directed to Medical Records where they were able to pour over his chart, but they learned nothing new, just as they had suspected. However, they planned to leave no stone unturned in their search.

From Medical Records they started hunting up the doctors, nurses, and CNAs that they knew had taken care of him. They learned nothing from the doctors, and then went in search of the nurses. They found Maura in the cafeteria eating lunch.

"Hi Maura, remember me?" Raven walked confidently up to the nurse, not caring if she was interrupting the woman's lunch or not.

Maura looked up, her eyes questioning before lighting up with recognition.

"Why yes, I do. Raven, isn't it? Aspen Windchase's sister?"

"That's right." She took a chair next to Maura's while Gus remained standing behind her. "I'm sorry to bother you while you're eating, but I'm desperate. I need to ask you a couple of questions if you don't mind."

"Sure, go ahead. What can I do for you? And how's your brother doing, anyway?"

"That's just it. We don't know where he is—we can't find him."

"What do you mean, 'you can't find him'?" Maura looked mystified.

"We can't find him. Anywhere. He left the Rescue Mission with a woman several months ago. He was continuing to attend that special school, and I managed to sort of keep up with his progress there, but all of a sudden he quit attending. He simply never showed up one day. No phone calls, no explanation, nothing. We thought maybe you might have some ideas since you had gotten to know him fairly well while he was a patient here."

"Gosh, I'm really sorry, but this is the first I've heard anything about his disappearance. I had no idea! But on the positive side, as awful as it sounds, he is in fact blind, so there's no way he simply took off on his own. Whoever that woman is, he must be with her. They didn't tell you anything over at the mission?"

"Nothing over the phone, and they were pretty mum about the whole thing. We're heading over there next to see what we can find out. We just thought we would check here first, and then work our way along the trail, so to speak."

Maura nodded her head slowly.

"We were hoping to talk to that Allie person while we were here, but she must not be working today, is that right?"

"Well, actually, she was on the schedule for today, but she never showed up for work, which is definitely not like her. She's usually very reliable, and has a great work ethic. She hasn't called in sick so we were thinking maybe her car broke down or something. Lots of people have cell phones these days but here, as in most of Montana, there's no reception anyway so I doubt she even has one of those. I'm sure she'll be in tomorrow. Do you want me to see if she's heard anything about your brother when I see her?"

"Oh, would you please? I'll leave you my phone number since we have to head back later today. There're horses to feed, so we can't be gone overnight." Raven's face showed obvious relief at Maura's offer to ask Allie about Pen, and she quickly wrote her full name and phone number on a piece of paper to leave with the nurse.

"OK. I'll call you as soon as I talk to Allie and find out whether she knows or has heard anything or not. I'll call you either way, how's that?"

"Wonderful. Thank you so much. Sorry again to interrupt your lunch. Talk to you later. Bye." Raven rose from the chair and, taking her husband's hand, walked out of the cafeteria.

From the rehab center they went to the Rescue Mission, and finally to the school. They had no luck at either place; no one seemed to know anything about Aspen Windchase. They headed back to Bozeman, defeated. But they were not giving up. They would wait until they heard something from Maura, and if there were still no leads, they would hire a private detective, though they had no idea how they would pay for one. Whether Pen wanted to see them again or not, they were going to find him.

Maura was unable to finish her lunch. Worry consumed her after Raven and Gus left. Pen was special, and hearing that he had disappeared was devastating to her. What had happened to him? Where was he? Fear began to gnaw at her as her mind raced through all the possibilities. She knew he had been profoundly depressed; goodness, who wouldn't be in his situation? Surely he hadn't done something foolish, had he? She would have read something in the newspaper or seen it on the news if that were the case. But there had been nothing.

She decided she needed to find Allie right away. Allie had been really fond of Pen, though she realized "fond" wasn't quite the right word. Maura had seen how Allie looked at Pen, and her feelings went way beyond fondness. She wondered if there was any chance Allie had been the woman to take Pen out of the Rescue Mission. But Allie hadn't come to work . . .

When her shift was over Maura looked up Allie's address and home phone number. She started by calling the phone number she had found, but there was no answer. In case she had misdialed, Maura tried three more times and let it ring about ten times with each attempt, but there was no answer. She decided to find Allie's apartment and see her at home, and picking up her car keys, she headed for the address the facility had kept on file.

The apartment was dark when Maura pulled up in front. It appeared no one was at home. Undaunted, she walked up the three steps to the front door and rang the bell. She rang it three more times, and then began banging on it, loudly, but no lights came on and no one came to the door. Allie was obviously not at home.

Maura wasn't going to get any answers today. Perhaps tomorrow Allie would be back at work and they could talk then. She turned away from the front door and walked back to her Blazer, and, starting the engine, drove away.

Inside the apartment Aspen lay on Allie's bed, stoned. He woke once when he thought he heard something like a bell, but he wasn't sure and he didn't care. It kept ringing, however, and he almost got up to see what was going on; the noise was disturbing his rest. But he decided it was more trouble that it was worth. He was busy in his own gray world and didn't want to be disturbed.

An hour or so later he was disturbed again, and this time it sounded like some sort of pounding. Who was making all the racket? Didn't they know people were trying to sleep around here? Where was Allie? Why wasn't she taking care of that noise? He turned on his side and ignored the pounding. They would go away soon enough.

For two days Pen lived alone in the apartment. Allie hadn't come home but he had no perception of time. There was no night or day for him. In his gray void, time was totally meaningless. He stumbled to the bathroom when he needed to, took his pills when he felt reality sliding back, and basically lived in Allie's rumpled and now dirty sheets. When he was hungry he simply took more pills and then it didn't matter. He made his way around very well with his cane and the walls that surrounded him. But in his stupor the dreams began recurring more frequently, and always, in every one, there was a raven-haired woman, a stunningly beautiful, smiling woman. He always smiled to himself when she appeared.

Allie was terrified. She had been picked up two nights ago when making her drug purchase. All of her excuses had fallen on totally deaf ears. The police wanted names and numbers, and until she gave them, she was going to be locked up. While she had been allowed to call someone, she was afraid to call anyone she knew. How was she going to explain herself? How was she going to tell any of her friends that she was buying drugs for the blind drug addict she had stashed in her apartment? What would happen to her? To him? To her baby? And her job, what about her job? Was this the end of her career as a CNA? She didn't know anything else. Heaven help her, how was she going to get out of this mess? And what about Pen? He was all alone in that apartment. He could get out, but he was totally helpless and had no idea where to go if he did walk out. Oh, God in heaven, what was she going to do?

She knew she was going to have to tell someone about Pen; she couldn't leave him there alone for too long. Finally, after going over the names of everyone she knew, she settled on Maura. Maura would know what to do, and she would for sure take care of Pen. She could have called his sister, but then she knew she would lose Pen for good. Raven would be right there to take him home with her, whether he wanted to go or not. And it wouldn't be too hard to figure out that Allie had enabled his drug addiction. But Maura, she was pretty sure she could trust Maura; Maura would help her. She would be sure Pen was taken care of and then she would give the police what they wanted. Hopefully she would be out in a matter of days. She called for the guard and then made the call to her friend.

There was a message on the answering machine when Maura got home from work the next day. Playing it back, she listened in stunned silence, replaying it several times, and then grabbing her keys and she headed downtown to the jail. She needed to talk to Allie in person, and she needed to get the key to the apartment.

Billings is basically still a cow town, and the police were friendly and cooperative. They bent the rules and allowed Maura to see Allie for a few minutes, which was long enough to get the whole story and the apartment key. Maura said very little to Allie; what was there to say? Allie wasn't stupid, even though her actions seemed to belie that fact, and words certainly weren't going to change anything now anyway. She left Allie and went straight to the apartment.

Pen was hungry, and when he was hungry he wanted pills, not food, and he needed water too. He was thirsty. Dragging himself out of bed he stumbled toward the door and crashed into the wall instead, banging his forehead. He moaned with the sudden pain. He had forgotten his cane, but the apartment was small enough that by now he was able to count his steps between the rooms and get around that way. He listed from one side to the other, one hand cradling the lump on his forehead, the other grasping for the walls on either side of the hall, his balance poor.

He made it to the bathroom, and, turning on the faucet, he slowly filled the plastic cup with cold water and drank deeply. Three times he filled the cup and quenched his thirst, then filled it one last time to facilitate getting his next few pills down. He set the cup on the counter and opened the drawer that held his pills, but when he went to put the pill container back, he misjudged the space, and the full cup of water crashed to the floor.

"Damn!" There was water all over the floor and he swore at the inconvenience of it. He would have to grab a towel and mop up the mess before Allie came home. Turning to reach for the towel, his foot slipped in the puddle of water, and instantly he found himself on the floor. He hit hard. There would be another bruise besides the one on his forehead. Trying to get up, he slipped and fell once more, and, lying there in the puddle of water, Aspen gave up. He didn't try to get up again. Reflexively, his arm went over his eyes as if to block out the light, but of course there was no light. There was nothing and no one.

Tears began to flow softly from the corners of his sightless eyes, as reality washed over him. He was in his stupor, but for some reason it wasn't the oblivious state he was used to. His personal reality had crept in, and it was overwhelming.

Aspen Windchase was totally alone. He was blind. He didn't remember his sister or any of his friends before the accident. He was as helpless as a baby and had to be led everywhere he went outside of this apartment. Allie, a woman he liked very much but did not love, said he was the father of her baby. He was lying on a cold bathroom floor in a puddle of water clad only in a pair of pajama bottoms, and he couldn't get up. He wanted to kill himself, but he lacked the courage to do even that, when it came right down to it. And for the first time he acknowledged that he was, in fact, a drug addict. Why couldn't he just die? He kept taking more and more pills, but he kept waking up, never sure if he really meant to take that final overdose or not. He was, in fact, a coward. The tears continued as he wallowed in self-pity and wished once more that he were dead.

Chapter 9

Maura pulled up in front of the apartment and nearly ran to the front door. She didn't bother with the doorbell but instead inserted the key, turned the knob and entered. Total darkness enveloped her and she quickly reached for the light switch. Turning it on, she scanned the room before her, searching, not knowing what awaited her in the darkened rooms down the hall.

"Aspen? Are you there?" She called his name frantically, but there was no answer. "Pen? Answer me, please!" Only silence echoed back at her call.

She walked quickly down the hall, turning on lights as she went. Peering into the bedroom, only rumpled sheets in the empty room greeted her. Where was he? He had to be here? Why wasn't he answering her?

She found her answer when she turned on the bathroom light, nearly falling over the inert body on the floor as she did so.

"Pen! Are you OK? Pen, answer me!" She sank to her knees on the bathroom floor beside her friend, terrified. He was so pale! But he was breathing, and that relieved her greatly. He was alive, but why was he on the floor? How long had he been there, she wondered.

She took the arm he had draped over his eyes and put it down to his side. He was so cold! Taking one of his hands in hers, she began to rub it. "Pen, wake up, Pen! It's Maura. I'm here. Wake up! What's wrong?"

She was nearly knocked over when a low moan escaped his dry lips and he suddenly swung his arm out to the side.

"What . . ?" He moaned again, louder this time, and began twisting his torso. "Allie?"

"No, Pen, it's me, Maura. Remember me? The nurse from the rehab center? You need to wake up, Pen. Come on, can you sit up for me? Do you need my help to sit up?"

"Maura, did you say? What are you doing here? Where's Allie? She's supposed to be here, not you." The words were slurred.

"We'll talk about that later, Pen. Right now, we need to get you up and back to bed, and then we need to get you dressed. Now, sit up until you get your bearings."

"OK, OK, I'm sitting up." He brushed her hand away. "I can do it myself. Well, I think I can." He made a rueful smile, but he managed to rise to a sitting position. He had been on the floor so long that the water had dried and the floor was no longer slick. His pajama bottoms were still damp, however.

"Pen, what happened here? How did you end up on the floor, for heaven's sake? And are you hurt anywhere?" Maura could see no obvious injuries other than a small lump on his forehead, but she needed to hear it from him. "Nothing broken?"

"No, nothing broken or injured except for my pride." His words were less slurred now as he woke up. "I'm not sure what happened exactly. No, wait, I do kind of remember. I came in here for some water and a couple of pills, and like the stupid blind man that I am I spilled the water when I went to take my pills, and then I slipped and fell, and when I tried to get up I fell again, so I just stayed here. What's the use of getting up anyway?"

"What do you mean, what's the use of getting up? Why wouldn't you want to get up?"

He turned his sightless eyes toward the sound of her voice. "Maura, look at me. Look real close."

She did as he asked and saw the dried traces of his tears streaking the corners of his eyes and cheeks. Tears filled her own eyes as she saw the marks for what they were, but she was careful to hide her feelings from Pen. She was sure he wouldn't want her feeling sorry for him. He may not even realize that he had been crying.

"I see a very handsome man sitting on the floor who definitely needs a shower and a shave." She smiled at him and her smile was evident in her voice.

"Maura, you're not looking close enough. Look again." His voice became very soft and low, his despair evident in its tone.

"I told you what I see, and unlike you, I can see very clearly at the moment."

"No, you must be as blind as I am." He took a deep breath and turned his head away. "What you're looking at is a pathetic half-naked man sitting in a pool of water on the bathroom floor, a blind, useless shell of a man that doesn't even know who he really is. And he's a drug addict, Maura, a lousy, pathetic, dirty drug addict. One of those people you want to avoid at all costs. And worst of all, he's a coward."

"Pen, you're wrong. You're not useless, you're not pathetic, and you're not a coward. And you aren't sitting in a pool of water either—it's all dried up. So there!" She got to her feet. "You are, however, correct about one thing."

"I'm correct about all of it, but what's the one thing I'm right about as far as you're concerned?"

"Well, you are in fact dirty. Frankly, you stink. You need a shower, so get yourself up off that cold floor and head for the shower, will you?"

"OK, OK. Look out. Get out of my way."

The water had, in fact, dried up and the floor was no longer slippery. He rose to his feet without difficulty, a little more sober with the cold and being so long without pills. He stood for a moment, leaning against the vanity, and then turned to use the commode. As he began to expose himself, Maura gasped audibly.

"What on earth are you doing? I'm standing right here, Pen!" She was a nurse and had seen it all before, but this wasn't a hospital or the rehab center and he wasn't her patient. She was actually embarrassed.

"Well, leave then, but I have to go to the bathroom."

Maura fled the room, shutting the door behind her.

When he was finished, she heard the door open behind her.

"Sorry. I tend to forget that just because I can't see, that doesn't mean that everyone else can't see either. Besides, things have gotten pretty casual around here between Allie and me. Nothing to get embarrassed about, anyway."

She realized that it was probably true: being blind put a whole new spin on things for him. It would be easy to forget that others could see him clearly.

"OK. Fine. Do you need any help from me or can you take that shower on your own?"

Pen scowled. He wanted to curse at her. He was blind, not totally incapacitated. He wasn't a toddler and he could certainly take a shower on his own.

"I think I can manage on my own," he said dryly, and shut the door in her face.

Well, she thought, guess he's coming around just fine! She turned and went to wait for him in the small living room.

He was gone for nearly half an hour, and just as she began to get worried, hoping he hadn't fallen in the shower or something, she heard the bathroom door open and footsteps coming down the hall. Seconds later he entered the living room, but promptly banged into the coffee table, hitting his knee hard.

"Damn!" he exclaimed. "That hurt like hell!" He bent to rub his kneecap where it had collided with the sharp edge of the coffee table.

"Pen?"

"Oh, sorry. I actually forgot for a moment that you were here. Sorry for the swearing. But it really hurts!"

"That's OK, I'm sure it does hurt. It looked like you hit it pretty hard. But where on earth is your cane? Why are you walking around without it?"

"Actually, I haven't used it for so long I forgot where I left it. I didn't need it to go just between the bedroom and the bathroom, you know?" His gait was still unsteady and his words were still slightly slurred. He was only a little more sober than before his shower, it seemed.

"I'll get it for you. Just sit down and wait here." She watched him as he gingerly groped his way to a chair and sat down heavily. She noticed that he was wearing the same dingy pajama bottoms that he was wearing when she had found him on the floor.

"Well, you certainly smell better, that's for sure. Thanks for taking the shower. But I need to get you into some clean clothes. Where are they?"

"These are just fine." He scowled again, obviously unhappy with her interference. "And what are you doing here?

Where's Allie?" His eyelids started drooping and his speech was starting to slow perceptibly.

"Pen, did you take more pills while you were in the bathroom?"

"Yeah. So what if I did?"

Maura sighed. She was going to have her hands full, that was certain. Well, first she would have to get him dressed and somehow convince him to come with her to her house. One step at a time, she thought.

"I think I need to go back to bed now. I can find my own way and you can leave. Allie should be here soon, so go." He rested his head on his arm as his eyes slowly closed into the familiar stupor.

"Oh no you don't, mister! You're going to wake up and you're going to get dressed in some real clothes. I'll go find something for you to wear so don't get too comfortable in that chair." She got up, intending to find some clothes for him.

"There's no need for me to get dressed. Just leave. I'm going back to bed." He started to rise but Maura was suddenly right in front of him and pushed him none too gently back into the chair.

"Nope. Sit. Stay. I'll be right back."

"Sit? Stay? I'm not a dog you know!"

"Then don't be acting like one." She left him sitting and went down the hall to find some clean clothes and his cane.

When she returned a few moments later, he was sound asleep in the chair. Well, at least he stayed like he was told, she thought. But how was she going to wake him up enough to get him dressed and out of here? She wondered what, and how much, he had taken.

The bedroom had been a regular pigsty. The sheets looked like they hadn't been changed in months, dirty clothes were all over the floor, and the room actually stank. The sight had nearly made her sick to her stomach. What on earth had Allie been thinking, anyway? She wasn't that kind of person, Maura knew, so what was going on?

She found his duffel bag and stuffed everything she found that seemed to be his into it; there wasn't much. She kept a pair of clean underwear, sweat pants, a sweatshirt, and a pair of moccasins out for him to wear. She wanted to throw those pajama bottoms in the garbage, they were so nasty.

"Pen, wake up and get dressed. I brought some clothes and a pair of moccasins for you to wear."

Pen mumbled something but barely stirred.

"Pen!" Maura actually yelled into his ear. He did raise his head at that invasion.

"What?"

"Wake up and get yourself dressed!"

"Oh, just go away. I want to sleep." He wasn't about to wake up now or in the near future.

"If you don't get up out of the chair I'm going to kick you in that knee you just whacked when you came in here, and I'll make sure it hurts you enough to wake you up! So get up now, do you hear me?"

"I told you to just go away. Leave me alone. I'm fine here until Allie gets back."

Maura made good on her threat. She hated to do it; she really didn't want to hurt this man, but she saw no other way to get through to him. Pain was usually a pretty good way to wake anybody up. She stood carefully to the side and then kicked him in his sore knee—hard. Swearing loudly, Pen nearly jumped out of the chair. His unseeing eyes were flashing fire.

Maura jumped away from him, not knowing what to expect, but he was awake, at least for the moment.

"I did warn you, Cowboy." She thrust the clothing into his reluctant arms. "Now put these on or I'll do it for you."

"Fine. Do it yourself because I'm not going to. I don't need these to go back to bed."

"You're not going back to bed, Pen, you're coming home with me." She wasn't sure how much of what she was saying would actually register in that drugged-up brain of his, but she had to start somewhere.

Apparently he heard what she said. He turned his head toward the sound of her voice.

"What did you just say?"

"I said you're going home with me, so get yourself dressed. You can't go outside wearing only those nasty pajama bottoms!"

"I'm not going anywhere except right back to bed, so forget it. Where's my cane?" His hands reached out, searching.

"If you don't stay right here and start getting dressed I'll hit you in that sore knee one more time!"

"You wouldn't!"

"I would!"

"Fine. You want me to be dressed so bad you do it yourself!" He stood, swaying slightly, with his hands outstretched, as it to see what she would do next.

"Have it your way, then." Maura was angry and the tone of her voice left no doubt about it. While she might have been embarrassed with him in the bathroom, the situation had now seemed to revert to a patient-nurse relationship. She had seen him naked before, and she began to realize she would probably have the great honor of seeing him again. Reaching over, she roughly yanked his pajama bottoms down to his ankles.

"Step out of them."

"And if I don't?"

"I'll pull your feet out from under you, that's what."

Reluctantly, Pen placed both hands on her shoulders for balance and stepped out of the confining material. He must have remembered her earlier embarrassment because he grinned broadly as he did so.

"Think you're funny, don't you. Go ahead and laugh. I don't much care because you are getting dressed no matter what you want." She tossed the pajama bottoms to the side and held the underwear for him to step into.

"Here. Put your feet into your underwear."

He did as she asked, but his smile got even broader if that were possible. He was apparently awake enough to realize that Maura was getting her way, but she was also getting a full, unrestricted frontal view of his private anatomy. Revenge can be sweet at times.

Maura was the professional nurse now, however, and she was unfazed by his display. Well, mostly unfazed. Pen had been more than a patient to her for months, and he was even more so now. She couldn't help the involuntary swallow as she finally got his underwear and then his sweatpants on.

The grin never left Pen's face.

She was infuriated.

When he was dressed, he sank quickly back into the chair, exhausted. It was more work than he had done in weeks.

Maura left him dozing while she took his things out to her Blazer. She returned in minutes, and picking up his filthy pajama bottoms, she stuffed them into the trash bin she found under the sink. They weren't worth the effort to even wash them.

"OK, you're dressed. Let's go."

"I told you I wasn't going anywhere with you."

"You don't get a choice, sorry. Get up and let's go. I'll take your arm so don't worry about using your cane." She reached out to him, but he shook her off.

"Fine. I'm going before you kick me in the knee again. But I don't need your help. Give me my cane; I can make it on my own."

She handed him his cane and walking slowly, swaying slightly, he followed her out of the front door to her vehicle. He slept all the way to her house.

Chapter 10

Maura had a small, two-bedroom home on the east side of town in a very quiet neighborhood. Getting Pen inside her house and into his bed proved much easier than it had been to get him out of Allie's apartment. He was so drugged he seemed beyond caring where he was or who he was with. He had spoken to her only once and that was to ask if she had brought his pills, which she had. She wished she could have left them at Allie's, but Pen would have to be weaned off of them slowly, she thought. For sure she couldn't stop them cold turkey unless she had some help with him. He couldn't be left alone while he was detoxing.

Which presented the next problem. She was going to have to find someone to stay with him while she was at work, or else she would have to take her vacation now, which she really didn't want to do. She decided the first thing to do was to let Raven know that she had found him and that he was OK.

She was so tired! It had been exhausting getting that mule-headed man out of Allie's apartment. She sighed deeply, and leaning back in her couch, she rested her head for a moment on its back. She really wanted to go to sleep herself, but she needed to call his sister before anything else. Pulling Raven's number out of her pocket, she roused herself and quickly made the call. Raven answered on the second ring.

"Hello?"

"Raven?"

"Yes, this is Raven."

"Raven, it's Maura. I found your brother and I brought him home with me. He's in my spare bed, sleeping soundly at the moment."

"Oh, thank you God!" Raven's relief echoed in her voice. "How is he? Is he OK?"

"Well, yes and no. I need to tell you everything, I think. Then we need to make some plans." She proceeded to fill Raven in on how she had found her brother, about Allie, and about his obvious drug addiction. She relayed the fact that she was going to need some help until he was clean again.

"Gus and I will come down in the morning and bring him home with us, so don't worry. Can he stay alone until then after you go to work?"

"Yes, he'll be OK I think. He just sleeps all the time anyway. But Raven, I have to warn you, something tells me he won't go home with you, at least not yet. He's mentally not in very good shape, which isn't surprising. But I want you to be prepared. He's OK, but he doesn't look too good. I think he's been trying to live off his pills instead of food. He's lost more weight and he's very pale." She went on to explain how she had found him on the bathroom floor and how he had been living.

"Maura, I can't thank you enough for all your help. Gus and I will be down to get him tomorrow. We'll talk again tomorrow when you get off work. Just give me a call when you get home, OK?"

Maura gave Raven her address and told her where she would hide the key, then hung up the phone. Putting her feet up on a footstool, she lay back, pondering the situation, and promptly fell asleep. Sometime later she was suddenly awakened by a bellow from another room.

"Where the hell is the bathroom?"

Pen was obviously awake.

"Coming!" Maura got to her feet and went in search of her new houseguest. She heard him before she saw him. He was trying to navigate without his cane again and was banging into walls and furniture.

"Pen! Stand still, will you? I'm coming! Let me bring you your cane . . ."

"Forget the stupid cane and get me to the bathroom or you're going to be sorry!"

She did as he asked, the urgency obvious in his voice. Taking his arm she led him to the bathroom, and placing his hand on the back of the toilet, left him and shut the door.

When he was finished he stumbled to the door and opened it.

"You were almost too late, you know that don't you? Next time be a little speedier, will you?"

"Whatever happened to that polite gentleman I took care of in the rehab center after he woke up? I seem to remember a very nice young man, but right now you don't bear much of a resemblance to him, let me tell you. Here." She handed him his cane. "Find your own way back to bed."

"And just how am I supposed to do that, pray tell?"

"I don't know and right now I don't much care. If you can't be nice to me I guess you don't need my help, do you!"

"OK, OK, I'm sorry I yelled at you. But I really had to go, you know? Can you just get me back to bed? Please?"

"Follow me." She turned and led the way to his bedroom.

She heard him clearing his throat, and then a soft voice asked cautiously, "Where're my pills? I think I need a couple."

"I'll bring them when you get back to bed." Tonight was not the time to start his rehab program.

She was true to her word and brought the bottles, leaving them at his bedside along with a glass of water.

"Think you can find your way to the bathroom now if you need it again during the night?"

"I'll be fine. You can go."

"Good night then. Sleep well." She turned to leave.

"Maura?"

"Yes?"

"Thanks. The shower really did feel good, and the clean sheets on this bed are pretty great too."

"You're welcome. See you in the morning." She was surprised he was alert enough to make any comments at all.

She headed for her own bed, wondering how this was all going to end up. How had this man ended up in the drugged, blind, lost state he was in? *God, I know you have a plan for each of us, but I really don't understand, Lord. This makes no sense to me. I do know one thing though; we're both going to need a lot of help from You. There's no way we're going to make it through this without You.*

Pen was dreaming again. There was that woman with the blue-black hair again. They were walking in the country, holding hands, chattering away to each other. And then there were horses, and a dog too. The dream ended abruptly.

Maura left for work at six the next morning. She didn't bother to wake Aspen, assuming he was too drugged to think about eating. Hopefully Raven and her husband would be there in good time and would be able to convince him to go home with them. She felt an unnatural attraction to Aspen Windchase; she wasn't sure exactly what it was that she felt for the man, but while she wanted him gone so she didn't have to deal with him, she also wanted to keep him near. If she could just see him sometimes . . . she couldn't forget the hug he had given her on that last day. It had meant something, something special to her. Lots of her patients had hugged her goodbye over the years, but Pen's had been different. Work soon demanded her full attention, however, and her guest was tucked away in the back of her mind for the rest of the day.

Raven and Gus were on the road to Billings by six-thirty, having taken care of the horses early. Raven was so excited she could hardly sit still for the long drive down. Gus, steady as always, did his best to calm her, but it wasn't easily done, and she chattered nonstop for the full two hours it took to get to Maura's house. They found the key right where Maura said she would leave it, and without bothering to knock, they unlocked the front door and walked right in.
"Pen? Where are you?" She didn't wait for an answer but went searching every room until she found her brother, sound asleep in the small bedroom. She hesitated only an instant before running over to sit near him on the edge of the bed, her hand on her twin's forehead. He roused only slightly at the unfamiliar touch.
"Pen? Pen, wake up. It's me, Raven."
Pen mumbled something unintelligible and turned on his side.
Raven stared hard at her brother, sick at heart. He was pale and gaunt; she knew the signs so well, having been in the same place only a couple of years ago, when she was drinking and then started doing drugs before finally taking control of herself and went through her own forced recovery. She thought back to those days, remembering how Pen tried so hard to intervene and get her to stop her lethal behavior. Is this how he had felt when he looked at his sister? She remembered

all too well her resistance to his pleas and offers of help. She had been angry and defensive, wanting only to be left alone to lead her own life as she saw fit. In her case, it had been simple willful behavior; in her brother's case, she could only try to imagine how he must feel, waking up from a coma with no memory and no sight.

Well, she was going to take charge now, and her brother was coming back to Bozeman with her and Gus. Raven was as stubborn and willful as she was beautiful, and she had no intention of taking "no" for an answer.

"OK, Pen, get up. We're going home." She shook his shoulder in an attempt to wake him. When that didn't work, she pinched him on his forearm, hard. That got his attention.

"What the . . . ?" He turned on his back, opening his sightless eyes trying to focus, and as always his eyes saw only gray.

"Get up, Pen, you're going back to Bozeman with me. So get up, get dressed, and let's get out of here."

"No."

"Here we go again with the 'no' thing. You don't get a choice here, brother dear; you're coming with me, so get yourself out of that bed.

"Coffee."

"You want coffee first?"

"Yeah. Strong coffee."

"You got it, Cowboy. Gus, think you can rustle up some coffee in the kitchen? I'm sure Maura won't mind, and actually I'd like a cup myself. How about you?"

"Sounds good to me. I'll bring it in here when it's ready." He turned and headed for the kitchen.

Pen was very slowly waking up, at least somewhat. He was so full of Valium it was impossible for him to be fully alert, but he should be at least somewhat coherent with a good cup of strong coffee inside him.

When Gus came back carrying a tray with three mugs, Pen sat up in bed and began sipping his cup while Raven and Gus sat on the bed with him drinking theirs. As the caffeine hit his system, he began trying to focus his thoughts.

"Raven, is your hair black?"

"Yes, it is. Don't you remember?" She bit her tongue at her lapse. "Sorry. I forgot for a moment that you don't remember anything from, well, from before. But yes, it's very black. Any special reason you're asking?"

"I've had some dreams, and there's always a woman with black hair in them. I can never see her face, but that hair is unique, I think. Guess I was wondering if that woman was a real person, or what. Maybe it's you in my dreams, if your hair is black." He turned his head away. "Is it long or short? Your hair?"

"Don't spill your coffee. I'm going to guide your free hand to my hair and you can see for yourself." She did as she said and put his hand to her head.

Pen stroked his sister's glorious head of thick, raven-hued hair from the crown to her shoulders, where it rested in loose waves.

"Can I?"

"What?"

"Can I touch your face? I want to see you."

"Of course you can. Touch whatever you want." She giggled at the face Gus made with that statement. "Well, almost anything you want! Careful with the hand, mister!"

Slowly, gently, his fingers barely making contact, Pen learned the contours of his twin's face. He didn't remember her, but suddenly, for the first time since waking from his coma, he wanted to. He felt her smooth forehead, the thick brows, her high cheekbones that hinted at their shared Crow ancestry, and the full lips, sensuous and curved upward in a smile.

"You're beautiful, aren't you." It was a statement, not a question. "Thanks for letting me . . . thanks."

"Pen, you have no idea just how beautiful your sister is." Gus smiled at his glowing wife. "She turns heads wherever she goes. How I got so lucky I'll never know, but I thank God every day for her, I'll tell you that."

Raven interjected, "And Pen, we're twins, remember? So you're the male equivalent, and trust me, when you walk into a room, women can't take their eyes off you. You really are a hunk, you know!"

The atmosphere was lightening with the conversation, and Pen started to relax a little, letting his guard down slightly.

They talked about the stable and work, and for a change Pen listened. He found he actually wanted to know about his sister and their life before his accident.

"Pen, do you happen to remember any of my visits while you were in that coma? I didn't come often, but I did tell you I was taking good care of your sister, and, other things." Gus hesitated slightly.

"I remember hearing voices at times, but so far, no, I don't remember anything specific. Sorry."

"That's OK. I was just wondering." Gus turned his head away and stared out the bedroom window.

They finished their coffee, but Pen wanted another cup. Gus obliged, and they sat a while longer, waiting until Pen was ready to get dressed and leave with them.

But Aspen had absolutely no intention of going anywhere with his sister and her husband. He was not leaving Billings. He didn't know where he was going to end up, but he was still adamant about not being a burden to his sister. If only he could actually remember her and their relationship, perhaps he might feel differently, but the fact was, even though they had talked and he had stroked her face, she was still a stranger to him. He knew Allie and Maura better than he did his own twin sister. God help him! God? Where was He, anyway?

"Raven, you and Gus can take off now. I'm not going back with you."

"What do you mean, 'you're not going back with us'? What do you think you're going to do? Where are you going to stay?"

"I don't know yet. Maybe I'll go back to the Rescue Mission. Maybe I'll find out about Allie and go back with her. I'll talk to Maura tonight when she gets home, but I'm definitely not going home with the two of you."

"Pen, please!" Raven was very close to tears. How could she leave her brother here again?

"Raven, I'm sorry. I really am. But I have my reasons and I'm not going with you. So drop it." His voice was firm.

It was time to get serious. Raven, having been where Pen now was, quit being nice.

"Pen, you and I both know you're an addict now. I can tell just by looking at you, let alone how you're acting. If I leave you're never going to get off the drugs, and I can't let that happen. I love you too much to let you slowly kill yourself like this. I won't do it!"

Pen surprised them both when he admitted. "I am well aware that I'm addicted to these pills. I don't need you to tell me. The fact is I like them. I like how they make me feel, which is nothing. When I take them nothing matters. I don't have to think or feel anything. It's my happy place."

"I understand how you feel, Pen, I really do, and you have to believe me when I say that. I know what that stuff can do to you, so please. Listen to me, will you?"

He turned his sightless eyes in the direction of her voice. "You have absolutely no idea how I feel so don't sit there all high and mighty and try to tell me that you do!" Pen was angry now.

"You're right. I don't know how it feels to have no memory or to be blind. But I do know about addiction. You don't remember but I went through it nearly two years ago. I finally recognized that I had a real problem, and I detoxed myself up in the hills. So yes, I DO know a lot about what you're going through. I'm your sister and I am not an idiot." She took a deep breath and went on. "There's a lot more that happened to me during the past year but I won't go into it with you now. Someday, we'll talk about all of that, but not today. But just for the record, you're not the only one with problems, so let's just quit the pity party, OK?"

"Sure, you've got problems, I can just imagine. What happened, your lipstick got smeared kissing your husband? Oh, wait, you lost an earring? What do you know? You've got your health and your looks. I've got nothing."

"Oh Pen, if you only knew how wrong you are!"

"Well then, sister dear, why don't you fill me in? What problems and troubles do you have?"

"Not today, I told you. When you're done with these pills we'll talk. But for now I want you to come home with me."

"I already told you to leave without me because I'm staying. Nothing you can do or say will change my mind so you're just wasting your time and your breath." He held his hand out with the empty cup. "Thanks for the coffee. I'm going back to sleep now." He went to lie back down, but thought better of it and reached over to the drawer at the bedside with his pills in it. Taking out the vial, he counted four out into his hand and deftly tossed them into his mouth. "Goodbye." He turned onto his side with his face to the wall.

Raven and Gus left the room, tears welling in Raven's beautiful eyes. This was her brother, the only family she had besides her husband. How could she possibly leave him like this? But what choice did she have? Pen might be a drug addict, but he still had a mind of his own. Impossible; simply an impossible situation.

Gus left a simple note for Maura on the kitchen table, then they left the house and headed back to Bozeman. There were still horses to feed and water.

Pen lay in his unending darkness, waiting for the pills to kick in. He wasn't sure just what he was actually feeling inside, but it occurred to him that he desperately wanted to remember someone, something, anything. Suddenly he knew: he wanted to belong, to someone? Somewhere? This vacuum he was living in was pointless, useless. He understood in that moment that he was going to have to make a decision. He was going to have to choose to live or to die. His oblivion would be permanent with death, or he was going to have to give that oblivion up and come alive once more. But he loved his drug-induced state—how he loved it! Why couldn't he just stay there and forget about everything else? Why was making a choice so strong in his mind?

The word "baby" echoed in the depths of his consciousness. "Baby." Who was having a baby? He tried hard to remember, but it was a supreme effort to recall anything of importance. Baby. Oh, right. Allie. Allie was pregnant with . . . no, it couldn't be his baby. Or could it? Was that even possible with the drugs he had been steadily taking? He didn't remember! He couldn't remember! Oh, that's right, he had awoken one morning to find himself in Allie's bed, and heaven help him, they had both been naked! She swore up and down that she was pregnant with his baby. His baby? He was going to be a father? If he had actually made a baby with someone, shouldn't he remember the act? Maybe he should, but he couldn't. He remembered absolutely nothing about that night. And where was Allie? He hadn't seen her for some time, and then Maura came and now he was here, at Maura's house.

But just the remote possibility of fatherhood was enough, in the end, to tip the scales on the side of life. If there was even a chance that he was actually going to be a father, how could he let the child grow up knowing his father was an addict and had chosen death over him? The hard fact was, he couldn't. He was going to have to live. He was going to have to somehow overcome his addiction and live, but how? He wasn't strong enough to do it on his own, he recognized that right up front. Oh, his saintly sister might have been strong enough to do it alone, but he knew he wasn't. He wondered if she had even told him the truth about being addicted once herself.

The stupor began to settle over him and he drifted slowly off to sleep once more. Sleep. Nothingness. Bliss.

Raven was silent most of the way back to Bozeman, in total contrast to her animated chatter on the drive to Billings. She had been so happy, anticipating bringing her brother home with her. And now? How could she just leave him there? Oh, Maura would do her best, but she had to work, and besides, it wasn't fair to leave her brother with anyone else.

"Gus?"

"Yeah?"

"What do we do, Gus? We can't leave him there like that! He's going to die if we don't do something, isn't he?"

"I know. I've been racking my brain trying to come up with something. There's got to be a way. There's got to . . . wait!"

"You have an idea?"

"What do you think about asking Pastor Benson to come down to Billings and stay with him? They were good friends before all of this, and he's a former addict so he knows the ropes, so to speak. What do you say we talk to him about it? If he can't come down to stay with Pen, maybe he'll at least have some ideas for us."

"Good thinking, my love. You're not only handsome, you're pretty smart, too! I knew there was a reason I married you!" She leaned across the cab of the pickup and planted a big kiss on her husband's cheek.

"Careful! I'm driving!" But he smiled broadly; he did so love his wife!

Chapter 11

Maura arrived home from work around seven forty-five that evening. She worked twelve-hour shifts, so she was scheduled three to four days on at a time and then the same off. Today was the last in a run of four straight days, so she had the next three off, and she was looking forward to her badly needed rest. Twelve-hour shifts were exhausting and at thirty-seven she wasn't getting any younger. It was exasperating to her that she didn't have the energy she did only a few years ago, and while she knew she would miss Pen after being with him for even that short period of time, she was also looking forward to some much needed down time.

Parking her car in front of her house, she turned off the ignition and leaned back in the seat, resting contentedly for a few moments before going inside. She had mixed emotions. While Aspen Windchase had been in her home only one night, she knew the house would already seem empty without him. There was something about that man, something she couldn't really identify, although in truth she hadn't tried too hard up until now to figure out her feelings. She realized that he was more than a patient to her; taking care of him over those months he spent in a coma had contributed to that awareness, and in fact he had never been far from her thoughts, especially after he had awakened that first day.

Sighing deeply, she gathered her purse and, opening the car door, gasped as the cold Montana night air hit her face. "Get over it, Maura. He's not your responsibility, and he's gone. You probably won't ever see him again." But she realized it would have been much easier for her if she hadn't had to rescue him from Allie's apartment. Her heart had melted within her when she had found him on the bathroom floor, the dried tracks of his tears mute evidence of his total despair.

She walked up to the front door, unlocked it, and walked in. The room was cool and dark. Not bothering to switch on the light, she removed her coat, draping it over a living room chair, and walked down the darkened hall to her bathroom. The house seemed abnormally cold and empty.

She switched on the bathroom table lamp with the soft lighting and proceeded to strip out of her uniform and underwear. Dropping the soiled garments in the laundry basket, she stepped into the shower, standing under the warm spray allowing the heat and steam to melt her tension away. When the water began to feel tepid, she quickly stepped out, toweled herself dry, and headed down the hall to her bedroom to get her nightgown and robe.

She screamed as she crashed into the warm, male body, and nearly fainted as strong arms caught her awkwardly around her waist.

"Oh! Hel . . . ! Aspen? Is that you? What on earth are you doing here? You scared me to death! I had no idea you were still here!" The adrenalin surge was quickly passing and her knees were suddenly weak. She began to sink to the floor, but Aspen tightened his grip and managed somehow to keep her upright.

"Sorry. I didn't see you coming." He smiled, apparently aware of his crude joke.

"You're not funny! Not one bit!" Maura was angry now.

"I'd slap you for that nasty trick if I thought I had the strength pull it off." She couldn't help it, she had been so scared, and then so relieved, that she started to cry.

Pen reacted in the only way he knew how; he gathered her close to him, one hand on her back while the other began to stroke her hair.

"It's OK. I'm here. I didn't mean to scare you, but I really didn't realize you were in the house. I can't see, you know that, but didn't you see me coming?"

"No, dummy, of course I didn't. I thought I was alone in the house and I was just walking along with my head down. And I hadn't turned on the hall light so it's kind of dark in here. Oh!"

It seemed to dawn on both of them at the same time that she was naked. Her body stiffened in his embrace and their faces turned scarlet in unison.

"Can you stand now?"

"Yes! Now let me go!"

He released her so suddenly she nearly fell and crashed into the wall. Pen reached for her again to steady her as he sensed her condition. He tried to be careful, but his hands managed to find places they shouldn't as he did his best to keep her upright.

"Sorry."

"You should be! Don't you realize I'm . . ."

"Naked? Yeah, I figured that out pretty quick." He smiled broadly at her.

"Oh!"

"Yeah, 'oh.' Hey, don't worry, I'm blind, remember? I didn't see a thing, so relax, Maura."

"Well, you may not have seen anything but you sure must have felt plenty, you creep!"

Pen laughed out loud at this. "Well, as a matter of fact, I have to admit you are correct about that, and I will confess it pretty well made my day."

She did slap him for that one. He released her and she stomped down the hall to her room. She couldn't remember being so frightened or embarrassed before in her life. How was she ever going to face him again? He would take one look at her and . . . oh, right, he couldn't see. Well, she was still embarrassed!

Pen used the bathroom, which was where he had been headed when he literally crashed into Maura, and then went to wait for her in the living room. He was pretty sure she would be fuming for a long time, and he knew she was going to want an explanation as to why he was still here.

His head was clearer than it had been in weeks. *Bumping into a naked, screaming woman will do that to a person.* He began smiling once more as he relived the incident in his head. It had been one of the few times in his blind state that he had really, really wished he could see, but he could smell, and Maura had smelled wonderful. The fresh, fragrant smell of her soaped body and clean hair had nearly overwhelmed his senses as he stood holding her, trying to calm her. He had spent countless nights naked in bed with Allie, but he didn't remember ever feeling with her the way he did with Maura. He wanted to feel this way forever. If only . . .

Maura marched into the living room completely covered from head to toe in a pale blue chenille robe buttoned up tightly at the neck. She had combed her hair out but hadn't bothered to dry it, and, unknown to her, its fragrance filled the air in the room. Flopping into a large easy chair, she crossed her legs and folded her arms protectively across her chest.

"OK, Pen, time to talk."

Pen had a somewhat dreamy look on his face, which was turned up toward the ceiling. He looked as if he were smelling something.

"What? Oh yeah, you want to talk." He lowered his head and turned his face toward the sound of Maura's voice.

"Why are you still here? Didn't your sister come down to get you?"

"She came, I told her I wasn't going, and I sent her home again." His face was set, rigid.

"So what do you think you're going to do? I can't take care of you, Pen. I have to work and you and I both know you can't be left alone anymore."

"I know. I know I'm an addict now." He turned his face away from her with that admission. "It didn't matter before, but now, I guess it does, doesn't it?"

"It always mattered, Pen. You just didn't know it. But tell me, why does it matter to you now? What's changed in your world?"

"A lot."

"Like what? Give me something here."

Just then the phone rang and Maura rose to answer it. Raven was on the other end and she was excited, her words spilling out in such rapid succession Maura had a little trouble keeping up with her. The call was short, however, and Maura thoughtfully hung up the receiver and then sat down again.

"That was Raven. She's coming down again in two days with your pastor, Dave Benson. Sounds like he's going to be staying with you when I'm at work."

"Sorry, but I don't remember anyone by that name."

That's part of the reason she'll be coming down with him. Somehow we're going to work all of this out. We're going to get you back, Pen, all the way back. Please don't fight us on this."

"I won't fight you. I won't stay with my sister, but someone I don't know, like this Benson person, well, that's OK I guess."

"You're willing to live with me or Allie, but not your twin sister? That makes no sense, you know."

"Maybe not to you, but it makes perfect sense to me. You, Allie, Benson—you're all nonthreatening to me. I can't really explain it, but Raven makes me nervous somehow. Gus, her husband is OK, but there's something about Raven I'm not comfortable with yet."

"OK, I'll accept that for now." She took a deep breath. "But before that phone call I think you were about to tell me what had changed for you and why you seem ready to face your addiction all of a sudden. What's going on, Pen? Most addicts are not willing to get help, but all of a sudden you're not fighting it. Why?"

"Allie's pregnant."

"What?" Maura gasped audibly. "She's pregnant? She never told me anything about that when I got the keys to her apartment!"

"Yeah, well, she is most definitely pregnant. By the way, where is Allie anyway? She just sort of disappeared and then you showed up."

"Allie ended up in jail. She got picked up buying your precious pills for you. You didn't know?"

"Of course I didn't know. How could I?"

"I guess you were pretty out of it for quite some time, weren't you? So why do you seem so alert right now? When was the last time you took some pills, anyway?"

"Well, I meant to take a few when I went to the bathroom, but running into a naked woman sort of diverted my attention and priorities, you know?" He smiled ruefully. "I really am sorry I scared you, but I have to admit I'm not sorry about keeping you from falling." The rueful smile morphed into a happy one.

"Don't remind me." Her face flushed once more at the memory. "Go on. What were you going to tell me earlier?"

"She says I'm the father." He closed his eyes tightly in his agony at this disclosure.

"What? You're the father? You and Allie . . . ?"

"I said that Allie says I'm the father. Frankly, I don't know how on earth that can be possible, but she swears up and down it's the truth, and if in fact I really am going to be a father, it seems I have to do some extreme sobering up, and fast."

Maura's face betrayed her shock at this news. Pen was lost to her forever with his announcement, and the emptiness she suddenly felt was devastating. She couldn't help herself; she wanted to know everything.

"How did this happen, Pen? Can you tell me the whole story?"

"Sure. I'll tell you everything." And he did.

"Allie took really good care of me, Maura. She didn't have to rescue me from the Rescue Mission," his lips curved upward at his lousy joke, "But she did, and I can't thank her enough for that. She took me home and disrupted her life for me. She was really good to me, and I have to confess, I like Allie. I like her a lot. But I'm also pretty sure that I never walked down the hall to her bedroom that night. It's true that I woke up in her bed one morning and we were both naked, but I still don't think it would have been possible for me to get down that hall by myself. Even with all the pills I've been taking, it doesn't make sense that I would forget crawling into bed with a woman and . . . well, I really think I would have some sort of memory about something like that."

Maura's forehead was pinched as she thought very carefully about all Pen had just related to her.

"Pen, I'm afraid I'm going to have to agree with you. Frankly I don't see why, let alone how, you could have gotten up after taking all those pills and made it down the hall to her bed. You should have been too stoned to even have a thought like that enter your head, you know? Even if you, well, I really doubt . . ."

"That I would have been able to perform? Is that what you want to say? Well, you're right. I don't think I could have. I told her all of that and she still insists the baby is mine." He lowered his head into his hands, his elbows resting on his knees.

"Maura, what on earth am I going to do? What if, in spite of all logic to the contrary, I really am going to be a father? I know I have to take responsibility, but how can I? Look at me! I'm blind; I crash into walls, knock over glasses, I can't even see if I shave clean or not! I have no memory, no job skills—there's no way I can support a family! And on top of that I have to face the fact that I am an addict. I haven't been clean for weeks, probably months. Who knows? I sure don't remember!" He sighed deeply. "And what's worse, I'd do just about anything for a few pills right now." He raised his head, staring in the direction of Maura's voice, the pleading look on his face unmistakable. Pen was lost and very desperate.

"I'll get you a few. Stay here and I'll be right back."

Very softly, she heard "Thank you" as she rose to get some pills and a glass of water for him. Detoxing could wait for another day.

It didn't take long. His unseeing eyes began to glaze over, the lids half shut. His speech became more slurred and he slumped in his chair. Maura was deeply saddened at the sight before her. Where was Aspen Windchase, the real Aspen Windchase? Sitting across from her now was only a mere shadow of the man she knew he really was, deep inside. Was the real person lost forever or could she, Raven, and Pastor Benson somehow get him back? *God, we're going to need a lot of help from you. A lot. Please Lord, be with us and especially with Pen. He needs your touch more than he will ever know. Thank you Lord for answered prayer.*

Pen was gaunt, pale, and listless. He had become somewhat animated as he told Maura all that had happened with Allie, but the Valium and Tylox were back in his system now, and the spark had left. She looked away from him and then back again. Tears sparkled in her eyes as she noticed the tremors now controlling his limbs.

"Pen, let's get you up and back to your bed while you can still move."

He waved his arm in the air in an act of dismissal. "I can just sleep here in the chair. Leave me alone"

Maura rose and, picking up his cane, she shoved it into his right hand.

"Now, Pen. Get up. I'll help you back to bed. You can't sit up here all night."

He tried to argue with her, but in the end her nursing experience won out and he was soon lumbering down the hall to his room. Listing from side to side, it was an effort for him to remain upright, but somehow he managed with Maura's help to make it back to his bed. He was asleep in moments, oblivious to Maura's presence.

She sat on the bed next to him, lost in thought. It was so sad. This handsome, once vibrant man was so very lost. He would be depressed enough at his condition when he awoke from the coma, but the drugs on top of it must surely render him suicidal. She couldn't even begin to comprehend all that he must be feeling when the drugs started to wear off. And now Allie was claiming he was the father of her baby? He couldn't take care of himself; what made her think he could be a father in any capacity? He was lucky to get himself to the bathroom at this moment in time. The muscle tremors she had seen earlier were a telltale sign that his addiction was slowly killing him. She hadn't noticed the tremors before today. She would have to watch closely; incontinence would be next. Somehow, some way, they had to get Pen, the real Pen, back.

She reached over to lightly stoke his stubble-roughened cheek. So very handsome, she thought. So beautiful. Her hand cupped his jaw and rested there lightly.

In what seemed like slow motion Pen's hand came up to cover hers. He held it there for a few seconds, seeming to want to keep the comfort there as long as he could, but the stupor overrode his desires and his hand fell back to the bed.

Maura rose and softly closed the door behind her as she left him sleeping.

Chapter 12

Maura left him alone when she went to work the next morning. He would probably be OK as long as he wasn't detoxing. He would just stay in his stupor, happy to be left alone. When they started cutting down on the pills it would be a different story altogether. Someone would probably need to be with him all the time.

A rehab center had been discussed, but none of them could afford it and when it was mentioned tactfully to Pen he had adamantly refused. If they tried to make him go he would overdose the first chance he got; he made that very plain. He was willing to go through his withdrawal but not in any "public" place. The only reason he was willing to even consider detoxing at all was that "baby" that hovered just beyond his reality. He actually vaguely remembered touching Allie's stomach and feeling the reality of her baby there. He had forgotten everything else in his life; why couldn't he forget that? But even though he remembered the baby, it remained surreal to him.

Sometime that afternoon while Maura was at work, Pen got up out of bed and stumbled his way to the bathroom. Lurching from side to side, careening off of one wall only to bang into the opposite wall in the hallway, he suddenly forgot why he was up and slid to the floor, his back against the wall.

He never noticed the tremors shaking his limbs or the liquid warmth spilling between his legs. Pen was more lost than he had ever been in his life.

Maura came home around seven-thirty that evening to find Aspen sprawled spread-eagled on the hallway floor, his pajama bottoms still wet. The odor of rank sweat and urine assaulted her nostrils. A tear slid silently down one cheek. She sighed as she turned and walked out of the house and back to her car. An hour later she returned with a supply of Texas catheters. Then she called in sick for the next day.

It took her nearly two hours to get Pen cleaned up and back to bed. She put a catheter on, attaching the bag to his leg and, neglecting his pajamas, pulled the covers up over him, and left him sleeping, snoring softly. He barely roused the whole time, and he was mostly dead weight.

The phone began ringing as she sank heavily, tiredly, into a chair in the living room. It was Raven.

"Maura, I'm sorry to tell you this, but we won't be able to get down to Billings for another few days. Something has come up with Pastor Benson and he just can't get away right now. Is there any chance at all that you can stay with my brother until we can get down there?"

Maura covered the receiver with her free hand, and then sighed deeply. She really had no choice unless she called an ambulance and simply had him transferred to the ER. Taking a deep breath, she plastered a smile on her face and spoke into the phone. "You do whatever you have to do, Raven. I've got some vacation time coming so I'll just take a week off. I don't think he should be left alone anymore."

"Has something changed? What's wrong?"

"Well, he seems to have gotten worse over the past couple of days. He's having muscle tremors more and more frequently, and I think we have to start detoxing him right away. I don't think we can wait until you get back down here, so I will just take some time off of work and start cutting back his pills right away." She did not tell Raven that her brother was now incontinent.

They talked for a few more moments before Maura replaced the receiver. Resting her head in her hands, she began planning her actions for the next few days. She would let him have whatever pills he wanted tonight, but tomorrow morning things were going to change. It was going to be pure hell at her house for a while.

Maura rose early and put on a pair of scrubs she kept to wear around the house. It was the beginning of several twenty-four hour shifts without pay. Fortifying herself with a strong cup of coffee, she began the new routine.

First things first. She went through any part of the house that Pen may have entered and gathered every pill container she could find. Valium, and Tylox, his favorites, and then every aspirin, Tylenol, and Advil bottle she kept on hand for her occasional head and body aches. If it remotely resembled a pill, she took it. Gathering them all up, she put all but two Valium containers into an empty shoebox and walked out to the garage. There she carefully hid the box behind some similar boxes that stored Christmas decorations on a high shelf. Standing back to survey her work, she was satisfied that even in a desperate search, which she knew would be coming, without going through every single nook and cranny in her house they would never be found. She thought about flushing them all down the toilet, but then thought better of it. There was time enough for that later, when he was totally detoxed, but for now, she was a little concerned that she might need them in an emergency.

Leaving the garage, she went to her office and deposited the two Valium bottles she had kept in reserve into a small fireproof safe where she stored her important papers. She kept seven Valium out and put them in her pocket. The rest she locked up in the safe. Exiting her office, she locked the door carefully behind her.

Pen had taken a handful of pills sometime during the night from the stash he kept on his nightstand. Mid-morning, he woke up, looking for his next fix.

Maura heard noises coming from his bedroom, took a deep breath, and went in to face the dragon in his lair.

Hearing her enter, he looked up. "Maura, I can't find my pills. Did they fall on the floor or something? Help me find them, will you?"

"They didn't fall on the floor, Pen, I took them. Do you remember that old saying, 'today is the first day of the rest of your life?'"

"No, I don't remember that," came his slurred response. "What's that supposed to mean? Doesn't matter, I just need my pills."

"It means just what it sounds like. You're starting a new life as of today."

Pen scowled. "What little memory I have tells me I already started a new life when I woke up from that coma. Isn't that new enough for you?"

"Remember when you told me about you and Allie and her baby?"

"So? What about it?"

"Well, don't you think it's about time you sobered up permanently?"

"I thought we were going to wait until my sister and that pastor person came down here. They aren't here so how about you find my pills for me?"

"They can't make it for a few days, so it's just you and me, and we're going to start without them. I took a week of vacation, so we're going to make a new man of you starting today."

"What's that supposed to mean? No more pills? You can't just shut me off, Maura, I can't do it."

"No, I won't just shut you off. But starting this morning, you're going to go an hour longer between your fixes, and I'm cutting the pill count one at a time."

"Maura, I don't . . . I don't think I can do it. I need them too badly. Let's wait a few more days."

"Pen, it's me and you, here, starting right now, or I call for transport and you go to the ER and then to a rehab facility. What's your pleasure?"

"No! No more hospitals or centers or whatever. I've had enough of those places." He smiled ruefully. "I probably don't even remember them all, do I?'

"It doesn't matter if you remember them or not. But the ride is over, Cowboy. You're getting clean if it kills us both in the process. You have a sister who loves you and wants you back. And whether or not Allie's baby is really yours, until that issue is resolved one way or the other, you're going to have to be stone cold sober to settle it."

Pen was angry. His face became flushed and his hands shook involuntarily. His jaw clenched.

"Give me the damn pills Maura! Now!"

She carefully counted out four Valium. There would be no more Tylox.

"Hold your hand out, Pen. I'm cutting you down, but I'm not cutting you off all at once. I'm not sure just how many you were taking at a time, but here's four Valium. You're all done with the Tylox. No more of that, sorry."

He held his hand out, palm up, like an obedient child. She dropped the four Valium into his hand and he closed his fist around them.

"There. And here's your water."

"Thanks." His hands were shaking so badly she had to steady the glass for him as he drank.

"Do you get it now, Pen? You're so far gone you can't even get them down anymore without help."

"Yes I can. You don't know what you're talking about so just shut up, will you? You can leave now. I don't need you for anything else, so go."

"Fine. I'll come check on you in a few hours. Go ahead and sleep for now. I'll be in the other room if you need me."

Pen was already lying on his back, somnolent, back in the void he loved so well. She drew the covers up over him before she left the room.

About four hours later she heard a thud as Aspen crashed into a wall. He was up, and looking for either the bathroom or more pills, or both.

She found him still in his bedroom, his sightless eyes glazed.

He heard her enter. "Maura? Is that you?"

"Yup, me and no other. What do you need, Pen?"

"I need to go to the bathroom and I need some more pills. And you'd better hurry!"

"Pen, you have an external catheter, remember? We talked about it yesterday." She had explained it all to him when she applied one after finding him incontinent in the hall. Obviously, he had forgotten.

"What are you talking about, anyway? I just need to get to the bathroom. Are you gonna help me or do I crash my own way there?"

"Pen, you have a catheter. I can help you to the bathroom, but if you don't make it in time, well, let's see how it goes."

"What?"

"Pen, run your hand down your left leg and you'll feel it. Then maybe you'll remember."

He proceeded to pat his right upper outer thigh.

"Here." She carefully took his free hand and placed it over the bag attached to his left inner thigh. "Feel it?"

"Yeah, I feel something." Suddenly it dawned on him that he was standing naked in front of her.

"Where's my pajama bottoms?"

"Do you remember passing out on the floor yesterday? When I got home from work I found you lying there, totally out of it and soaking wet. It was just too much trouble to put pajamas back on your uncooperative bull-headed self. I got you cleaned up and the catheter on, but I couldn't handle much more after I finally got you back to bed." She laughed at the incongruity of the whole thing. "It's not like I haven't seen you naked before, is it? I took care of you in the rehab center for months."

"Well, we aren't there now, are we, so I think I'd like to be covered, thank you very much! It may not matter to you but it does me, at least right now!"

"OK. Stand still and I'll be right back" She turned to leave him.

"Hold it! What happened with getting me to the bathroom? I told you I need to go now!"

"Fine. Come with me and we'll get you covered later." She took his arm and led him down the hall to the bathroom. She helped him undo the catheter and left him, listening closely, hoping he was oriented enough to stay upright. He apparently was.

When he was finished, he called for her to help him back to bed, but Maura had a different idea. The wash up she had given him yesterday had been OK in a pinch, but the stinky man needed a shower pretty bad.

"Pen, let's get you into the shower before you go back to bed, OK?"

"I don't want a stupid shower. I just want my pills and to go back to bed."

"Well, here's the deal, Pen. You take a good soaking shower or bath, your preference, and I'll get you some of your precious pills. How's that for a trade?"

He scowled quite fiercely at the sound of her voice, but he could tell from her tone that she wasn't going to negotiate, no matter what he said.

"Fine. Give me the pills first, then."

"Nope. Shower or bath first. What's your pleasure? I don't want you passing out and making more work for me. While you're soaking I'll get some clean sheets on the bed for you. So what do you want? Shower or bath?"

"Shower."

"Fine. Sit on the stool and wait here for me. I'll be right back."

He did as he was told. She returned in seconds with a plastic lawn chair that she placed in the tub. Taking his hand, she guided him to the tub and helped him in.

"I put a lawn chair in here for you to sit on, just in case you get faint or something. Here's a washcloth and the soap's just to your left. Anything else you need?"

"I don't need any stupid chair. You can take that away."

"The chair stays. You might feel differently after you stand in hot water for a few minutes. When was the last time you took a shower, anyway?"

"I have no idea. Don't know. Don't much care. Now go."

"I'll listen for the water and come back when you shut it off. Bye."

He turned the water on, slowly increasing the temperature until the water was steaming hot. It did actually feel good. He had forgotten how nice a good hot shower could feel. He found the soap and lathered up all over, finishing by washing his glossy black hair, a gift he shared with his twin from their half-Crow Indian father. But he wanted his pills. He wanted . . . what did he want? He couldn't think clearly enough to focus on anything. Pills. He wanted more of his pills.

Slowly, imperceptibly, he began to feel light-headed. Maura had been right; he did need to sit down. He sat with his head down, basking in the hot spray. Eventually the water lost its heat and became tepid. He roused enough to shut the water off, but remained seated, waiting. For what? Pills. And Maura.

She had been listening for the water to shut off. Several times she leaned against the bathroom door, her ear close, trying to determine if he needed help or not, and then left again when she heard nothing.

"Are you finished? Ready to get out?"

"Yup, all done. You were right. It did actually feel pretty good. But my pills, did you bring my pills?"

"They're right here in my pocket."

"Good. Let me have them."

"As soon as you eat something, I'll give them to you."

"I don't want anything to eat. Just the pills."

"You haven't been eating much of anything lately, and you've got to start getting some food into you. You've been losing weight, and frankly, you look terrible. I never knew such a handsome man could look so awful!"

"I said I don't want . . ."

"Too bad. Here's your towel. Why don't you just wrap it around yourself after you've dried off and use it for a robe of sorts? I leaned your cane against the vanity. When you're finished in here, come on to the kitchen and I'll have breakfast for you. Bacon and eggs, how's that sound? Most men like bacon and eggs."

He wished he could remember if he liked bacon and eggs or not. Right now he didn't much care. He just wanted his pills and would do whatever he needed to do to get them. If it meant eating, so be it. He would eat. At least a few bites to make his keeper happy.

Wrapping the towel around his waist and securing it, he found his cane and tapped his way to the kitchen where the smell of fresh bacon should have tempted his taste buds, but today smelled nearly repulsive. It had been so long since he had eaten real food that his stomach was already in rebellion mode.

"Maura, I'm sorry but I don't think I can eat anything. I really can't. I don't think my stomach is going to let me."

"Three bites each of everything, that's all I ask. Then you get your pills. Here, find a chair and sit down."

He sat and she put a plate in front of him. He found it with his hand, and like a child, dutifully put one forkful after another into his mouth until he had eaten his required three bites of poached egg and three bites of bacon. There was also a piece of toast which he ate as instructed. His stomach immediately cramped up on him, but he kept it down.

"Want to sit up in a chair for a while and let that food settle?"

"No. I want to go back to bed. Give me my pills."

"I'll give them to you when you get back to bed. By the way, I have to tell you, you smell a whole lot better now than you have since you got here. Thanks for taking the shower. I appreciate it."

"Sure. I'd say anytime, but let's not push it. I'll see you later, I guess. I'm pretty tired. That shower wore me out more than I thought it would."

He headed for his room, and Maura followed close behind. She had a pretty good idea what was coming over the next few days, and it was time to be prepared.

"Why are you following me? Don't you think I can even get myself to bed? Just put my pills on the bedside table and then go away. I can get to bed and take my pills by myself. I learned a few things at that school."

Maura put on her professional nurse persona, removing her attitude of friend.

"One more thing. We need to put another one of those Texas caths on you before you go to sleep."

"What? Are you crazy or something? I'm blind, not a little bedwetting baby! I don't need one of those!"

"Pen, you were incontinent yesterday, and the odds are pretty high you are going to be again, so just put this on for me and save us both a lot of embarrassment and work later."

"I will not!"

She played her trump card. "You will if you want those pills! Here." She removed a catheter from its bag and held it out to him. "Can you put it on yourself or do you want me to do it for you? I think I can walk you through it if you would prefer to not have my help."

"Leave me a little dignity, will you? Just tell me what to do and let me try to get this thing on. If this is the only way I'm getting my pills, then I guess I have to do what I'm told. At least for now."

With her instruction he was able to get the catheter in place but was having a little trouble figuring out how to secure it to his leg. She leaned over, and guiding his hands, between the two of them it was soon secured.

"OK. You can go back to bed. At least now I don't have to worry about changing the bed later!"

"Whatever."

"Hold out your hand. Here are your pills."

He took them gratefully and sank back into the pillows. Oblivion. He wanted oblivion; no, he NEEDED oblivion! He needed that awful, depressing, grayness to surround not only his physical body, but also to permeate his brain, to the point that there was room for nothing else. Just the void. His friend.

Chapter 13

Three days passed with little change in Pen, and then on the fourth day the real horror began for both of them. In two more days Raven and Gus were driving down with Dave Benson, who would be staying with Pen while Maura worked. She wondered if she was going to survive until then.

Being a nurse, Maura pretty well knew what to expect, but even with her experience and knowledge, that fourth day alone in the house with Pen was beyond anything she had actually imagined or dealt with before.

Pen was waking up. She had cut his pills way down in number and frequency, and it wasn't going well. Pen was no longer able to retreat into his favorite place of nothingness, and he was mad. He also ached pretty much all over, and the good Christian man who had seldom sworn since he was a little kid on the Reserve in Canada spit out expletives non-stop.

That afternoon he began sweating profusely, drenching the sheets in minutes. Soon after that the seizures began. Maura would have done almost anything to send the man off to rehab somewhere, anywhere, but she was stuck with him, and it wasn't pleasant.

She had been expecting the seizures, but it was still disconcerting when he started having them. They began with petit-mals; he became suddenly very still, his vacant eyes staring straight ahead into nothingness. These usually lasted less than a minute, but it wasn't long before they accelerated and he began to thrash uncontrollably. She managed to restrain him with bed sheets that she tore into strips. Never leaving his side, she became exhausted; but she stayed, knowing it was far worse for him than it was for her.

She was glad she had brought the catheters home as he had become totally incontinent. He was not eating or drinking, and probably wouldn't for another day or two. She began nearly forcing him to drink water whenever he was physically able to do so. She had to keep him hydrated or he could end up with even more problems.

Later in the afternoon the hallucinations began as the seizures tapered off. He was mumbling: there were men in the room. Once there was a huge bear and he couldn't figure out why no one was chasing him away. Then there were butterflies all over the room; butterflies of all things! His mind took him many other places she couldn't understand, but she stayed with him. And at times her tears flowed unnoticed.

Aspen was somewhere. He was nowhere. His world wasn't gray now, it was nearly black. He was lost. *Where are you? No, wait! Don't leave me! Please don't go! Please! I'm . . . I'm . . . what am I? Where am I? Mom? Please come back, Mom. I'm all alone in here and I'm scared. Please don't leave me!*

His hands and legs were free now. It seemed like not long ago that he couldn't move at all. It felt good to be able to move, but now he didn't want to. He wanted . . . what did he want? He didn't know. No, that wasn't true. He wanted his mother. His right arm extended into the empty air, fingers outstretched, reaching.

"Mom? Mom, please don't leave me! Not again. Please!"

Maura took his cold, clammy hand into her own and held it to her chest. "I'm here, Pen. It's OK. You're going to be OK, just hang in there."

"Mom?"

"No, it's Maura. But I've got you Pen. You're OK and I won't leave you. It's scary, I know, but I'm with you, so hang in there, Cowboy."

Pen was once again a little boy of nine, before his parents had passed away in that awful flood. Before his world had crashed around him and the life he had known that had been filled with loving parents and stability was gone forever. Before he was left with only his twin sister for comfort, but who was also left bereft.

He missed being tucked into bed at night by his parents. He missed home-cooked meals. He missed the shine in his parents' eyes when they gazed at him. He missed . . .

He was alone, all alone. His world was dark, empty, and cold. Clasping Maura's hand tightly he reached out with his other arm.

"Mom, please hold me just once more." He was sobbing now.

Maura leaned over to lie beside him on his sweat-soaked sheets. Wrapping her arms around him, she comforted him as any mother might comfort her child. She hugged him and sang to him. She stroked his hair and his cheek, and the more she mothered him, the closer he nestled, seeking even more warmth.

Finally, finally, he slept, but the dreams haunted him still.

When he woke several hours later, he remembered nothing but a couple of his dreams. He definitely ached all over and felt exhausted rather than rested, but he was thinking at least a little more clearly; his speech remained very slurred. But the dreams—he remembered two of them. One was about a birthday party. A beautiful woman with blue-black hair swirling around her shoulders, and she was holding a squirming puppy. There was a birthday cake with a black bird in icing decorating the top. Was this real? Had this actually happened or was it just a stupid dream that meant nothing, as most dreams do? In the other, he and a little girl were walking through the hills hand in hand, kicking rocks as kids do, laughing together. He wished he knew what was real and what was not. Was it an actual memory from his past or just a meaningless trick his brain was playing?

Maura left him and returned with a couple of cold meat sandwiches.

"Here, you haven't eaten anything all day, and you really do need to eat at least a little, so why don't you sit up and see if you can wrap yourself around one of these."

He stared vacantly in her direction.

"Need help to sit up? Here, I'll help you." She sat next to him on the bed, and taking both of his hands in hers helped him into a sitting position.

"Hold your hand out for me?"

He did as she asked and she placed half a sandwich onto his open palm.

"I don't think I can eat anything, sorry. I don't feel too good right now."

"Pen, you really need to eat at least a little. Just this half, please? I . . ." The phone began ringing in the other room

"I'll be right back. See how much of this you can get down while I'm gone, will you? There's a glass of water on the table "

He tried, he really did. He ate quickly, trying his best to do as she asked, but within seconds after the last bite was swallowed it all came back up. He swore violently.

Why hadn't he just died? It would have better for everyone if he had. Why hadn't they pulled that plug and let him go months ago? His memory of recent weeks and months was very fuzzy, but he remembered enough to know he truly wished he had killed himself when he had the chance. Death would have been better than this. His sister had told him he had been kicked in the head by a horse. Why hadn't it just killed him? Instead here he was, a blind, useless, piece of baggage. All he did was cause work for everyone around him. He didn't even remember who he was, for heaven's sake! What kind of a life is that? And now, he smelled the vomit that soiled his chest and upper thighs. He couldn't even see to clean himself up. He groaned as he acknowledged that even if he could see, he didn't have the strength to do it. *God! Can't you take me home now? I'm nothing anymore. Please just let me die. Please!* Tears trailed unheeded once again down his cheeks. Aspen Windchase was a totally broken man.

Maura entered the bedroom, relief evident in her voice.

"Pen, that was Raven. They're all coming down in the morning, a couple of days sooner than they had expected. We're going to get . . ." her voice trailed off as she took in the source of the sour smell.

"Told you I couldn't eat. Sorry. Couldn't help it." He turned his head away, facing the wall. He was sick, he reeked of vomit and sweat, and he was embarrassed. "Sorry."

She handed him three Kleenexes and left the room to return shortly with a couple of wet cloths and a towel.

"I'll get the majority of this cleaned up here, but you really need another shower. Think you can manage one or not?"

He shook his head. "No way. I'd never make it down the hall."

"OK. I'll just get you cleaned up in here."

"I . . ." He suddenly started seizing violently once more. Pen was still a long way from being detoxed.

When the seizure passed he lay as one dead. He hadn't thought he could be any more tired than he was after he tried to keep that sandwich down, but now he was so exhausted he didn't know if he could even make one finger twitch. He wanted to take a deep breath and give a big self-pitying sigh, but he couldn't even manage that. Once again a single tear escaped from beneath his closed lids.

Maura left him long enough to rinse a wash cloth in cold water, and returning to his room, she sat on the bed, placing the carefully folded cloth across his forehead, covering his eyes, and then covered one of his hands with her own.

Pen mouthed the word, "Thanks." Too exhausted to speak, he drifted off into a deep sleep.

While he slept, Maura gave him a complete bed bath and changed the sheets, rolling him from side to side as she tucked the sheets under him. It was a lot of work; emaciated as he now was, Pen was still a big man, and Maura was only average size. When she had finished and cleaned up the room again, she sat in the chair that guarded one corner of the room. It wasn't long before her head drooped and she began to doze off. Tired, uncomfortable, but unwilling to leave her patient alone, Maura considered her options and decided that as long as Pen was sleeping, she needed to sleep also. Rising from the chair, she crossed over to the bed and stood for a moment, watching him sleep. Then, before she could change her mind, she walked around the bed and lay down next to him, careful not to touch him anywhere.

She wanted to touch him, however. She wanted to curl up next to him with her arms around him and sleep in that position for weeks. But common sense reigned, and she kept her place. A girl couldn't help but dream a little sometimes, though.

The sad truth was, Maura was in love with Pen. She knew there was no future for her with this man, but love is never a respecter of proprieties or feelings. Maura was a very nice girl. She was smart, honest, and loyal. She was also very plain. Only two men in her past had ever found her worthy of dating, and they had both been former patients who had actually confused gratitude with attraction. Neither relationship had lasted very long.

Average height, average weight, and less than average looks; that was Maura Anderson. Medium brown hair, dull brown eyes, a nose that was too large for her face, and freckles that made her look like someone had spattered paint all over her did not make a physically appealing picture, and men seldom gave her a second glance. Her lips were her one redeeming feature: they were full and generous, but even they were not enough to detract from the overall dull visage she presented.

While Maura was plain, Allie was, well, men would probably describe her as "adorable." Allie was a natural strawberry blond with a perfect figure. She had a quick wit and was just fun to be around. She was also a very nice person and made friends easily. The simple truth was that Maura would never be able to compete with Allie on a physical level. It didn't matter that Pen was blind; there was simply no competition.

Aside from her lack of physical attributes and the reality that she was several years older than Pen, there was Allie and her baby to consider. She agreed with Pen that it didn't seem possible for him to be the father, but the fact that he had found himself naked in bed with her one morning and she had subsequently given him credit for the pregnancy left it a possibility. There was simply no way to disprove it. Maura was a Christian, and no matter how much she loved Pen, she would never come between him and Allie, especially where there was a baby involved. A relationship with this man was totally impossible and out of the question. But she could still daydream, so she did.

His blindness was not an issue for her; it didn't matter. She knew it was different for him, but for her it was simply part of who he was. She had never known him any other way. She had never seen him in a physically fit condition, but she loved the skinny, pale, morose man that he was anyway.

Was it really love she felt? Was she confusing pity for love? It was very easy to do that, she knew. But Maura had dealt with pity for others for years, and while she did feel sorry for Pen, it was far more than that. Maura had never been in love before, not once in her entire life, and because of that, she knew the difference. What she felt for Aspen was far more than pity, it wasn't going to fade when he left her house, and there was not one single thing she could do about it. Feeling sorry for herself, something she never did, she fell asleep.

Sometime during the next hour, Pen roused enough to turn over.

Someone, a woman, was lying next to him, he could tell by her scent, but that was all he could tell, and he didn't care to know any more. His mind remained in a fog and he was still having dreams, flashbacks, and hallucinations off and on during his now restless sleep. Reaching out to the woman, he wrapped his arm around her waist and pulled her to himself, resting his head on her chest. *Mom, you came back. Please don't leave me again! Please!* Comforted by her presence, he relaxed and sank into a deeper, curative sleep.

Maura was instantly awake at his touch, and nearly terrified as his arm pulled her close to his side. What . . . ? Rigid, she kept herself as still as possible, not wanting to disturb him any further. She felt him relax as soon as his head rested on her chest and knew he was sleeping, and in fact had never awakened. He had clasped her in his sleep. As his breathing deepened and slowed further, she also relaxed and allowed herself to enjoy this once-in-a-lifetime experience. Resting her chin on the top of his head, she drank in his scent. While his hair wasn't clean, her bed bath had him smelling a whole lot better than he had before. He smelled good. He smelled like Pen. Smiling, she returned his embrace and drifted off to sleep once more.

Pen was seizing again. Maura was roughly awakened by his clenching hands, grabbing her with a viselike grip as the seizure wracked his body. She tried to get free, but escape was not possible. She called out to him, hoping to break through, knowing even as she did so that it was useless. The bed shook as he seized, his unseeing eyes rolled in his head, and drool slid from the corners of his mouth through his clenched teeth. Unable to do anything else, Maura grabbed him back and held on as tightly as she could. While she couldn't stop the seizure, she could in fact keep him from injuring himself by keeping him tightly in her embrace. It was over in less than a minute, but that minute seemed more like an hour. Exhausted, he went limp in her arms as he slept once more.

Maura smiled to herself ruefully. Sure, she had allowed herself to daydream a little, but somehow this recent embrace they had shared in no way resembled the ones in her fantasies. He had sweated profusely as he seized, and he didn't smell nearly as good as he had earlier. But this man in her arms was still the one she loved, and safe in the realization that he was totally unaware of his surroundings, she slept once more along with him.

They stayed entwined off and on until early the next morning. Pen alternately seized, hallucinated, picked at unseen objects in the air, called out for his mother, and slept. Maura couldn't remember when she had been this tired; even when she slept, it was only dozing as she stayed ever on the alert for whatever he might do next. She had to admit that while holding the man she loved in her arms was pure bliss for her, she could hardly wait for Raven and Pastor Benson to arrive and relieve her.

Chapter 14

Maura had hoped to get a hot shower before Raven showed up, but there was no way she could leave Pen for even that long. She was tired, irritable, dirty, and fed up. Pen should have gone to a rehab center. That certainly would have been the best thing for all of them. But, well, "woulda, shoulda, coulda"—it wasn't happening. Oh, but she needed some time alone!

Raven, Gus, and Pastor Benson showed up around eight-thirty that morning. Raven flew out of the pickup, with the two men following close behind. They rang the doorbell and Maura nearly ran to let them in. Shift change! She was so very ready! She couldn't help herself; she grabbed Raven in a big hug, she was so happy to see her.

"Raven, I am so glad to see you—trust me, you have no idea. Your brother is definitely not an easy case. Sorry, I'm sure you don't want to hear that, but I'm just about done in. Thank you so much for coming."

"I'm sorry it took us so long to get down here, Maura, but we just couldn't make it any sooner. Anyway, I can't thank you enough for what you're doing for my brother."

"That's OK, better late than never."

"Anyway, let me introduce Dave Benson. Dave, Maura. Maura, Dave."

"Hi Mr. Benson, I'm more than happy to meet you."

"Nice to meet you too, Maura." He set the duffel bag down that was carrying his things and put his hand out to shake hers in greeting.

"By the way, do I call you Mr. Benson, or Pastor, or what?"

Raven interrupted, "Oh, I'm sorry, Dave. I just have a hard time calling you 'Pastor.' You're always going to be just Dave to me. Sorry. You know me. I have this thing about church and religion and pastors, but I'm getting a lot better, don't you think?" She flashed him a radiant smile.

"It's OK, Raven. I don't mind in the least. And Maura, just call me Dave, OK?"

"Whatever you say." She studied the pastor briefly, wondering if this man could actually be of any help or was he one of those pastors that was good behind the pulpit but useless in the real world.

At six feet tall, Dave Benson was well-built and straight. Bright blue eyes complemented the well-worn face, lined and tanned, that greeted the world. Pastor Benson looked nothing like the average pastor. He looked more like a cowboy who had been out on the range for two months. His smile, however, could thaw a glacier. Maura suspected there was a whole lot more to this man than she would ever know.

"Well, I'm sure glad you're here, all of you. I've about had it, let me tell you." She started when she heard Pen begin yelling in the other room. "Guess he's awake again. I'll be right back. I can't really leave him alone." She walked quickly to Pen's room, leaving her guests standing awkwardly in the front hall.

Dave gave a lopsided smile to his friends. "Looks like we're none too early, doesn't it?"

"I think I . . ." Raven started for Pen's bedroom.

Dave put a hand on her arm, stopping her from leaving. "No, Raven, you stay here."

"But I . . ."

"No, you shouldn't see him when he's like this. Trust me, you really don't want to, and I know for a fact he wouldn't want you to. Maura and I will take care of this."

"Gus, do something! I need to see my brother!"

"No, Raven, just do as the man says. That's why he's here, after all. When you were drying out, would you have wanted Pen to be there?"

Raven shook her head violently in the negative.

"Then let's give Pen the same courtesy." Gus gave his wife a warm hug, softening the blow.

Dave was ready to begin his part in the detox program. "I'll leave you two and go spell Maura now. She needs a rest, and I'm geared up and ready. I'll say good-byee, and I'll see you again in a few days, right?"

"Good luck, Dave. Hang in there, will you? We'll be in touch and whenever you two say it's the right time, we'll be back." Gus spoke for the two of them.

"OK, then. See you." Dave picked up his duffel bag, turned, and squaring his shoulders, walked quickly down the hall to Pen's room.

Raven and Gus, unsure, stood with their arms wound around each other for support. They needed to talk to Maura before they left, so they waited until she came out of Pen's room. It took only a few minutes.

"Sorry about that, but he can't be left alone, and when I heard him making some noise down there I had to go." Maura ran her fingers through her hair, looking very obviously exhausted. "I think Dave knows what he's doing; he managed to take right over and didn't need any instructions. Thank you so much for bringing him. There's no way I could get him through this detoxing on my own. I simply don't have the time or the strength to handle this."

Gus spoke up. "We're just sorry we couldn't get him down here any sooner, but as we told you, he had some personal things to clear up before he could leave for more than a few hours."

"How about a cup of coffee before you go?" Maura asked.

"Sounds good, if you're sure you don't mind. You look like you've been 'rode hard and put away wet,' if you know what I mean." Gus smiled warmly at her.

"I feel that way, too. Come on and follow me into the kitchen while I make that coffee."

Sitting around the kitchen table, each nursing a steaming mug, the question and answer session began. Maura tried to be careful in her descriptions, not wanting to alarm Pen's family nor present him as less a man than he really was. It was a delicate, fine line to walk.

Raven began. "So how is he doing? Is he going to be OK?"

"Oh, sure, he's going to get through this, but it's not an easy or quick thing, Raven. The side effects of withdrawal are not pleasant, and they're uncontrollable. Not only that, but they take a very long time to recede."

"What do you mean by a long time? Days? Weeks?" Raven was frowning.

"Well actually, sometimes it can takes months. You have to remember that Pen was taking both Valium and Tylox in very large doses. Since you didn't want him in a rehab center to detox, it's probably going to take close to a month at the very least."

"Maura, please believe me, it's not that we didn't want him in a center; we just couldn't afford it. We would do it if we had to, but the odds are pretty good we would lose the stable in the process. I love my brother more than anyone," she looked at her husband, smiled, and amended her statement. "Well, almost more than anyone."

Appeased, Gus gave her hand a loving squeeze.

"And Maura, we plan to pay you for all you're doing, we sure don't expect you to put yourself through all of this for nothing. We can't afford a licensed facility, but I'm pretty sure we can afford to pay you pretty well."

"You don't have to pay me anything at all, Raven, I . . ."

Raven cut her off. "No way, you're not doing this for nothing. We'll make it right with you, somehow, we promise."

Maura sighed. "Let's talk about this some other time, but not today, OK?"

"OK. But back to what's going on with him now. Just what is he going through, anyway? Can you tell us?" Raven leaned forward in her anxiety.

"Well, it's not pleasant and it's not easy. I started by cutting his dosages and increasing the times between letting him have anything. He's not doing too well, but that can't be helped. He had been taking so much of both pills that he built up quite a tolerance, so it's going to take longer to get the drugs completely out of his system, unfortunately."

"What do you mean by 'not doing too well'?" asked Gus.

How much to tell them? "Well, he's starting to hallucinate for one thing. And he's been having some mild seizures also." She didn't mention the grand mal seizures or his incontinence. "He's also having some nausea so it's hard for him to keep any food down. Oh, and he's started sweating profusely so I have to keep pushing fluids to keep him from getting dehydrated."

"Is all of this normal? Are these things to be expected?" Raven asked.

"Oh, they're perfectly normal, but then again, you have to remember that Pen as an addict was taking far more pills than the average addict, and getting away with it. But normal or not, he could hurt himself if he's left alone when he's awake, so someone has to be with him at all times. And as the drugs slowly leave his system he's going to have more and more trouble sleeping, so there's a lot less time off for whoever is watching him. That's why I needed someone to help me; there's no way I could do it twenty-four hours a day by myself."

"Got it. Maura, we can't thank you enough for all you're doing, can we Gus?"

Gus nodded in agreement with his wife, and then asked, "So what's the plan now that Dave is here? How are you going to work this?"

"Well, I took my two weeks' vacation so I still have about ten days off. Dave and I can work opposite each other; while he sleeps I can stay with Pen and vice versa. That should get us through the worst of this, and we'll just see how it goes from there. How long can Dave stay?"

"I think he was planning on at least two weeks, so it's coming out about right, isn't it?" Raven explained.

"Sounds good to me." Maura smiled ruefully. "All I know is that I need a good hot shower and a full uninterrupted night's sleep in my own bed! And that's where I'm headed as soon as you folks leave."

"We can take a hint," said Raven. "Are you sure we can't look in on him? I'd feel a lot better if I could see him, you know?"

"I do know, but I really think we should respect Pen's privacy on this one. You have to remember that in essence you're still strangers to him, and he would be very embarrassed to know you had seen him in this state."

"OK. You're the boss. We'll respect your wishes. But when CAN we see him?" Raven's eyes glistened with her disappointment.

"I'll keep in touch by phone, and just as soon as he's alert enough to know what's really going on and is willing to see you, I'll let you know. But stay realistic and don't be in too big of a hurry for that to happen. It's going to be a while. Remember that."

They rose from the table in unison and Raven walked around to give Maura a big hug.

"Thanks again, Maura. May God richly bless you for all you're doing. We'll talk again soon. Take care."

Maura kept back her own tears as emotions rose between them all.

"I will. Drive safely home, you two."

She walked them to the door, and after closing it carefully behind them, she sank into a chair in the living room and, resting her head on the back of the chair, fell instantly asleep.

She awoke nearly two hours later to loud moans echoing down the hallway. She had taken several steps toward her patient before she remembered that Dave was there now and she didn't have to worry. The responsibility for his care had shifted to her new assistant. *Thank you, God. Thank you for sending help for me.*

She decided to check in on the two of them anyway. While Dave Benson seemed to be competent, she really had no idea what qualifications, if any, he possessed to help in this situation. Being willing to help was nearly good enough, but she needed to know how he would handle some of the extremes Pen was very likely to be throwing his way.

She knocked softly before entering and found Dave sitting on the bed with Pen, holding his friend like a baby. Pen was rocking back and forth, moaning in pain.

Dave looked up at her approach. "Our friend has the mother of all headaches right now. I feel bad for him, but I also know there's nothing we can give him for relief, is there?"

"No, you're right. We can't give him anything right now. He's going to have to suffer through it. However . . ."

"Pen, it's Maura."

A low moan was his response.

"Pen, I'm sorry we can't give you anything for that headache, but I can get you a cup of strong coffee. Do you think you might be able to sip a cup?" She placed a hand on his shoulder, trying to connect with him.

"I . . ."

"The caffeine might help the headache a little. It's worth a try if you're willing. What do you think?"

Dave looked up at her questioningly. "Can we give him coffee? And do you really think it might help?"

"I know caffeine is actually a drug of sorts, but he's not going to live the rest of his life without coffee, I'm sure. And there's been some studies that suggest caffeine, by constricting the blood vessels in the brain, may help relieve headaches, at least a little. Works better in some people than others, but we won't know until we try."

"Pen, willing to try the coffee? I'm not going to make it if you're not going to drink it."

"I'll try. Anything's better than this!" His words were still slurred, but somewhat less than two days ago.

"Be right back, then. Hang tight, Cowboy." Glancing at Dave before she left the room, she asked, "Want a cup too?"

"That would be great, if you don't mind."

"Cream or sugar?"

"Straight black, please. And thanks."

She returned in about ten minutes with a tray holding three steaming mugs of hot, black coffee, one for each of them.

"Here you go. Hold your hand out, Pen."

He released the side of his head with one hand and held it out to grasp the cup. He was shaking so Maura handed him the mug and then kept her hand covering his to help control the tremors.

"I'll help you. Try to relax and believe this will help. Sometimes believing something seems to help it be true."

Dave released Pen and took his own cup of coffee.

"You've had your hands full here, haven't you, Maura?"

"You could say that. Even when you know what to expect it still surprises you sometimes. The worst of it is that I'm so tired now. It's been pretty much nonstop for the last four days. I can't tell you how relieved I am that you're here."

Pen was sipping the coffee a little faster as it cooled, and when the mug was half empty, Maura removed her steadying hand from his. "I think you can manage it yourself now, right?"

"Yeah, I can. But oh, my head! When will this stop?"

"I really don't know, but I do know that eventually it will go away. You have to remember that you were taking a LOT of pills on a regular basis, actually nearly around the clock, so it's going to take time to get it all out of your system."

While they drank their coffee Dave and Maura made small talk, providing a distraction for Pen. Twenty minutes after the first sip, Pen's breathing slowed and became more regular.

"Feeling better now, Cowboy?"

"Yeah, better. Here." He held his mug out for someone to take, which Maura did. Then he laid back down and was instantly asleep once more.

"Good job, nurse Maura," Dave complimented her. "I'll have to remember the coffee trick. Looks like it helped quite a bit."

"Thanks. Again, you just never know what's going to work and what isn't." She cocked her head to the side and then inquired, "Can we talk for a minute?"

"Sure. What would you like to talk about?"

"About you, actually. Do you mind?"

"Nope. Don't mind at all. What would you like to know?"

"Let me take this tray back to the kitchen and I'll be right back. I'd say let's get comfortable in the living room but I don't think leaving him alone even for ten minutes is a good idea right now. Maybe if he wasn't blind . . . but anyway, I'll be right back."

When she returned she made herself comfortable in one of the two chairs in the room while Dave took the other, crossing his legs comfortably while waiting for her to begin."

"OK, for a start, are you really a pastor? You sure don't look like any pastor I've ever met before. Not to be rude, just stating a fact."

Dave Benson laughed out loud. "I've heard that before, so don't worry about being rude. But yes, I really am a pastor. One of those 'born-again, washed in the blood, saved by grace preacher-men.' I'll admit I haven't been one all that long, only about five years now, but it's the best thing I've ever done in my life hands down."

Maura shook her head; it was hard to believe.

"OK, next question; you're here and you're willing to stay for two weeks, but do you have any idea at all what sitting with this man is going to entail? Have you ever helped to detox anyone before? It can get pretty wild, let me tell you."

Dave's smile left his face as memories seemed to wash over him, and he turned his head away from her. "No, I've never sat through this with anyone before. But I'm a former addict myself, so I've been through it. I know what's coming, Maura. I know all too well what's ahead for all of us here, and let me assure you, I can handle it."

Maura was silent. Perhaps she should have guessed that truth; his face betrayed that part of his story if one looked closely enough.

"I'm sorry, Dave. I didn't know."

"Of course you didn't. I haven't told that many people. There's not a lot in my life that I'm proud of before giving my life to Jesus, so I try not to talk about it too much. I suppose I could use it as a testimony for others, but I'm not there yet. I'm just thankful God forgives anyone, anyone at all, no matter what they're guilty of, as long as they repent. Let me tell you, once I 'saw the light' as they say, I repented, big time."

Maura didn't really know what to say to that confession.

"That's really as much as I prefer to say about myself, if that's all right with you. I figure you needed to know I was an addict and that I understand all of this, but the rest is private, if you don't mind."

"Got it. No questions about your past. However . . ."

Dave's winning smile was back. "However, what?"

"Well, I know a lot of men don't do well with sick people. I mean more than aches and pains, you know, well, for instance, if he throws up. Can you handle it?"

"I can take anything, Nurse Maura. I told you, I know what's probably coming and I'm here anyway. And no, I won't be calling you if he can't make it to the bathroom in time."

"But what if it's . . . it's diarrhea? Can you . . . ?"

Dave laughed. "I can and I will. I won't be calling you for anything unless I need something I can't find, how's that? I'm not squeamish and I won't quit on you. Trust me, I know what

I'm doing and I won't need any help. Your 'time off' is all yours and you can relax. I'll be fine."

"I'll take your word for it then."

"Good. Glad that's settled. Now, where do I sleep and when?"

"I only have the two bedrooms, so how about when I'm with Pen you sleep in my bed and vice versa. I can just change the sheets every morning when I get up. Oh—I'm assuming you won't mind doing nights. I normally work day shifts at the rehab center and it's hard to switch back and forth. Twelve-hour shifts OK with you? Except for today. I know it will be extra-long for you, but I really am beat."

"That will be fine. It's what I expected, actually. And don't worry about the sheets on your bed. If you have an extra blanket or two I can just roll up on top of the bed in that. No need to keep changing bedding."

"But . . ."

He smiled broadly at Maura. "No buts. Trust me, I've slept in some pretty rough places. A real bed with a blanket will do just fine."

"Well, if you're sure."

"I'm sure. Why don't you quickly show me around a little, like where you keep everything I'm going to need for him, and then go get some rest."

"Thanks. Come on and I'll show you where you can stash your toothbrush and where everything for Pen is kept."

She pointed out where she kept clean linens, a basin, soap, and clean pajamas, as well as where to stow his duffel bag. Then Dave went back to his post in Pen's room, and Maura headed for that hot shower.

It didn't take long after the shower for her to snuggle into her bed. *Thanks again, Lord. I think you sent just the right person for this job. Maybe it really is going to be OK.*

She slept for twelve hours straight.

Chapter 15

Dave Benson had actually hoped he would never have to deal with any detoxing in any way, shape or form, ever again. His own experience had been more than enough to last a lifetime. But Aspen Windchase was his friend, even if his friend had no memory of him, and if Pen needed him, then he would be there. The cost, whether physical or emotional, was of no consequence. But it was very hard to watch anyone go through this agony, let alone someone he cared so much about.

It was all so sad. Pen had been such a good, strong, honest man with his whole life ahead of him, and here he was blind, no memory, and detoxing. *I know life isn't fair, Lord. I understand that. But Lord, please help us get through this! We need you and your help; please enfold us in your promised peace, and help Pen, Lord. Thank you, Amen.*

That afternoon Pen started to wake up. From somnolence to agitation, he was running the gamut as the sedating effects of his chosen drugs wore off. At times he was loudly vocal, and at others he would simply sit up and stare out into his nothingness. He began wanting to walk anywhere and everywhere, but he was still too weak to manage more than a few steps. Dave kept pushing fluids as Pen continued to sweat profusely off and on. Conversation remained at a minimum due to Pen's hallucinations.

Through it all Dave kept calm and non-judgmental. While it was hard to watch, he knew Pen had to go through it, and he would have to go through it on his own. Dave and Maura could be there for support, but in the end the outcome totally depended on Pen himself.

Around five o'clock that afternoon Dave heard persistent knocking at the front door. Telling Pen to wait quietly, he left to see who was there since whoever it was obviously wasn't leaving. Opening the door a crack, he found a desperate-looking young woman.

"Can I help you?" Dave asked cautiously.

"I'm looking for Aspen Windchase, and I know he's here. I want to see him, please."

"Sorry, but he's not accepting any visitors. You'll have to come back in a couple of weeks." Dave started to close the door.

She wedged her foot in the doorway so Dave was unable to close it.

"I'm not leaving until I see him so let me in!"

"Look, I told you, you can't see him right now. Please leave." Dave was firm.

"He's the father of my baby and I'm not going anywhere! Now let me in!"

Dave's face paled. Father of her baby? *Pen, what have you done?*

"Look, if I can't see Pen, is Maura here? Let me talk to her. Tell her Allie's here. She'll see me, I'm sure."

"Nice to meet you, Allie, but Maura's sleeping right now. Come back later, as I said."

"Well, go wake her up. Now. I told you I'm not leaving until I talk to either her or Pen."

Dave sighed heavily. "OK. Come in and wait in the living room. I'll go get Maura. But you stay in the living room, do you understand? Step one foot down the hallway and I'm calling the police."

"Fine. I'll stay. Go get Maura."

After seeing Allie settled in the living room, Dave nearly ran down the hall to Maura's room. Entering without knocking, he shook her sleeping form gently.

"Maura, some weird girl named Allie is here to see Pen and she won't leave. I had to let her in. She's waiting in the living room; said she's not leaving until she sees either Pen or you."

Maura groaned and opened one eye.

"One more thing. She says Pen is her baby's father. Obviously, we're going to need to talk. You coming?"

"Yeah. Give me a second to get my bearings. Tell her I'll be there in a minute."

"OK. I'll tell her and then I'm going back in the room with Pen." He left.

Maura forced herself awake, then got out of bed, put on a robe and headed to the living room where Allie was waiting. She took a chair opposite Allie.

"What do you want, Allie? Why are you here?"

"Why do you think I'm here, Maura? I want to see Pen, of course. How is he?"

Maura liked Allie, she really did, and although she didn't like the fact that Allie had enabled Pen's addiction, she could understand how it had happened. Allie was not a bad girl, she had just made some stupid mistakes, and Maura knew that Allie really did care about Pen. Maybe she even loved him.

"Sorry, but he's not seeing anyone for a while. Didn't Dave tell you that?"

"I'm not just anyone, though, am I?'

"No, you're not just anyone." Maura lowered her gaze to Allie's abdomen.

"Why didn't you tell me you were pregnant when I saw you at the jail, Allie?"

"I didn't think it was a necessary piece of information for you, that's why. This baby is between me and Pen and has nothing to do with you."

"Let's back this whole thing up for a moment, OK? First of all, how long did you have to spend in jail and how long have you been out? I thought nowadays it was automatic prison time for what you were doing?"

"Let's just say I had a pretty sad story and a really good lawyer. Two weeks in the slammer and they let me go. I'm lucky, I know. Really lucky."

"I'm not sure lucky is the right word. I think perhaps God was watching out for you, don't you?" Maura paused, then, "How about your job? Are you going to be able to keep it? I'm worried about you, you know?"

Allie lowered her head. "Yes, they're letting me keep my job." She raised her head again, her eyes glistening with unshed tears.

"Maura, I know I did a really stupid thing by getting those pills for Pen, but I really didn't know what else to do! He wanted them so very badly, and I couldn't blame him. I can only imagine how I'd feel if I woke up one day with no memory and no sight. I wouldn't want to live either. At least if

I got him the pills, he was going to stay alive to take them. I wasn't sure what he would do if he got cut off. I knew he was depressed and suicidal, and I couldn't let that happen. I just couldn't. Can you understand at all?"

Maura sighed. She actually did understand. She may not like it, but she understood. "I think I do, in fact, understand. But you do realize how foolish it was, don't you? Please tell me you do."

"Yes, now I get it, and I'm sorry. But all of that aside, I need to know how Pen's doing. What's going on with him? Is he OK or not? And when can I see him?" She sounded desperate.

"He's detoxing and it's not pleasant. It's going to take some time; he's a pretty bad addict."

"But I want to see him, Maura. I NEED to see him! Please?"

Maura shook her head firmly in the negative. "Sorry, but no."

"He's going to be a father; we need to see each other."

"Are you in love with Pen, Allie?" Maura decided not to dance around the subject, and got right to the point.

"I'm having his baby aren't I? What do you think?"

"Actually, I don't think the baby you're carrying is Pen's. I don't see how that's possible."

"Well I don't really care what you think. It's my baby and I think I know who the father is."

Maura decided to let the question of paternity pass for now. Right at the moment it was not the most important item on the agenda. "Well, it doesn't matter because you can't see him now. Maybe in a couple of weeks. I can let you know, how's that?"

"You're really not going to let me see him?"

"No, I'm not. I will tell you that he is detoxing and having a rough time of it. Whatever your relationship is with him, I'm pretty sure he wouldn't want you to see him like he is right now. No one sees him except for me and Dave until he's done with the roughest part at least."

"Dave? Is that the man who answered the door?"

"Yes. Dave Benson. He's actually Pen's pastor from Bozeman. I couldn't do this myself and needed help; he agreed to come down and lend a hand, thank goodness. Now, I really need to get back to bed. Do you mind?" Maura rose from her chair and headed for the front door.

"Allie?"

"Yes?"

"I really am happy you're out of jail. You're a good kid, and I've always liked you. Be careful, will you?"

"I will. Thanks for seeing me, Maura. Will I be seeing you at work?"

"I took some vacation time to be with Pen, so it's going to be another week or so, but eventually I'll see you there."

"And you'll let me know when I can come back?"

"I will, I promise." Maura opened the door for her guest, then closed it firmly behind her after her exit.

Baby. Allie. Drugs. Pen. Lord, how much worse can things get? She shuffled down the hall and crawled back into bed. Morning would come soon enough.

Chapter 16

Maura and Dave settled into a routine that worked well for both of them. Maura stood her watch from six in the morning until six at night, when Dave took over for her until six the next morning. If Pen noticed any change in his care he never mentioned it. He was so focused on himself, on his body and all it was going through, he had no time or energy for anything else.

He was still hallucinating, raving, swearing, sweating, and becoming more agitated with each passing day. While still incontinent, the frequency was decreasing. He had only one episode of stool incontinence, which was a relief for all involved, and it happened while Maura was with him. She took it in stride like the professional she was. Pen was devastated.

His speech became clearer, with less slurring, and his concentration span was lengthening. He was increasingly more aware of his surroundings. He was also more aware of his condition, and he didn't like it. He began begging for pills. After begging came his attempts at bartering; he was willing to trade anything for a couple of Valium, but his pleas went unanswered.

As his agitation increased, so did his stamina. It was several days before he was strong enough to walk to the bathroom for a much-needed shower, but when he finally did, he enjoyed it so much he stood under the hot stream until the water began to run cold. He was sad about that; he would have stood under that shower for hours if he could. He began taking hot showers on a daily basis, happy to lose himself in the steamy environment, to feel good if even for a short while. Long showers helped him kill some time, taking his mind far away from his aches and nerves as long as he stood there.

He began to pace, wanting to walk constantly, unable to sleep. Being blind, night and day were indistinguishable for him, and he soon had them confused. He slept only when he became exhausted, usually mid-morning, and then it was never longer than two hours at a stretch.

Dave tried everything he knew to divert Pen's attention, but it was tough. With no memories, they couldn't talk about the past. Being blind and severely depressed, Pen didn't want to talk about any possible future. What future was there for a blind addict? He couldn't read, he couldn't play any games, and he couldn't reminisce. What could he do to pass the time? He paced and he swore.

Dave tried reading to him, but Pen wasn't interested in that. He couldn't focus on anything Dave tried to read to him. And always, he wanted his pills. If he couldn't have his pills, he wanted, again, to die.

And then, just when he thought he couldn't go even another minute, *"baby"* would sneak into his thoughts. *Baby. I'm going to be a father. I can't leave, can I? God help me, I have to get clean somehow! But God, I feel like there are bugs crawling all over me, I can't sleep—Lord I just want to die. Ah, but there's the baby . . .*

One evening while Pen was agitated and pacing the room, he miscounted his steps and crashed into a wall in the bedroom. Instantly angry, he barely hesitated before punching a hole in the wall with his fist.

"Pen! Hold up there, friend!" Dave was instantly at his friend's side.

Pen shrugged him off and prepared to take another swing at the offending wall.

"Aspen, stop! You can't tell me that putting a hole in that wall made you feel any better, so calm down. Don't do it again, for heaven's sake!"

"Leave me alone," came the growl. Just leave me alone."

"Pen, come over here and sit down. Let's talk a bit, shall we?" Dave was doing his best to divert his friend's attention.

"Why talk? What good's that going to do? I feel better punching the wall, I tell you."

"This is Maura's house and that's her wall. She's been pretty good to you, you know? Do you really want to pay her back by putting holes in her walls?"

"You don't understand, Dave. You have no idea how I feel, what I'm going through. I need . . . I don't even know what I need. I'm going nuts inside my head!"

"That's where you're wrong, Pen. I know all too well what you're going through."

"You're a preacher, so don't try to tell me you have any idea at all what's going on up here," Pen sneered at Dave as he pointed a finger at his forehead.

"That's where you're dead wrong, Pen." Dave lowered his head, remembering, and spoke softly. "I haven't always been a preacher, Pen. I was—no, I am—an addict, just like you. So yes, I do know what you're going through.

That confession brought Pen up short. He turned his head in Dave's direction.

"You're an addict? You? A preacher?" His obvious shock at Dave's confession echoed in his questions.

"Pen, my friend, I'm not perfect, just saved by God's infinite love and grace. Yes, I'm an addict. Heroin was my drug of choice for many years. You think Valium is tough? Try coming off of heroin. I know only too well what you're going through, and I also know punching holes in walls won't help anything. Why don't you sit down and we'll talk for a while?"

Pen didn't answer, but his hands dropped to his sides, and, turning, he counted the steps he had memorized to find his way to one of the two chairs in the room.

"OK, start talking. Let's hear your story." For the first time in over a week Pen was able to think about someone other than himself.

"Not today, Pen. I'm not up to it today. It's pretty personal and it's not pretty. So, some other time."

The fact that Pen had actually asked about someone else was a first. He was making progress at last.

Maura's two weeks of vacation were coming to an end. With only four days left before she needed to return to work, she and Dave decided it was time to switch Pen's nights and days around again. Pen would need to start sleeping at night like the rest of the world.

He was still agitated and restless, and it was difficult for him to sleep at all, but as he continued to process his thoughts more clearly and rationally, he did realize the necessity of keeping normal hours. While it made no difference to him, he understood it did to others. And something else was happening to him. He liked Dave. Dave was easy to get along with, easy to talk to, and after learning the man was an addict like himself, Dave became more of a friend. But he found that while he was comfortable with the pastor, he missed Maura; missed the sound of her footsteps coming down the hall, her subtle scent, the sound of her voice. As he slowly became aware that he preferred to be awake when she was around, he started doing his best to sleep more during the night and stay awake for longer periods during the day. He didn't care if he talked to Maura or not, he just wanted her around. Something about her relaxed him, soothed his nerves. But still the heightened agitation made it almost impossible for him to actually remain calm for any period of time.

One day as he was fidgeting and picking at the air, Maura had an idea.

"Pen, what kind of music do you like?"

"Stupid question. I don't remember anything, remember?" He smiled wryly at his attempt at making a joke.

"Well, if you don't care, why don't I put some music on? OK with you?"

"Whatever you say. Play whatever you like. If I can't stand it I'll say so and you can change it."

"Fair enough. I'll be right back." She left him just long enough to retrieve a boom box and several CDs.

"This is one of my favorites. Hope you don't mind it too much." She inserted a disc of classic hymns by the Oak Ridge Boys, and sat back as the first song began to play.

The soft sounds of "It Is Well with My Soul" filled the room, washing over them both. Maura glanced over at Pen and was amazed at the peaceful expression that appeared on his face. His eyes were closed, his face relaxed, his hands resting on his knees. She almost thought he had fallen asleep when suddenly his lips began to move. Shocked, she watched in awe as Pen began to whisper the words along with the song.

He remembered.

Maura's hands flew to her cheeks as she fully registered the fact that Pen was whispering the words in perfect sync with the CD. She said nothing but remained motionless as the next song, "Be Thou My Vision," began to play. Pen continued whispering the words, his countenance almost serene as he did so, his sightless eyes seeming to focus on something in the distance.

With no planned intent, she began to hum along with the singers. She was no more a singer than she was a beauty queen; in fact the Bible verse *"Make a joyful noise unto the Lord"* described her singing attempts perfectly. As she hummed along, totally out of tune, she watched Pen carefully.

He started to sing out loud, his voice pitch-perfect, deep, and clear.

Tears coursed silently down Maura's face. Finally, she could stand it no longer and rose impulsively to her feet. Four big steps had her inches from her patient, and she reached out to give him a true "bear hug."

"Pen, you're singing!"

At her touch he stopped immediately, apparently coming back to reality.

"Yeah, I guess I was, wasn't I." He rose to his feet and hugged Maura back. Hugs felt so good! SHE felt so good!

"Pen, don't you get it?"

"Get what? What's got you so excited, anyway? You like my singing or something? I don't think I sing all that great." He smiled at her.

"You stupid man! You were singing along with the Oak Ridge Boys!" She released him only to thump him on his chest.

"Well, I liked the song I guess. So what?" He looked truly puzzled.

"Pen, you were remembering the words! Don't you see? Your memory must be coming back!" She sniffled and wiped her nose with the back of her hand. "You big dummy! You remembered the words to the song! Two songs in fact!"

He sank back onto the chair in shock as the reality hit him. He had, in fact, remembered the words to those old hymns. *Lord God in heaven, thank you! Thank you, thank you, thank you!* He closed his eyes in silent prayer, acknowledging the source of this miracle, for in fact, that's what it was to him, a miracle. He sat there quietly, listening as the CD played to the end. There were twelve songs on it, and he knew the words to every one. Silence filled the room.

"Maura, can you play that CD again? Do you mind?" He wanted to hear the words once more, the words that sprang from somewhere deep within him as they became sound.

"Sure, anything you want, Pen. Your wish is my command." She started the boom box up again.

"I cannot describe to you what this is like for me, Maura. All I can do is thank you for playing this music. I think, no I am positive, that people have no idea how precious their memories are. They are taken for granted, and they shouldn't be. Ever. I realize words to songs aren't that big a deal in the grand scheme of things, but they're huge to me. Huge." He clapped his hands while grinning from ear to ear.

"Will you do me a favor?"

"Sure, what do you want?"

"I want another big hug from you, if you don't mind. I'm so high right now I need to share it somehow, and a hug seems like the best way there is. OK?"

If you only knew, Cowboy. She hugged him once more, a bittersweet smile on her face.

They stood that way for some time as the hymns played on. Pen hummed along from time to time, but he never released her. Finally, the room was quiet once more, and emotion was thick.

"Maura, will you do me one more favor, please?"

"What would you like now?"

"I want to 'see' you, like they taught me at that school. Do you mind?"

"No, I don't mind. Go ahead."

"You do realize it means I will be tracing you with my hands. It means touching you much differently than a hug. Still OK?"

She took his right hand in her own and raised it to her cheek. "Go ahead. But I warn you ahead of time, this is not a face to stop a crowd by any means. Hope you're not too disappointed."

He did not respond to that comment, but began slowly to trace the contours of her face, her forehead, her eyebrows . . . She closed her eyes as he gently ran his fingers across her closed lids. She held her breath as he learned the shape of her too large nose, and then, so softly she barely felt it, he outlined her mouth. Her eyes remained closed as he learned what she looked like.

Then, in slow motion, as one finger rested on the outer curve of her lips, he bent his head and kissed her. Gently, slowly, he learned her mouth with his own as he breathed in her scent. One hand found her waist as the other left her mouth to cradle the back of her head.

She remained still in his embrace, not returning it, but her lips soft and pliant under his. Then, suddenly, she pulled away, shock registering in her brown eyes.

"Sorry. Guess I shouldn't have done that. I took advantage of you and I'm sorry. It won't happen again, I promise."

She uttered only one word in response to his apology. "Allie."

Sucking in her breath, she turned from him, intending to leave the room, but he caught her arm, restraining her.

"Maura, don't go. Please. I said I was sorry. I don't know what came over me."

"Is that what you did with Allie? Did you just get carried away a little with her too?" Then softly, barely audible, "I thought you were different." She refused to turn back and look at him.

"No."

"What's that supposed to mean? Maybe that's what happened that night you and she . . ." Pain showed on her face, unseen by the one who caused it.

He heard the pain in her voice. "No, I never hugged her like I just hugged you. And no, I never traced her face. And most definitely no, I never kissed her. You've got to believe me; I'm telling you the truth."

She turned back to him then. "But you must have. You slept with her, remember? How dumb do you think I am? I should believe you never touched her?"

"Yes, you should believe that. Maura, I was completely stoned the whole time I stayed with her, remember? I didn't care about anything or anyone except for those pills I was taking. I didn't care what she looked like. Oh, I'll admit I like Allie. I like her a lot. She's a really nice girl, and she did her best to help me, but that's the end of it."

"And the baby?"

He raked his hands through his hair. "I still don't think that baby she's carrying is mine, but I can't prove it. I do remember waking up next to her in her bed, but that's all I remember. I'm still a man, even though I'm an addict, but I wasn't the least bit interested in anything beyond taking more pills. And I'm actually ashamed to admit I didn't care what she thought or what she looked like."

"So, what . . . why . . . ?"

"I honestly don't know. I was so elated about remembering something from my past, even if it was only words to songs . . . I guess I just got carried away. And I'm sobering up, as you well know. I was just so happy, and well . . ." He turned his head away as he released her arm. "I said I was sorry, and I am. No, let me rephrase that. I'm sorry I upset you, but I'm actually not sorry I kissed you. I didn't mean to, it just sort of happened. But whether you enjoyed it or not, I sure did. But I do promise it won't happen again."

Her silence was deafening.

"Maura? Can we still be friends or have I ruined it for good?"

She sighed deeply. "We're still friends. I'll get over it. I just need a little space right now. I don't want to leave you in case you, well, you know, you're still . . . But I need to get out of this room and I think you do too. Why don't you come with me to the kitchen while I fix us something to eat?"

He reached out for her once more. "Take my hand?"

"Nope. Take your cane." She left the room, Aspen tapping close behind her.

She fixed a couple of fried egg sandwiches. They ate together in silence, after which Pen tapped his way back to his room for a nap.

Maura made sure he was settled, and then went back to the kitchen to clean up the dishes.

Aspen Windchase was definitely sobering up.

Chapter 17

Pen couldn't go to sleep for the life of him. He heard Maura leave his room, assuming he was well settled. How could he possibly relax after what had just happened? No way! What had he been thinking? How could he go and kiss her like that? *Stupid! Stupid! Stupid!*

He had no answers to those questions, no matter how hard he tried to rationalize his actions. He tried to tell himself that while he was blind and coming out of detox, he was a long way from dead. He was still a man, after all, and with a woman he liked that close to him, well . . . He squeezed his eyes shut tightly, and then pounded the bed with one closed fist.

What was it she had said? "I thought you were different?" Why did it hurt so much that she had said that to him? Why did it nearly suck the air right out of him? If only he had just been content to learn her face with his fingers. He could have run his hand over her hair. He could have done almost anything but kiss her.

But he had. Kissed her. He had apologized; what more did she want? He had said he was sorry. But was he really sorry? No, he had to admit that just as he had confessed to Maura, he wasn't in the least bit sorry he had kissed her. While he had no memory of anything before his accident, he somehow felt in his gut that there was no lost memory of anything in his past that compared to that kiss. He was only sorry he might have permanently ruined any possibility of anything more in the future with her.

Future? What on earth was he thinking? There was no future with anyone for him! He was an addict, and once an addict always an addict. Oh, he might kick the pills, but the temptation would always be there for him. He still had no memory, although he smiled once again as he thought about singing along with that CD, how he had remembered words to the songs. Maybe there was at least a little hope that more would come back to him. But even if he managed to regain his memory, he was still blind. He couldn't work, couldn't ever support a family, he was still . . . useless. Not a man any woman would want on a permanent basis. Not a man any woman could ever truly love; and he now admitted to himself that he wanted that more than he wanted even his sight. He wanted someone to love him, to hold him when he felt so lost. He wanted . . . he wanted Maura. And he had just driven her away for good.

He lay there, going over every aspect of his relationship with his nurse friend. Why Maura? Why not Allie, who claimed he fathered her baby? Allie was a perfectly nice girl who obviously liked him and had taken her into her own home to help him out. So, why not her? He liked both women. What was the difference? Why had he kissed Maura but not Allie? Had he ever wanted to kiss Allie?

Yes, he had to admit to himself, he had wanted to kiss Allie a time or two, but only because he was a man and she was a great girl. They got along well together and liked each other. But kissing her would have been for fun and not really for any other reason. And the fact was that even though the thought had occurred to him, he had wanted his pills much more than he had wanted anything physical with her. He remembered her lying next to him, naked, in bed. He hadn't even been interested enough to touch her in any way, not even once. He knew she was there and that she was obviously willing, but he simply wasn't interested.

So that brought him back to the present conundrum: Why on earth had he kissed Maura?

Because he liked her, that's why. He liked her, he finally admitted to himself, the way a man likes a woman as a woman, not just as a friend. Was he confusing her generosity and kindness with something else? No. No, he wasn't. Did he love Maura? He didn't know for sure. He only knew he wanted to be around her whenever he could. He wanted to hear her voice, breathe in her unique scent, and listen to her footsteps as she walked through her home. He wanted to hug her again, to hold her close and feel her warmth. He wanted . . . what did he really want after all this introspection? He wanted to kiss her again, that's what he wanted. He wanted her.

Maura was beside herself. Her freckled cheeks were flaming red, and she was more than thankful the man was blind and had no idea what effect he had on her. *Lord, he actually kissed me, and I let him! How could I be so stupid?* Aspen Windchase was a man who had been deprived of everything normal in this world for nearly a year. Give any man in that condition a good, tight hug and see what happens! What had she expected?

The problem for her was not that he had kissed her, it was that she was in love with the man and he had no idea that she felt that way. She was not a stupid woman. He hadn't kissed her because she was special in any way, he kissed her because she was there and convenient. If he felt anything more than that for her he wouldn't have promised never to do it again, would he? Oh, he had admitted he enjoyed that kiss, but he was pretty quick to vow he would never do it again. Well, it was probably for the best. She was several years older than him, she was definitely not attractive, and there was still Allie and the baby to consider. There was positively no future for her with him. None at all.

But oh! That kiss, while a total surprise, was something she knew she would never, ever forget, and she certainly didn't want to.

While he had been learning how she looked with his fingers, she had been essentially mesmerized, frozen in place. She had never in her life experienced anything like it; the feelings he had aroused in her could not be expressed in words. She had come to the realization that she was in love with him before that kiss, but just how far gone she was had not been apparent. Now, she was simply lost. And it was all so hopeless.

Was she happy or sad that she had to be around him now on a daily basis for the next few weeks at the very least? It was going to be torture for her on the one hand, but when he left she didn't know how she was going to bear the emptiness his leaving would bring to her and her home. *Why, Lord? Why did you allow this to happen? Nothing good can ever come from it and I know that all too well.* She sighed deeply; the weight she felt on her shoulders seemed a physical reality. How would she ever be able to act normally around him now? Impossible. Simply impossible. But somehow, some way, she would have to pull it off.

After cleaning up the kitchen, she returned to his room with a book. Settling herself in a chair in the corner, she did her best to occupy herself by reading, but the words ran together and she found herself watching Pen as he slept instead of reading. Secure in the knowledge that he couldn't tell she was watching him, she allowed herself that luxury with no guilt. The blush returned to her face from time to time as the memory of that shared kiss washed over her, but no one saw, and she was thankful for that.

At six that evening a soft rap on the door announced Dave Benson's arrival for his night shift. He opened the door softy, carefully so as not to awaken Pen if he was sleeping.

Maura came fully to her senses with Dave's arrival. Putting her fingers to her lips to signal "quiet," she rose from her chair and motioned for Dave to follow her out of the room.

"Dave, I have the most exciting news!" Holding tightly onto his arm, she related to him how Pen had remembered the words to the hymns earlier that day.

"Dave, he's getting his memory back! I don't know why those hymns triggered his memory, but maybe, just maybe, he'll be able to remember everything in time. Won't that be wonderful?"

Dave's eyes misted with the joy he obviously felt with this wonderful news. "God is truly good, isn't He?"

"Amen and amen! I was beginning to wonder if he was ever going to get anything back, but now I know there's hope. Should we call his sister and let her know or do you think it's too soon?"

"Oh, if it was your brother, you'd want to know, wouldn't you?"

"I sure would. I'll go give her a call before I go to bed. I'm so excited I can hardly stand it! Oh, and I also think he's turned a corner in other ways today. His speech was definitely less slurred, almost normal actually, and, well, if you didn't know what was going on with him you might think he was perfectly well. I know he's going to continue to have some bad days and the occasional episode of heavy sweating or agitation, but I really think we're over the hump, so to speak. Thank God!" Her elation was contagious.

Dave was grinning from ear to ear. "I almost want to dance, I'm so happy Maura."

Sobering as she thought about calling Raven, she said, "I'm going to have to call Allie also. I promised her she could see him when he was doing better. I don't want to, but you saw that she was definitely pregnant. If Pen is, in fact, the father of her baby, she has every right to see him, I think."

"Before you call Allie, I think you need to talk it over with Pen tomorrow and see what he wants to do, don't you? What if he doesn't want to see her, or at least not yet?"

"I think he's going to have to see her. The baby isn't going away, and I think she's close to four months along now. They're going to have to start making some plans. Pen is still adamant that her baby isn't his, but he in fact has no way of knowing for sure. Those two are going to have to sort this whole mess out somehow."

"Well, you're certainly right about that. Maybe you should go ahead and see how he is tomorrow; talk to him and see what he wants to do, and we can go from there. How does that sound?"

"Perfect. I'll talk to him tomorrow. He was actually up most of the day today, so I expect he'll probably sleep pretty well tonight; well, at least better than he has been. An easy night for you, perhaps." She smiled. "I'll go call Raven and I'll see you in the morning, OK?"

"Good night. Sleep well. And thanks for the good news." He turned and went back into Pen's room for the night.

Maura fixed herself a bowl of soup and then called Raven. She filled her in on all that had happened and could hear his sister crying with relief. Pen remembering anything at all was absolutely huge, and everyone around him knew it.

"Shall we come down tomorrow, Maura? I can't wait to see him! Is he really doing so much better that maybe he'll agree to see us?"

"Let me see how he does tomorrow before we decide about that. If he regresses in some way it's not a good plan.

Besides, I want to get his permission now that he seems to be thinking more rationally. I would hate for you to drive all the way down here and then have him refuse to see you. Why don't I give you a call tomorrow evening and let you know how his day went, and if he's willing to see you now? How would that be?"

"That would be great. I'll wait to hear from you tomorrow, then. But Maura, I'm so excited right now I can hardly stand it! My brother may be coming back to me! Thank you God!"

"Yes, thank you, God. Talk to you tomorrow. Sleep well, Raven. Good-night."

"Good-night and thanks again." Raven hung up the phone.

Chapter 18

Pen woke slowly the next morning. It had taken what seemed like most of the night to settle into a restful sleep. His agitation was still a problem, and compounded with his concerns related to his improper actions the day before, sleep was a long time in coming. He had faked it with Dave in the room. Whether he had fooled the man or not, it didn't really matter to him. At least he hadn't had to make conversation, and that was really all he cared about.

He wondered if Maura had said anything to Dave about what had happened, but the more he thought about it, the more he was convinced she had not. He thought perhaps she was too embarrassed to say anything. He hoped so. He still wasn't sorry he had kissed her, and as the memory of it came back to him, he smiled to himself. It HAD been good!

Keeping his eyes shut, he pretended to still be sleeping. His mind began to wander from his kiss with Maura to . . . Raven? Why did she pop into his head all of a sudden? Raven—*Oh dear Lord in heaven—I remember!* Memories of his sister began to wash over him. Pictures, sounds, places and memories bombarded his brain with shards and vivid colors that alternately pierced and soothed.

He sat bolt upright in bed.

"Dave! Dave are you there?"

Dave had been dozing in the chair and was startled into abrupt wakefulness with Pen's exclamation. Rubbing his eyes, he looked at his patient questioningly.

"Yeah, I'm here. What is it? What's wrong?"

"Nothing's wrong! Everything's all right! Perfect, in fact. Dave, I remember! I think I remember everything!"

"You what? You remember?"

Pen began laughing, giddy with joy. "Yup. Dave, I know who I am, can you believe that? And I know who you are. I know who my sister is. I don't know if I have it all back, but Dave, I remember an awful lot! Oh Lord! Thank you God!"

Dave took the few steps to Pen's bed in record time.

"Really Pen? You're not just saying that to make me feel better or something, are you?"

"No way. I love you like a brother, Dave, and I'm telling you the truth here. I remember you and I even remember that some of your sermons weren't all that great. I remember I wanted to tell you that before, but, well, how do you tell your preacher that his messages aren't always top of the line? That in fact some were pretty boring!"

Dave laughed out loud, and grabbed both of Pen's hands in his own. "So tell me what else do you remember? How about—how about Gus? Remember him?"

"Sure do. He used to work at the church and then he came to work for my sister and me at the stable. I don't remember anything about them getting together, but they seem to have gotten married while I was 'out,' am I right?"

"You sure are. Holy Cow! Wait until Maura hears about this!" Without thinking he released Pen's hands and clasped him in a big bear hug.

"Pen, I have to admit, I was worried you might never get any of your memory back. After Maura told me you came up with the words to those hymns I had a little hope, but this is nothing short of a miracle. Yup, a bona fide, genuine miracle!"

"Guess it really is, isn't it, Dave?"

"And Pen, if you've gotten this far, you're going to make it all the way, I'm sure of it."

"Does that mean you think I'll be able to see again?"

Dave hesitated, hating to dampen Pen's enthusiasm.

"Pen, I have to be honest here. Will you ever see again? That's truly doubtful."

"Hey sourpuss, God just worked one heck of a miracle, why would you think He wouldn't work one more for me?"

"It's true, He sure could. But reality says it probably won't happen, and we're going to have to face that. But Pen, you ARE going to beat this drug thing. You're actually almost there now, you know. With you getting totally sober and having your memory back, why, you're going to be a whole new man! I'm happy for you, brother—you have no idea just how happy I am."

"Sure, I know. You just want to go home, don't you!"

Dave slapped Pen's back playfully. "You got it. I've got a church to take care of. You just lost first place with me."

"Dave, what time is it right now?"

He looked at his watch. "It's morning, about 5:45. Maura will be here soon. I can't wait to tell her the good news, can you?"

"Do me a favor, will you Dave?"

"Sure, what do you want?"

"Don't tell Maura. Let me tell her myself. Do you mind?"

Dave looked quizzically at his friend. "Why? Any special reason?"

"Not really. I just want to surprise her, that's all. And I want it to come straight from me. I don't remember much of what I put her through when she first brought me home with her, but I'm pretty sure I made her life a living hell. I'm right, aren't I?"

"Yup. That's a pretty accurate description I think."

"Thought so." Pen grimaced as he imagined all sorts of things that had happened in his stupor. "I don't know. I feel like maybe I owe her that. For me to tell her personally. Do you mind too much?"

"Not at all. You go right ahead and do what you think is right. It's gonna be awful hard for me to keep my mouth shut, though. If I can keep this sick grin off my face maybe I'll pretend I have a headache and just leave when she shows up."

"Thanks, Dave. See you tonight? Maybe we can go over things as I remember them. Sound OK to you?"

"Sounds great."

A knock sounded softly on the door.

"She's here. See you tonight, buddy." Dave rose from the bed and went to let Maura in.

The door opened slowly, quietly, as Maura entered the room. If Pen was sleeping she certainly didn't want to wake him up. Dave swiftly put his hand to his forehead, partially covering his eyes.

"Hi Maura. See you tonight." He passed her quickly and sped out of the room.

Maura turned to watch him leave. *What's wrong with him?* As the door closed behind him, she went to take up her position on one of the chairs in the room. Pen seemed to be asleep. Picking up the book she had been reading, she found the page where she had left off the day before and was soon engrossed in the story; at least she pretended to be. No pages were turned, no words or ideas entered her brain. She was in the same room with Pen, the man she loved, and all she could think about was the kiss he had stolen. Was stolen the right word? She certainly hadn't pulled away. What on earth must he think of her! Did he think she was easy, like Allie? Was he feeling so much better that any woman would do for him? She wanted so badly to think that perhaps she was special to him, but that was just a dream, just wishful thinking. But oh how she wished.

The voice startled her; she had thought him asleep.

"Did you know my folks died when I was nine?"

"What? What did you say?"

"I said, my parents passed away in a flood when I was only nine years old. Had you heard about that?"

"No, I don't think I knew that. A flood you say?"

"Spring run-off from the rain and melting snow up in Canada on the Reserve. One of my mom's mares was stuck in the mud and she was trying to get her out. My dad came to help and they were all washed away. You hadn't heard about that, huh?"

"No." Maura was shaking her head in the negative when it suddenly hit her. Without thinking she shot out of her chair and was sitting on the edge of the bed in seconds.

"You remembered something! Pen, you actually remembered something from your past? Oh my! I'm . . ."

Pen laughed as his hands came out from under the covers, searching for hers. Instinctively, Maura took his hands in hers as joy washed through her.

"Maura, I remember everything. Everything, do you understand?"

"Pen, I . . ." She was speechless. What does one say at a time like this?

"Everything, Maura. I remember what Raven looks like, I remember Gus. I remember our stable in Bozeman. I remember the man Raven almost married, and that special Appaloosa stallion that she loved so much. I remember growing up on the Reserve in Canada, just me and Raven, pretty much on our own. I lost some time recently, but I think I'm thirty years old, and I know when my birthday is." Tears began streaming unheeded down his cheeks.

Not thinking, but only responding to the wonderful news, Maura released his hands and embraced him in a tight hug.

"Pen, I'm so happy for you! When? How? Oh, it doesn't matter, I guess, I just thank God you have your memory back." Suddenly she realized what she was doing and pulled abruptly away. "Sorry. I didn't mean to do that. I'm just so happy for you. It's exciting, isn't it?"

"No, don't pull away from me, please." His hand was reaching for her again. "Please. Just hold my hand for a moment, OK? I promise to be good. I won't . . ." He grinned sheepishly. "I'm so happy I just have to hold on to someone right now."

Hesitating only briefly, she took his outstretched hand in her own. Pen's relief was evident in his face as his pinched brows relaxed.

"Thank you."

"Pen, what about Dave? Does he know? And why did he leave so suddenly?"

"Yeah, he knows. I woke up with my memories flooding back, so of course I told him, but I asked him not to say anything to you. I wanted to tell you myself, so he was pretending he had a headache."

"Well, I guess that explains his quick exit." She smiled again, happy at the new turn of events. Random thoughts were racing through her head. Excitement permeated the room.

"What do you say we celebrate all of this good news with a big breakfast? Are you hungry?"

"As a momma bear coming out of hibernation, woman! If you're willing to cook, I'm ready to eat!"

"Then follow me, Cowboy. Let's put some more meat on those bones."

He held his hand out again. "Take my hand?"

"Nope. Take your cane."

"Drat. Your hand is a lot nicer than that cane."

"Why don't you go shower and get dressed while I get breakfast going?"

"Fine. I can take a hint. See you in the kitchen in a few minutes."

She left the room humming softly to herself.

Pen was quick with the shower and returned to the kitchen in record time. He was happy, he was clean, and he was hungrier than he could remember in a very long time.

Breakfast over, they sat companionably sipping coffee. When they were sated, Maura broke the silence that had descended.

"Pen, I called Raven last night and told her about you remembering the words to those hymns. She wants to come see you today, if that's OK with you." She took a sip, uncertain of his response.

"That would be great, Maura. I think we have a lot of catching up to do now that I remember her." His brows furrowed as he continued: "But make it plain I'm still not going home with her."

"Why on earth not? At least after a few more days when those drugs are completely out of your system? You're doing great; there's no reason you couldn't go back to Bozeman with her." As the words left her mouth the realization that he might actually be leaving hit her, hard. She didn't want him to leave. Ever.

"Because I'm still blind and useless. What earthly good would I be at a stable? I'd just be in the way. You know that's true." He paused, seeming uncertain. "Unless, well . . . are you kicking me out?"

"You want to stay here, in this house?" She held her breath, waiting. What if he wanted to go home with Dave, or heaven forbid, back with Allie? The thought of him leaving her was an actual physical pain, like a knife slicing through her chest, sharp and piercing.

"I want to stay here, with you, if you'll let me, that is. I know I'm in the way but I, well, I'd like to stay."

"Sure, you can stay if you want. I'm going to have to be starting back to work in a few days so you'll be alone in the house after Dave leaves. Can you handle that?"

"Well, I've been thinking, maybe I should go back to that school. What do you think? Life seems a little less hopeless this morning." His face was nearly radiant.

"I think that's a great idea. Good for you. I don't know what your future will be like, Pen, but I know it can be good, if you'll let it all happen. God has a plan, you know? We may not understand it all, but He really is in control, and we just have to trust Him."

"Yeah, but that's a lot easier said than done!" He smiled at her yet again. "You sound a lot like Dave with that little speech, by the way."

"I do, huh? I'm in pretty good company then, aren't I?"

"Yes, you most definitely are."

Maura hesitated before bringing up the next subject that they needed to discuss.

"Pen, what about Allie?"

"What about her?"

"I promised her that I would let her know when you were feeling better and would see her."

"Well, I'm definitely feeling a whole lot better, but I still don't want to see the girl. Sorry."

"You're going to have to, though. You do understand that, don't you?"

Aspen sighed deeply. "You had to go and ruin a perfectly wonderful morning, didn't you?"

Maura's face looked stricken. "I'm sorry."

"Nothing to be sorry about, Maura. I don't want to see her, but I guess I'm going to have to, aren't I? But I still say that's not my baby!"

"Well, I guess you two are going to have to sort it all out somehow, but obviously you can't just walk away from her. And she was awfully good to you, taking you out of the mission and letting you stay with her."

"I know, I know. I just don't want to . . ." his voice trailed off and he turned his face away. "I for sure don't want to see her alone. Will you be with me while I talk to her?"

"No, I don't really think that's a good idea. Maybe Dave will stay with you." Maura didn't think there was any way she could sit through a discussion between Allie and Pen. No way. Her heart constricted at the thought.

"OK. I'll ask Dave to sit in with me. You can call her whenever you want. I might as well get it over with. But do me a favor and make it a different day than when Raven comes. Fair enough?"

"Fine. I'll call them both and take care of it. And you're sure you want to stay here? You're positive you won't go home with your sister?"

"Positive. It's not happening. Sorry. I'll go back to the Rescue Mission first."

She knew by the tone of his voice and the look on his face that he meant every word he was saying.

"I'll take care of everything then. Want some more coffee?"

"Sure. Thanks. Thanks for everything, Maura."

Chapter 19

Maura called Raven moments later and told her the good news; her brother was willing to see her at last. Raven was nearly hysterical with joy and anticipation, and planned to arrive at Maura's sometime that afternoon.

"Well, I made the call, and your sister and brother-in-law will be down right after lunch. Raven was so excited her words were running together and I could barely understand her. I'm not sure you really know just how much your sister loves and needs you, Pen. You might want to rethink your plan to stay here in Billings, what do you say?" Her words were altruistic, but her heart constricted at the mere thought of his leaving. It was the last thing she wanted, but she sincerely did want Pen to do what was best for him, and going with his sister might be just that.

"No. I won't go back to Bozeman with her. I would just be more work and a big hazard around the stable. Blind people shouldn't be anywhere around young horses, and my presence would be too much of a distraction on top of everything else. Besides, I told you I think I should go back to that school, and it's better to stay right here where they already know me—and I know them."

"Pen, be reasonable here. Your sister wants you home with her. She wants to look out for you, especially now that you remember her."

"What did I just tell you, Maura? Did I not say I was not going back with her?"

"Yes, but . . ."

"Maura, I don't want to hear another word about it! My decision is final." Pen's jaw was set, rigid. He lowered his voice to add, "I'm not your patient anymore, Nurse Maura, and I'm not a child. I'm sober enough to make some rational decisions on my own now."

Properly chastised, Maura lowered her head, relieved that Pen couldn't see her cheeks turning bright pink between the freckles. He was right; he was sober and an adult, and she actually had been treating him like a little kid. Being blind didn't make one stupid.

"Got it. I won't mention it again. When you're ready to go back to Bozeman you let me know and I'll call Raven for you. Am I forgiven for being so pushy?"

"Forgiven. And forgotten." He smiled in her direction. "Any coffee left?"

"Sure. Hand me your cup."

Gus and Raven showed up around twelve-thirty, just as Pen and Maura were finishing up their lunch. Maura had to caution them to keep the noise down since Dave was sleeping, but Raven was nearly uncontrollable in her excitement.

"OK, OK, OK, I got it, but where's my handsome brother?" she rambled on as she naturally headed for the kitchen. Where else would a man be at this hour? Seeing him seated at the table, her brother never had a chance. Raven ran the last few steps to him and nearly smothered the poor soul with her arms, her kisses, and her hair, which swirled unrestrained around his face as she grabbed him and held on tightly.

"You remember me now? Maura said you remembered everything? True? How about Gus? Remember him too?" Words tumbled out of her mouth, one after another, never giving Pen a chance to reply. She began kissing her brother's face all over, from hairline to chin and ear-to-ear.

"Raven, quit slobbering all over me, will you? And could you close your mouth for just a moment and give me a little room to breathe? You're smothering me, for heaven's sake!" But he was smiling broadly at her obvious enthusiasm as he wiped his face with his shirtsleeve.

Gus and Maura glanced at each other and by mutual unspoken consent, left the twins and went to the living room. Gus had brought his checkbook and while his wife was catching up with her brother, he intended to get a full report from Maura and do some settling up at the same time.

"Pen, you're looking almost like your old self again. Just as handsome as ever, but still a little thin, I think. Haven't you been eating? Doesn't Maura feed you enough?"

"She feeds me plenty, or at least she's been trying to. It's only been the last few days that I actually had any appetite for anything other than my pills. And don't give me any junk about looking like my old self. I know darn good and well that's not even a little bit true. I may not be able to see what I look like in a mirror, but I have a fair idea. I can feel my bones poking through here and there." He flexed an arm. "See? Used to have some muscle, but not much there now. Oh well."

"Pen, you look wonderful to me. You always have."

He could hear the sincerity in her voice and knew she meant every word.

"OK, now that the mushy stuff is out of the way, I have a lot of questions for you, sister dear. I seem to have missed out on a lot of events while I was 'asleep'."

"Sure; where would you like me to start? What's the last thing you remember?"

"Well, I remember working a colt with the running W rope, and that's it. I don't remember anything at all about the accident. I just woke up one day and 'was,' so to speak. Didn't even know my name."

"Do we have to talk about that day, Pen? You got a good hard kick in the head and that's most of the story. If it's all the same to you I'd rather not go into more details. On my list of bad days, that one ranks right up there, you know? If you really want to know more maybe we can get back to it some other time?"

"Sure. That's fine with me. But I still have an awful lot of questions for you."

"Ask away and I'll do the best I can to give you answers."

"Well, to start with, how in the world did you end up marrying Gus Whittaker? The way I remember it you were all set to marry Tom Martin. Oh, and what about that beautiful Appaloosa stud of his, Osage was his name, wasn't it?"

Raven's face became clouded as memories of her former fiancé were recalled. Her lids lowered as she remembered that terrible time in her life.

"Well, I . . ."

Pen interrupted her explanation. "Gus is a Christian, Raven, and I know how you feel about Christians. Well, except for me, of course." He smiled. "But how on earth?"

"I love Christians; I'm one of those crazy people now too. Can you believe it? Me! Of all people, me, a Christian." She laughed out loud at the puzzled look on her brother's face.

"No way. You? Spill, Raven. What on earth happened to you while I was gone?"

"A lot, Pen. An awful lot." She proceeded to fill her brother in on the life-changing events of the past year. About the horrific accident, her colostomy, and Tom's rejection of her. She left out the part about his betrayal with Caroline; there was no need to go into that with anyone. Gus knew and that was enough. But she told him how Gus had taken such good care of her, how she had tried so very hard to manipulate him into a life of servitude, and her eventual capitulation with God when Gus left her. She omitted as much of the really disturbing parts as she could, not wanting to relive the moments herself as well as not wanting to distress her brother. He had enough to worry about.

"Get this, Pen. I even got baptized! Dave did it for me, and I've been in church ever since." Her gaze drifted off into a distance that only she seemed to perceive, unseen by her brother. "I only wish I had listened, really listened, to our parents and you over the years when you all tried so hard to get me to really see God. Life would have been so much different for me, easier maybe. But then again, I may never have seen Gus for who he is, so in the end God really does work things out for the best for those who love Him. And I got to come along for the ride as He took care of Gus, who loved Him when I didn't. The old me would never have accepted being second best to anyone in a man's eyes, but I guess being second to God is OK."

"Gosh, I'm sorry, sis. Sounds like you had a really rough year, and I wasn't there for you. I guess I should have been more careful when I was working with that colt; maybe a lot of trouble could have been avoided for both of us." He shook his head slowly from side to side, trying to absorb everything Raven had just told him, a look of profound bitterness etched on his face. *Unbelievable. Simply unbelievable.*

Intense longing registered on Raven's face as she watched her brother raise his head toward the sound of her voice, his sightless eyes unfocused, vacant. Would he ever be able to see her again?

"Raven, what about Jesse? How's he doing through all of this? And what are your plans? When are you and Gus hoping to start a family? Soon, I hope. I'd kind of like to be an uncle I think. At least the idea sounds kind of good."

Pain replaced the look of longing on her face.

"My dog died in the crash. Glass from the broken windshield, I guess. No one told me for a long time, but when I came home and he wasn't there . . ."

"Sorry to hear that. I know you loved him. Do you plan to get another one soon or should I not ask?"

She smiled broadly. "Gus brought me another puppy when he came back to Bozeman. He's such a good man, Pen. I can never thank you enough for hiring him when you did. He literally saved my life, I think."

"Glad to hear I did something right!" he joked with her. "And what about that family, those kids you wanted so much when you were planning to marry Tom? You haven't said anything about that; hey, you're not pregnant already or something are you? Were you waiting to surprise me?"

A tear slipped unseen as she softly replied, "No. I'm not pregnant. I'm sorry, but you're never going to be an uncle. I can't have any children. The accident . . ." her words trailed off into silence.

"Oh Raven, I'm so sorry! Are you sure? Miracles still happen, you know. Look at me; I know who you are and three days ago I didn't even know who *I* was! I'm learning that anything's possible in this world. Want more proof? You became a Christian! How much more proof of miracles do you need?"

"No, Pen. There won't be any miracles in that department for Gus and me. I'd have to grow some new body parts for that to happen, so I just have to accept the fact that Gus and I will get to grow old together all by ourselves. But maybe one of these days you'll find that special someone and have some kids of your own and I can be an aunt."

Pen snorted in total denial of that idea. "Raven, I'm lucky when I can get myself to the bathroom. What woman would ever look at me? Marriage? Kids? I could only wish."

"Why are you so sure it won't happen? "

"Look at me, Raven. Look hard. I'm your brother and I know that you love me unconditionally. But as husband material? I have nothing but a high school education, and I'm blind. I can't drive, I can't . . . actually, there's precious little I can do. I certainly won't ever be able to support a family. No good woman wants a man that she has to take care of. And to top it all off, I'm an addict."

"Recovering addict," Raven broke in. "You're sober now as far as I can tell. Don't sell yourself short, please. You're still quite a catch for any woman."

Pen snorted again in derision. "Thou shalt not bear false witness, woman. Don't lie. It doesn't become you."

"I'm not lying. There's a couple of things you're missing here, Pen."

"Yeah, like what? I don't think I've missed anything at all."

"Like you're smart. Really smart. You've got guts and brains, and when you want something, you've got determination. Once you set a goal for yourself you pursue it until you reach it. I've seen you do that all your life. You just need to find and set some new goals for yourself. Oh, and one more thing."

"What's that?'

"You're still one of the most handsome men I've ever seen. You're tall and you stand out. . ."

Pen laughed out loud at that. "Like you, you mean?"

She smiled. "Yeah, like me. We're twins, remember? We're good-looking and smart, and neither of us does well without the other, so, welcome back brother. I love you."

"I love you too, Raven. And I guess it really is good to be back. Now, tell me what else is new. How's the stable going?"

They talked for most of the afternoon, catching up, remembering, planning, and just being together again. It was true; neither of them did very well without the other. Even with Gus as her husband, Raven never felt complete without her twin, and she was sure Pen felt the same.

When it was time for them to head back to Bozeman, Raven brought up the forbidden subject; she couldn't help herself.

"Pen, will you come back with us tonight? Please? We need you."

"No, I'm going to stay here for now. Maybe later but not now."

"But Pen . . ."

"Raven, no! I mean it and I don't want to hear any more about it. For one thing, I think I'm going back to school in a few days. Maura has said it's OK if I stay here for the time being, and the school is here. Besides, you can't run the stable and watch me all at the same time. You and Gus are too busy."

Raven gave in. It was obvious from his tone of voice that Pen was not going budge on this, and though she hated to admit it, he was right about her not being able to take good care of him.

After his sister left, Pen told Maura he wanted to spend some time alone. He needed to think and rest. She told him she would call him when supper was ready.

Alone in his room, lying on the bed, Pen closed his eyes and went over the afternoon's conversations with his sister. His heart ached for her as he came to terms with all she had gone through in the past year. It was easy to gloss over words, but sincere contemplation revealed the true enormity of it all. His sister had a permanent colostomy. He had only a vague idea as to what that actually was, and had no conception as to how it might affect a person in their daily life. He had never known anyone with a colostomy, and now his beautiful sister had one.

And no children? He remembered the plans she had so carefully made. She was going to marry Tom Martin and have the perfect life with the perfect children, and it had all crashed into nothingness for her. At least she had finally found God, and men didn't come any better than Gus, he knew.

Damn his sightless eyes! He wanted so much to know if his sister had been scarred in the accident, but there was no way he could ask her, or anyone else for that matter. He sure couldn't ask Raven; what if she had in fact been badly scarred? He knew how he felt about being blind, how he felt when anyone brought it up. How would she feel if her face was indeed badly disfigured and he asked her about it? Her looks had always been so important to her. He couldn't do it. And he wouldn't ask anyone else either, which begged the question of why not? Why didn't he just ask Maura or Dave? Because in truth he didn't want to know. His blindness was enough; he couldn't bear the thought of his beautiful sister with her beauty gone. It was better not to know, to remember her as she was before her accident.

He had told Maura and Raven that he thought he might go back to school soon. Was he sure he wanted to do that? Thinking carefully about his situation and his life . . . life? What life? Finding your way around with a cane and getting yourself to the bathroom on your own did not constitute a life. An existence, perhaps, but not a life. But did he really want a life, so to speak? He had been content for months with just existing, just him and his pills; why was he thinking about anything more now?

He didn't know for sure, but it seemed he had reached a turning point of some sort, because he suddenly felt adrenaline surging throughout his body, and he realized that he did, in fact, want something more. Oh, he hated what he had become. He hated his blindness and his constant feelings of uselessness. He hated banging into walls, spilling glasses of water, hated not being able to tell which of his clothes were clean and which were dirty without help from someone else. Hated not knowing if he had gotten all his whiskers when he shaved because he couldn't see in the mirror. Hated not being able to just go out for a walk without worrying about getting lost. But he also suddenly realized that he didn't really want to die anymore. He wanted to live. He just didn't know how he was going to do it.

What was it his sister had said? That he had always been good at setting and accomplishing goals? That he just needed to set some new goals for himself? Maybe she was right; maybe that was exactly what he needed. He almost wished he had accepted the counseling the rehab center had tried to set up for him, but he had been adamant in his refusal. He had only wanted to die and no amount of cajoling had convinced him to go to the psychiatrist. He wasn't crazy, after all, he was . . . what was he? He was sick, he thought. Very, very sick in many ways. It was hard to admit to what he considered a weakness, but there it was. Now what was he going to do about it?

It came back to the school. It was the best place to start. He would ask Maura to get him lined up there again before she went back to work. He could take a cab as he had at Allie's.

Allie. How had she come back into the picture? He wished she hadn't popped into his head. He had other things to think about besides her, and by association that baby she was carrying that she still insisted was his. What was he going to do about Allie? Maura was right; he was going to have to talk it out with her.

Allie was a nice girl. Pregnant, but nice. He really did like her, but he definitely did not love her. He thought deeply and honestly about his feelings for her. Just what did he feel for Allie?

Honestly? He thought of her as a friend, a buddy. Someone he could laugh and joke with. A friend who would do anything for him. Was she cute? Pretty? He had no idea, and he found that he really didn't care. She was a woman, but he just wasn't interested in her that way, even though she very obviously wanted him to be. Why wasn't he?

He had no idea why he wasn't. Perhaps a blind man shouldn't be so picky; after all, his prospects with women were pretty slim now. She was nice, she liked him, she wanted him, and . . . and she was simply not the woman for him. What was missing?

Ah, finally, the missing piece of the puzzle. Even when he was at his worst, in his stupor and haze from the pills, even then, he realized that God had been protecting him. Allie was not a believer; she was not a Christian, and even when Pen didn't remember God, God had remembered him. *Thank you Heavenly Father, for unseen blessings. You are ever faithful.*

Well, whenever Maura set it up for Allie to come over, he would be as kind as he could, but he was not going to yield. Baby or no baby, it would be wrong for him to make a life with her. Besides, she needed a good man who could love her and fully commit to her. He sincerely wanted Allie to be happy, and he knew full well she would never be truly happy with him. It was sad, but it was reality.

His thoughts shifted from Allie to other things his sister had discussed with him. She told him he would find that special someone and have the children she never would. Yeah, right. Like some normal woman would ever fall for him. He had absolutely nothing to offer a woman. But . . .

There was Maura. Once again, there was Maura. He remembered her being with him when he first woke up from his coma; her compassion and reassurance, her ability to calm him when his fears began to incapacitate him; her endless patience with him. The sound of her voice and the rhythm of her footsteps. How she felt when she hugged him. Her scent.

He remembered running into her in her hallway when he first came. How embarrassed they had both been at the encounter. True, he had reminded her that he couldn't see anything, but he could not forget how good she had smelled, fresh from the shower, how warm she had felt in his arms.

He thought about the kiss he had surprised her with. He was sorry he had overstepped the obvious bounds, but he in fact was not at all sorry he had kissed her. Was it worth her alienation? He smiled at the memory. *Oh yes, it was worth it. If I never have another, that one kiss was well worth it.*

His blood seemed warmer coursing through him as he thought of Maura. He liked Allie. He liked Maura. He had no future with any woman, but he wanted one, he decided. Things had changed. He found that he did indeed want a future, and that future included a wife. He wanted a wife. He admitted that he wanted Maura, and finally he admitted to himself that he was in love with her.

He closed his lids tightly, trying to force the pain away he couldn't help but feel when he thought about the hopelessness of his situation. What was he thinking? Did he really think he would ever have any sort of a future with Maura? Impossible. That woman could have any man she wanted, and he was sure it was never going to be him. She had made that pretty plain when she had pushed him away. He couldn't blame her. But why did it have to hurt so much?

At least she was going to let him stay with her for now. If he was careful, maybe he could stay for a very long time.

Lord, I know you're in control, but sometimes it's sure hard to understand what you're doing. None of this makes any sense at all. But I will trust You, all the way. I have no other choice.

Chapter 20

Two days later, Allie came. Dave had agreed to stay with Pen while he sorted things out with her, and it was he who answered the knock at the front door when she arrived. He took her coat and motioned for her to take a seat in the living room, where Pen was already waiting for her. Maura had left to run errands more than half an hour ago, not wanting any part of this discussion.

Allie flashed her megawatt smile at Dave as she took a seat across from Aspen. She was most definitely, obviously, pregnant, and her complexion was blooming. She always looked good; she was a cute girl. But the pregnancy had enhanced her natural beauty, and that beauty did not go unnoticed by any man.

"You sure you want me here for this, Pen?" Dave sounded like he didn't really want to be involved.

"Yup, I'm sure. Take a seat. I want a witness for everything that is said today."

Allie looked at Pen quizzically. "Are you expecting some sort of trouble, Pen? You know I'm not like that. We can talk alone, I think. It's not like I'm going to threaten you or anything." Her feelings were hurt a little. What must Pen think of her if he wanted his pastor here?

"No, I'm not expecting any trouble, but Dave's my friend as well as my pastor, and I just think he should hear the whole story. Is that a problem for you?"

"No, not really, but some of this is pretty personal, don't you think? I'm not sure I'm comfortable talking about everything in front of a stranger."

"Well, I want him to hear the whole story you're telling about how you got pregnant. Maybe we can talk in private for a while after that. OK with you?"

"OK. I guess." She lowered her head, unsure where and how to start this conversation. She was desperate, however, and ready to do whatever it took to make Pen marry her. She wanted to keep her baby, but there was no way her parents would ever accept her pregnancy if she was a single mother; they would promptly disown her. She sighed deeply, and looked over at Dave Benson.

"Want me to start, then?"

"Yup," Pen replied. "You go right ahead and tell him your story. Tell him why you think this is my baby."

"OK." She took a deep breath and began.

"Well, Pen slept on the living room floor. I only have a one-bedroom apartment and he either had to sleep with me in my bed or on the floor. I offered to share the bed with him. I told him I wasn't expecting anything beyond a good night's sleep, but he chose the floor. Said it wouldn't be right to share the bed. I let him make his own decision, but I wouldn't have minded either way." She looked over at him. "He is after all, quite a handsome man. And he's nice, too. Don't you agree?"

"Yes, I agree with both of those statements. He is pretty easy to look at and I know for a fact that he's a nice person." Dave smiled at her assessment of his friend. "Go on."

"Well, one night I was sound asleep when . . . well . . . he came into my room, and . . . and . . . now as you can plainly see, I am definitely pregnant. He keeps trying to tell me that this baby isn't his, but I know that it is. He came to my room. Ask him. He'll tell you he was sleeping right next to me the next morning. And he was naked, too." She turned her gaze to Pen. "I'm telling him the truth, aren't I? You were naked in my bed that next morning and no man climbs into a woman's bed just to sleep!" Allie had to make her case, and make it strong enough to convince the pastor, who was obviously no fool.

"Why didn't you stop him, Allie? There's no way Pen would have forced himself on you. I know him too well for that to be a possibility, drugs or not."

"Why didn't I stop him?" She lowered her lashes coyly for Dave's benefit. He was, after all, still a man even if he was a pastor. "To begin with, I was awakened from a very deep sleep, so I wasn't fully in my right mind. I was drowsy, it was dark, and, well, look at him. Aspen Windchase is very handsome, and besides, I liked him a lot. I was already half in love with him when he came to me, so no, I guess I really didn't want to stop him. I wanted him to make love to me. There, I admit it. I wanted him. I was glad he had come to me." She patted her swollen abdomen. "I'm still glad. I want my baby, but I want the father of my baby also. I don't want to do this alone, and I shouldn't have to. Don't you agree?"

"Well, yes, I do agree that you shouldn't have to be going through this alone. If Pen's the father, then he should be taking responsibility."

"There's no 'if' about it. He's the father!" Allie wasn't going to give an inch on this. This little chat was her one chance to make Pen come around, and Allie was nothing if not determined.

Dave turned his head toward Aspen. "OK, friend, let's hear your side of the story. How much of what she just said are you going to dispute? How badly is she lying, or is she even lying at all?"

Pen's face registered his dismay that his friend might doubt him. He shook his head.

"Well, a lot of what she just said is, in fact, true. We did talk about sharing her bed, which she graciously offered, but I declined and slept on the living room floor. It just wasn't right to be sleeping with her, even if nothing was going on between us. I may not have had any memory of anything, but I instinctively knew that much." He paused.

"Go on. I'm listening."

"It is also true that one morning I woke up naked in her bed. She was naked also. But that's all I remember, Dave. I have no memory at all of making my way down the hall to her room. I always sleep in pajama bottoms and I don't remember ever taking them off the whole time I stayed at her house. I remember being horrified when I woke up and discovered where I was. Horrified."

Allie interjected, "Thanks a lot, Pen. Horrified? Really? After what we had just shared? I think not, my friend! You most definitely were not horrified! Tell the truth."

"No, I was, in fact horrified, Dave. When it finally registered in my pickled brain where I was, yes, I was really upset. I will admit that it didn't take long for me to settle back into my nice, comfortable, safe little fog, though. Allie kept telling me how wonderful it had been, how much she had enjoyed it. But somehow I think I might have had at least some memory of the event, however small, if it had in fact taken place. But it didn't."

"Why are you so sure nothing happened, Pen? You admit you were naked in her bed. Maybe you were just more asleep than you thought."

"Dave, you know what I've been going through. That's why you're here, staying with me in this house. I'm telling you that with all the pills I was taking it was impossible for me to get up off that floor and find my way to her room. And even if by some remote chance I was able to do that, it would have been impossible for me to perform. There is simply no way I could have made this girl pregnant. No way."

Dave nodded his head as he considered both stories.

"One more thing, Dave. One more thing that hasn't been mentioned here."

"What's that? What else can there be?"

"Allie had a boyfriend when I first came to stay with her. She broke it off within days of my arrival, and I don't know how long she had been dating him before I came, but I know he definitely existed because I have a faint memory of him coming to the house one night."

Dave's head spun around to face Allie at this news.

"I admit I don't remember much about that. In fact I guess I could have been dreaming. But it sure seemed like there was a man in the room with us one night. And I thought I heard some yelling after he and Allie left the room."

"Wait a minute, Pen. Are you telling me you continued to sleep with Allie after that first night?"

Pen hung his head sheepishly. He was obviously embarrassed. "Yes, that's exactly what I'm telling you. It was so much nicer than the floor, and I was already there, and she said I should just stay—so I did."

"Oh, Pen!"

"I know, I know, it was pretty stupid of me. But I was so drugged up I barely knew up from down. I was completely stoned for weeks. It was all I could to do get myself to the bathroom." He turned his face toward Dave, his brows furrowed.

"I don't want to be telling anything confidential here, Dave, but you do understand what I'm telling you, don't you?"

"Yes, I do, and I have to say that I believe you, Pen." He turned to face Allie once more.

"I believe him, Allie. I think he's telling me the truth. I'm sorry."

"You're only siding with him because he's your friend, I can tell. You're a preacher—you're supposed to be honest! I feel like the two of you are just ganging up on me. What am I supposed to do, anyway? Don't you two understand? I'm pregnant! I'm going to have a baby in just a few months. And I'm not married! All of that aside, there's no way with my wages I can afford child care and raise this baby on my own! I'm going to need help, and Pen's the one that needs to help me!" She started to cry now as anger and fear began to overwhelm her.

"Can I just talk to Pen alone for a few minutes, please? Pen? Please, just for a few minutes?"

Dave looked over at his friend. "Want me to stay or leave, Pen? I'll do whatever you say."

"It's OK. I guess you can leave now. I think you've heard what I needed you to hear. I'll talk to her alone for a bit."

Dave rose to leave the room. "Just call if you need me; I'll be just down the hall in Maura's room. Play nice, you two."

"Allie, I . . ."

"Pen, we . . ."

Pen smiled at her. Relief showed on his face since his friend had confessed that he believed him. "Allie, it's going to be OK, you know. I'm sure you're scared and all, but this sort of thing happens all the time. You certainly aren't the first one to find yourself an unwed mother."

"Thanks a lot, Pen. You really think that helps me any?"

"No, I guess not. I just don't know what else to say. We both know that baby's not mine, and while I like you a lot, and I sure thank you for all you've done for me, I'm not in love with you, and I'm not ready to take responsibility for another man's child. I just can't do it. I'm sorry." She began to cry.

Pen heard her sniffling. "There's a box of tissues over on that other table, I think. Sounds like you need a couple. Help yourself."

"Thanks."

He rose to escort her out, but after grabbing a couple of tissues, Allie turned and enfolded herself into Pen's arms. He did not refuse her.

"Allie, I'm sorry. I really am sorry. I hate to hurt you like this, but I just can't do what you want me to do. You understand, don't you?"

She sniffled, and pressed herself closer, needing what comfort he could give her.

"Pen, what am I going to do? It's too late for an abortion, and I didn't want to do that anyway. I really want to keep my baby, but I can't, can I." It was a statement not a question.

"I don't see why you can't keep him or her. Lots of women do these days."

"But my parents—they are old-fashioned and very strict. I will be totally cast out. They'll never speak to me again."

"No, Allie, they'll come to love their grandchild in time. You just have to have faith. They won't abandon you, I'm sure."

Sobbing harder, she replied, "Pen, you really don't understand. My parents aren't like other parents. They will not ever come to love my baby. I will be nothing but a monumental shame to them. I won't ever be allowed to go home again."

Pen hugged her tighter in her misery. "Well, then, how about adopting the baby out? If you're really sure about all of this, why not put the baby up for adoption? Your parents will never know."

"How can I let this baby go, not knowing where it is? I don't know if I can do it. They keep adoption records sealed. All I would know is that he or she went to a well-screened home. I don't know if I can bear that."

"Well, there's still time, Allie. We'll come up with something between the three of us. Dave will help, I know he will."

"The man probably hates me, since he believes I'm lying."

"Dave hasn't got a mean or biased bone in his body, Allie. He doesn't hate you, and he will definitely help." He began to stroke her head soothingly.

"Do you really think so?"

"Yes, I really think so. Now, are you still going to stick to that ridiculous story that I'm the father?"

"Yup, I sure am."

"Allie, please don't. Do you have any idea how that makes me look? Don't you think I have enough trouble right now without that?"

"I still don't know what else to do, Pen. I just don't know what else to do." She disengaged herself to leave.

"Wait."

"What?"

"Here." Pen leaned over and gave her a gentle kiss on her forehead as a parting gesture. "I still like you a lot, Allie, and I thank you for everything you've done for me. I hope we're still friends. And we really will figure something out, soon. Don't worry, OK?"

She sniffled again. "OK. And Pen?"

"Yes?"

"Thanks. Thanks for being you. We might have made a good couple, you know?" She picked up her coat and left the house.

Outside, she stood on the front step for a few moments, leaning her back against the front door. What was she going to do? Her plan had failed. She had tried so hard, so very hard, and she was still pregnant and alone. She could only hope that Pen would do as he had promised, that he and his pastor friend would help her in some way. The future looked terribly bleak.

She sighed, and walked to her car.

Chapter 21

Maura returned nearly an hour after Allie had left the house. It had taken a great deal of willpower to stay away, but she had no desire to be anywhere near Allie right now. While she liked the girl, very much in fact, Allie had laid a strong claim on Pen. While dreams about Pen and herself were just that anyway, dreams not even remotely possible to come true, they were still Maura's dreams, and she was not willing to give them up quite yet. As long as Pen had not been accepted as the father of Allie's baby, there was still that small shred of hope for her. Pen's undisputed fatherhood would cement the end of all hope.

And yet, as much as she didn't want to hear the truth of the matter, she needed desperately to know. She knew she had no hold whatsoever over Pen, but she had to admit that she was jealous of Allie's claim on him. Why was it always the other girl that got the man? Why was Maura still alone at her age? She'd lost count of how many of her friends weddings she had attended over the years. Why had she never met someone like Aspen Windchase before? Why had she met him now, when it was all so hopeless?

Allie's car was nowhere to be seen. *Good. At least I won't have to face her today.* She carried the two bags of groceries to the front door; Dave heard her fumbling with the latch and opened the door for her, taking the bags from her arms and carrying them into the kitchen.

"Anything else you need help with?"

"No, thanks Dave. I'll just put these away and get supper started for you two. Are you hungry yet?"

"We're men; we're always hungry!" He smiled at her. "We'll just be in the living room. Holler when you're ready for us."

"Will do. Now shoo while I work my magic!"

She set about getting supper together but it wasn't long before she found herself listening in on the conversation in the other room. She couldn't help herself; she didn't want to know—she needed to know. The voices were soft, but she was able to get most of what was said.

"Dave, thanks for believing me. I wasn't sure you would. The evidence is pretty strong against me, I will admit. And I wouldn't blame you if you had your doubts. You're only human after all."

"But I know you, Pen. I think I know you pretty well, in fact."

"You might think you know me, but we both know that drugs can change a person a lot. I'll admit to having quite a few not so pure thoughts over the past few weeks. Guess I'll have to do a little repenting!" He laughed.

"The evidence was actually pretty damning, Pen. Waking up naked with a woman in bed, well, it's pretty hard to refute a pregnancy claim with that one. And you admitted to it!"

"I know, I know. Bad enough that first time, but then I kept right on staying with her. I know I should have moved back to the living room floor, but that bed was a lot more comfortable, and, well, I was drugged up enough I was barely thinking at all, let alone rationally. But I'm telling you the truth here; I never touched her, Dave. Maybe a hug once in a while, I really don't remember, but nothing, ever, not one time, more than that. Don't ask me how I know it, I just do." Pen was adamant in his denial.

"I believe you, I believe you. Want to know why I believe you?"

"I'll bite, why? Why are you so sure I'm telling the truth?"

"Because I've been there, remember? I know how I was and if there had been ten naked women in my bed it still would have been hopeless. Not much works when you're that drugged." He wasn't smiling at that one. "But, thank God, that was another lifetime ago."

Pen grimaced. "You know, I've never been serious about any woman, ever, but that doesn't mean I haven't had some improper thoughts about a few over the years. Sad, isn't it? Here I was, sex offered on the proverbial silver platter at a time in my life when morality meant nothing and I couldn't do a thing about it. Yup, just sad." He shook his head.

"But Dave, what can we do to help Allie? We both said we would try to help her, but I don't know how, do you?"

"No, I really don't. I'll check into adoption and see what I can come up with for a start. I feel sorry for her, Pen. I don't think she was ever really, truly in love with you, but you were her only hope of legitimacy with this pregnancy. She's really scared, and lost in more ways than one." He looked down at his hands, clasped in his lap as a confession passed his lips.

"I have to tell you, Pen, Allie is one good-looking woman. Did you know that?"

"Dave, come on! How would I know that and even if I did, what difference would it make?" He laughed out loud. "Like it matters to me what someone looks like! That's a good one, friend!"

In the kitchen, Maura's face registered sadness when she heard Pen's remark.

"Well, I suppose I shouldn't have noticed, being a pastor and all, but I couldn't help it. I wouldn't be human if I didn't. I guess it's not a sin or anything; I'm not married, but I have to admit it's been a long time since I've looked twice at a female."

"So, how does she stack up against my sister? I remember what Raven looks like and she's a knock-out."

"Well, it's hard to compare the two. Apples to oranges, you know? Raven has dark hair, for one thing, and Allie is a strawberry blond. Different builds, different . . . I think I'd still have to put Raven on top, but Allie's a close second. I might have to watch myself around her!"

Pen sucked in his breath. "Dave, you didn't mention anything about Raven's face. Is she, does she, does she look . . . ?"

Dave didn't seem to understand what Pen was trying to find out without actually asking. "Pen, your sister is still the most strikingly beautiful woman I have ever seen in my life. I know the accident left her with some problems, but to see her you would never know there had been an accident at all. We can thank God for His grace in that event."

Relief was evident on Pen's face. His question had been answered. "Thank you, God." He exhaled loudly.

In the kitchen Maura leaned heavily against the counter by the sink. *He never slept with her. The baby really isn't his. Thank you Heavenly Father, thank you.* She knew the chances of anything developing between her and Pen were slim, but at least she didn't have to worry about potentially breaking up a family in the future. She was free to continue dreaming without guilt.

Dave made his announcement over dinner that night.

"Well, Pen, it looks like you're finally about as good as you're going to get. I think you're dried out enough for me to go back home. What do you think?"

Emotions flickered across Pen's face: joy, sadness, doubt—they all seemed to register one after the other, as the thought of his friend leaving became reality. "I have really mixed emotions about that, Dave. You know I love you like a brother and I hate to see you go. On the other hand, I'm so relieved to finally be out from under those pills I can hardly stand it. Oh, I still miss that wonderful, comforting fog they put me in, but if I'm going to get on with my life at all, I know I can never take another one. Ever. Hard choices, you know? I really do love those pills!"

"How well I understand. But I'm so happy to hear you say you're ready to get on with your life. I know none of this has been easy in any way, shape, or form, and it's not over yet, I understand that. But if you've made up your mind to get well, then I know you'll make it the rest of the way. So, what are your plans?"

"I think I'm going to start by going back to that school. I actually learned a lot while I was there, in spite of myself." He chuckled as he remembered his first days there. "If I could learn that much in so little time without putting any real effort into it, I should be an outstanding student now!" He turned his face toward Maura. "What do you have to say about all of this, Maura? Can I still live here with you while I go back to that school? Would it be OK with you?"

"That would be fine with me. When do you think you want to start?"

"You're sure you don't mind my staying on longer? It could be for quite some time, you know?"

"I'm good with it. As long as you continue to be neat in the bathroom; don't make extra work for me and we'll get along fine. That means you're going to be learning how to cook and clean, you understand? I'm not going to be your maid." It hurt her to say that; in reality, she wouldn't mind being his maid. She just wanted to be around him, and help him in any way that she could.

"Sorry, but I can't promise I won't make any extra work for you. I am blind, remember, and the chances are pretty good I'm going to mess up once in a while, but I promise to do my best not to make your life miserable." He hung his head. "Not like before, anyway."

"Fair enough, then. You can stay as long as you like. If you learn to cook dinner for me you can stay forever!" A girl could only wish.

"How soon will you be leaving, Dave?" Maura questioned. "There's no rush, you know. You can stay as long as you like also."

"Well," Dave began, "probably sometime in the next few days. I think I want to get together with Allie at least once before I go and talk some more things out with her. I'll probably head back this way once or twice a week for a while just to be sure everything's going OK, but if Pen's back in school and behaving himself there's really no need for me to stick around. I do have a church to get back to."

"Well, I think I speak for Pen as well as myself, but we're going to miss you, Dave. You've been a huge help to both of us, and I'm sure you realize that. Just remember, you're welcome here anytime." Maura smiled sincerely as she spoke.

"Thanks. I'll remember that."

"OK, we've got that settled. I'll call the school in the morning and see about getting Pen back in classes. Now, how about some dessert?"

Pen was scheduled to start back to school the next Monday. Maura called the cab company and arranged for a cab to pick Pen up every morning and bring him home after classes every day. She and Dave took turns escorting him out the front door to the curb and back again until they were all confident he would be able to make his way on his own with his cane. They made a trip to the school and repeated the process until they were all comfortable with his ability to negotiate his way to and from the school.

Chapter 22

Dave spent the next two days taking long walks, stalling for time. He went to the phone several times a day with the intent of calling Allie to set up a meeting, but lost his courage each time. The fact was, Dave was attracted to Allie. It took him quite some time to admit it to himself, but there it was. That first night when she had come to the house he had been so tied up with Pen that he hadn't really looked at her. They had spoken few words to each other, and she had never taken her coat off. But the other day when she had come to really talk, it was a different story.

Dave couldn't remember ever being this interested in a woman, and he wasn't happy about it. Everything about her was wrong for him, and he knew it. In the first place, she was not a Christian, and for a pastor that was the number one requirement. Oh, that could change, it was true, but that was only one of the problems. She was pregnant. She was . . . she was an impossible candidate for a pastor's wife. End of story. And he couldn't get her out of his mind. He was in trouble and he knew it.

At the end of the second day he finally gathered up his courage and made the call. She sounded surprised to hear his voice.

"Allie?"

"Yes."

"This is Pastor Dave Benson. We met the other day with Pen."

"Yes, I remember you very well. How can I help you?"

He cleared his throat. "Pen and I said we would help you in any way that we could. I was wondering if you'd like to meet me for coffee somewhere when you have some free time and we can talk. Maybe we can come up with some ideas. What do you say?" He didn't realize he was holding his breath as he waited for her answer. Would she have coffee with him?

"Well, OK. Actually, that sounds like a good idea. I'd love to have coffee with you." She laughed, a light-hearted sound. "I'll try not to corrupt you too badly."

Dave exhaled, slowly. "Are you free tomorrow afternoon, say, about three?"

"Make it three-thirty and tell me where. I have to work until three."

He mentioned a café not far from the rehab center and they agreed to meet the next afternoon. He hung up the phone and noticed his hands were shaking.

He arrived at the café fifteen minutes early, his heart pounding. He felt like he had walked into the proverbial lion's den and was about to be lunch. He didn't like the feeling, but nothing could have dragged him out of that café. Allie was coming. He felt like he was sixteen again, giddy, and scared to death.

He told himself that if he just spent some time with her, the appeal and hold she seemed to have would evaporate. Reality would set in and he would see her for the woman she really was, a nice girl but totally unsuitable for him, and he could go back to Bozeman with no lingering feelings.

But when he saw her walking across the floor to the table where he was waiting, all rational thought flew out of his mind. She was here. He smiled.

"Hi. Were you waiting long? I came as quickly as I could."

"No, I just got here myself. Thanks for coming. I have some ideas I want to run past you, and, well, first, what would you like? Coffee? A sandwich? My treat."

"Just coffee will be fine. Black. And thanks." She smiled broadly at him.

He ordered for her, willing himself to relax and not stare. He lowered his head for a moment, then looked at her and began.

"Allie, I've been thinking about you a lot over the past few days, and I may have a solution that might work out well for all concerned."

Worry was etched on her pretty face as she leaned toward him across the table, anxious for any hope he could give her. "You're really going to try to help me? I thought maybe it was just all talk. You know, like a lot of preachers do. They talk a good show but it's all fancy words. I've been around a few in my time. But then, I think I may have told you, you don't look like a preacher. Sorry."

"That's OK, you're not the first one that's told me that. But just what is a pastor supposed to look like?"

"Well, I don't know, but not like you. You look like a regular guy. Normal, you know?"

Dave threw his head back and laughed out loud. "I'll take that as a compliment, if that's OK with you." It was getting easier; he started to relax a little more.

They made some more small talk, getting comfortable with each other before Dave got around to voicing his proposition.

"Allie, are you sure you don't want to keep your baby? That's the first thing that absolutely must be decided, and you've got to be very, very sure about your answer, so think carefully."

"Dave, I've done nothing but think about that, and I'm sure. There's no way I can keep this baby and my family too. If my parents ever find out, they'll never speak to me again, and I can't disappoint them like that. I just can't. I don't want to give my baby away. It breaks my heart to think about it, even though I know it's the best thing for all of us. But Dave, adoption is so final! They usually seal the records and I'll never know how, where . . ." She choked back a sob.

"OK, if you're absolutely sure, I think I have an idea." He reached across the table and took her hand in an effort to comfort and steady her.

"Allie, Pen has a sister; I'm sure you've met her, Raven?"

"Yes, I remember her. What about her?"

"Raven was in a terrible accident last year, and it left her unable to have children. She and her husband, Gus, haven't been married all that long, and I know they really wanted to have kids someday, but of course, now that will never happen."

Allie's head snapped up, her eyes riveted on Dave's face.

"Mind you, I haven't talked to them yet, but I'm pretty sure they would love to adopt your baby. They would give him or her a wonderful, loving home, and you would know where the baby is. The three of you could work out how often, if ever, you want to see the baby. I think it would be best if you never did, but you would still be able to keep in touch and know that all is going well. What do you think?"

Her face nearly glowed. "It sounds perfect! Do you really think . . . ?"

"I'll talk to them in the next day or so if you think you might be interested in doing this. I can't believe they won't be excited about the whole thing, but again, nothing's for sure until I talk to them."

"Yes! Yes! Yes! Dave, how can I ever thank you? Does Pen know about this? Did you talk it over with him?"

Dave sighed. "No, I haven't mentioned this to him at all. I wanted to see how you felt about it before I went any further. I think he'll be OK with it, though. We both know he's not the father, but he likes you, Allie, and he really does want only the best for you. So do I." He smiled at her again.

"How soon can you find out? Tonight? Tomorrow?" Her eyes glistened with unshed tears.

Dave thought he had never seen a more beautiful woman.

"I'll try to catch up with them tomorrow, and I'll let you know what they say as soon as I can."

"You know, I really thought I'd never hear from you again. I thought you'd just write me off and forget about me. I can't thank you enough for not doing that."

"I'm a man of my word, Allie. Believe it. I won't let you down." He meant every word he spoke to her.

They made some more small talk over a second cup of coffee, enjoying each other's company. When they stood up to leave, Allie couldn't help herself. She went to Dave and enveloped him in a true bear hug.

"Thank you, thank you, thank you, Dave Benson."

Dave hugged her back against his better judgment, loving the feel of this woman in his arms. And then, suddenly, she was gone.

The emptiness he felt was chilling.

He called Raven that evening and asked if he could come to Bozeman the next day to discuss something with them. Then he went to talk to Pen and Maura.

"Pen, I'm going to Bozeman tomorrow to discuss something with your sister and Gus. Why don't you ride along with me? It will be good for you to get out, and it's not like I'm going to drop you off there and leave you. I'll bring you back to Maura's afterward. What do you think, Maura?"

"Sounds like a great idea to me. It'll be good for you, Pen."

"You promise you'll bring me back here? You won't pull a fast one on me and just sort of forget to take me along when you leave?"

"No, I promise. I won't leave you there. I just think it would be really good for you to get out. What do you say?"

"OK. I think I'd like to. What time are we leaving?"

"I'd like to head out about nine in the morning, so be ready."

Chapter 23

Dave and Pen were finally on the road at nine-thirty the next morning. The air was clear and fresh, though brisk, and the cloudless sky gave their spirits a lift. While Pen couldn't see the brilliant brightness of the day, he could feel the sun on his face through the passenger window, and he basked in the warmth he hadn't felt in so many months.

"You know, Dave, it's been so long since I've been outside and sober at the same time, I'd forgotten how wonderful and warm the sun can feel on a person. I didn't realize how much I had missed this, the sunshine."

"Funny, isn't it, how a person takes everyday things like sunshine for granted until you've been denied it for so long. The Bible says, *"the rain falls on the just and the unjust,"* and it goes the same for the sunshine. The sun shines on the just and the unjust. One of God's free and bountiful blessings, isn't it?" He glanced over at his traveling companion.

"Did you get a good taste of that fresh Montana air, Pen?"

"Not really. Guess I'll breathe some in when we get to the stable."

"Why don't you roll your window down right now and soak some of that in along with the sunshine?"

"Won't it be too cold for you?"

"A little fresh air never hurt anybody. Go ahead."

Pen hit the power button and the window glided down silently. He inhaled the fresh Montana air deeply, and as he did so, a huge smile spread across his face. "I can't get enough of this, Dave. Thanks for the suggestion."

"My pleasure. Now roll that window back up before I freeze to death!"

Pen laughed and rolled the window up. It felt so good to be outside again. While he missed his pills, this was an altogether different "high," and he had to admit to himself that this high was far better. Life was good again. He still had a very long way to go in his battle for his new life, but at least he felt now that he had real hope. He had his sanity back, good friends, some goals, and yes, a woman that he found himself thinking more and more about on a daily basis. Was it possible for him, even in his new physically challenged state, to have a relationship with Maura? He knew blind people fell in love and got married all the time. Why not him? Would Maura ever consider him in her future? He had no idea, but he planned to find out. Somehow, some way, he would have to become someone she could love. He was mostly silent the rest of the way to Bozeman.

Raven and Gus were expecting them, and they both came out to meet the pickup when it pulled in. Raven was actually jumping up and down in her excitement, while Gus stood patiently at her side, smiling at his wife's exuberance.

She was pulling the passenger door open before Dave was able to kill the engine.

"Oh, Pen! You're here, finally! Get out here and let me give you a hug! Hurry up—why are you so slow? Come on, I've got a lot to show you."

"Slow down Raven, slow down. I'm here for a while so there's no big rush."

She grabbed his arm and started pulling him out of the seat. "Come with me. Just take my arm."

"Wait, sis. I need my cane."

"You don't need that since you have me. I'll see that you get around fine, just hang on to my arm."

"No, you don't understand. If I'm ever going to be independent I need to use this cane. I have to be able to learn my way around on my own. Just walk with me, but slow it down a little, OK?"

'Fine. Whatever you want. But you're here!"

"Yes, I'm here." Just then his cane hit something right in front of him. "What?"

"Oh, sorry, Brandi, get out of the way! It's my dog. Gus got me a new puppy right before we got married. I think I told you that Jesse died in my accident. Brandi's a good dog, but she's still pretty young and tends to get underfoot a lot. Shoo dog!"

"See, just another reason I need this cane." He laughed. "It's OK, though." He squatted down, holding his hand out, and called to the dog. "Brandi? Come here, girl, come here." The dog came up readily, sniffing Pen from head to toe, and deciding he was no threat, began licking his face. Pen laughed in pleasure.

"I'm glad you got another dog, Raven. She might not be Jesse, but I think she's a good one all the same."

Dave interrupted the reunion. "Can we go inside and sit down for a bit? I have something I want to discuss with all of you. It's kind of important, so I'm going to want your full attention."

"What? You brought Pen back to stay?" Hope echoed in Raven's voice.

"No, not that. He's . . ."

"I'm not ready yet. I told you that. I'm going to go back to school and that's going to take several months, I'm sure. I have to learn to be independent, Raven. I've got to find some way to support myself and live on my own before I come back here, if I ever do."

Raven's face showed her dismay and disappointment at this news, but she didn't push the issue. "OK, whatever you say. I'm just glad you came today."

Gus waved his arm with the invitation to follow him into the kitchen. "Unless you'd rather sit out by the arena where you can hear and smell the horses better?"

"You know, Gus, I think I'd actually like that, if it's not too much trouble. I know it was a horse that did this to me, but I do love them, and the smell of them. Yes, I think I'd like that. Thanks for the suggestion."

Gus and Dave grabbed some folding chairs and set them up in the arena. The noise of horses in their stalls, their breathing and the occasional nickers were welcome, comforting sounds to all of them. Pen raised his face, breathing in and listening to all the smells and sounds he had been away from for so long. He smiled, happy to be home once more. It would be nice to just stay here, with Raven and Gus and the horses. It would be much easier than going back to school. But if he did that, where would he be a year from now? Where would Maura be? Not with him, that was for sure. No, he had set some goals and he would have to see this thing through to the end. Somehow he had to get through it.

Dave cleared his throat and started in.

"I told you I had something I wanted to discuss with all of you, and I felt it needed to be talked over in person, not on the phone. This is important and will affect all of you, so you need to think this all over among yourselves carefully and honestly. If there is not full agreement, I don't think we need to go any farther."

"For heaven's sake will you spit it out, Dave? Just get to the point, will you?" Raven was impatient. She had things to do with her brother in the short time he was there.

"OK." Dave took a deep breath and started in. "You all know who Allie is, and how she still insists that Pen is the father of her baby, right?"

Heads all nodded in agreement.

"Yes, we know." Raven spoke for all of them.

"Well, she has decided she cannot keep her baby and she is reluctant to give him or her up for adoption, since she will never know what happens to him. The records at this point in time are always sealed. So, I was wondering . . . well, Raven, you and Gus had told me you can never have children, am I correct?"

Raven's head sank. "That's right. The accident fixed that permanently."

"Raven, Gus, would you possibly consider adopting Allie's baby? A legal agreement between the three of you where you would become the legal adoptive parents, but giving Allie the right to at least keep track of her child? Maybe see a picture now and then? I don't think she will want to be involved in any way in the child's life; she just wants to watch from a distance. For various reasons, she doesn't feel that there is any way she can keep her baby. What do you think?"

Raven grabbed Gus's hand in a death grip. Looking over at her brother, she had to ask, "Pen, what about you? What do you say to this? Aren't you the father?"

"No, I most definitely am not the father of Allie's baby. I'll grant you that she had at least some grounds to name me as the father, but I'm telling you that I'm not. I like Allie, and I feel sorry for her, but that's as far as my relationship with her goes. The baby is not mine. I don't want to go into any more details with you; some things are better left unspoken. But you can ask Dave. He knows."

"Dave?" Raven had to know.

"He's telling you the truth, Raven. The baby is not his. I'm positive of that. She's not telling anyone who the father really is; she was hoping that if she could convince Pen and everyone else that he was the father that he would marry her and things would work out for her. But Pen refuses to marry her, and I agree with him on this. I also want to add here that having met and talked with Allie, I'm pretty sure this baby will be a healthy, normal child. She's not a drinker and she doesn't do drugs as far as I know. She's a good kid, really, but like so many others over the centuries, she managed to get herself into the proverbial 'trouble.' So, you can think this over since there's no big rush. She has a few months to go before her due date. You can think about it and let me know what you decide." He rose from his chair.

"I think I'll go take a walk around the place while you folks talk it over. You don't need me around for this decision. I'll be back a little later. Take your time, and remember, you don't need to make a firm decision right now. There's time." He turned and walked away from the small group, who sat now in silence.

"Well, Raven, what do you think?" Gus had taken her other hand in his, holding his breath as he waited for her answer.

"Pen, what do you think about all of this? If we adopt her baby she may be in your life to some extent over the years, and of course we have no idea how often she'll be around. There's just no way to tell how firm her resolve will be. How do you feel about that?"

"I think the main thing is what you and Gus think about this, not me. But I think I can hear a lot of excitement in your voice, am I right?"

Raven's face was positively glowing at the thought of having a baby in her arms to complete her family with Gus. "Gus, what do you think?"

"Raven, honey, you know I was fine with the fact that we would never have any children of our own. I love you so much that it didn't matter to me in the end. But would I like some? Yes, you know I would, but it's up to you in the end."

"Gus, I want a baby more than almost anything else in the world right now. This is the chance of a lifetime for us! Oh Gus, a baby! Can you wrap your mind around that? Can you?"

"So, no second thoughts at all? You want to go ahead with this?" Gus wanted her to be positively sure.

Tears were shimmering in Raven's beautiful eyes. "Gus, no second thoughts on my part, but how about you? Let's stop if you aren't sure."

"I'm sure. I'm positive. I don't think we need any more time to think about it. Let's do it, if you're sure too, Pen?"

"Sounds like a wonderful solution for everyone. You two go for it, and I'll get to be an uncle! Wow. What a difference a year makes! Goes to show you never know when you wake up in the morning just what lies ahead. The best laid plans and all of that." He shook his head, but he was smiling.

Gus went to find Dave and give him the good news about their decision. There was no need to think about anything further; Allie had found a good home for her baby. The two men spent the rest of the afternoon visiting while Raven and Pen walked around the stable and the living quarters, catching up, hugging, and enjoying being together again. Too soon it was time to start the long drive back to Billings.

"Will you come back another day, Pen? Please? I've missed you so much!" Raven held onto her brother until the last moment.

"Sure, I'll come again, but right now I don't know just when that will be. I may not make it back for a few weeks what with school and all. But if I can hitch a ride, I'll come back."

"Maybe if Gus and I come to get you, you could spend a night or two? Maybe on a weekend?"

"I don't know about . . ."

Raven interrupted him abruptly. "Just think about it. You don't have to decide right now. But a weekend; think about a night or two back in your own bed. No one has slept in it since you left, you know. I'm saving your room for you."

"OK, I'll think about it. That's all I'll say for now." He found the door handle, and opening it, placed his cane inside then slid onto the seat, closing the door after him.

Dave took his seat on the driver's side. "OK, we're off! Thanks again for listening and making what I think is a good decision. Allie is going to be elated." He started the engine and, waving, drove out of the yard.

"Did you have a good day, Pen? Glad you came?"

"Yup. I did. Thanks for bringing me. And thanks for keeping your promise to take me back to Billings."

"Sure thing. I did promise you."

Pen slid down in the seat and pulled his hat down over his eyes. "I think I'll just take a little rest while you do all the work, if you don't mind. I'm pretty tired. This little jaunt seems to have worn me out." The reality was he had a lot to think about, but he was asleep in minutes.

Dave drove in silence all the way back to Maura's house in Billings; it was after dark when they arrived.

They spent some time going over the day's events with Maura, who voiced her enthusiasm for the decision Gus and Raven had made regarding Allie's baby, and then Pen excused himself to retire early.

Lying in bed that evening, Pen reflected on the day; his excitement about being outside in the fresh Montana air, the exquisite feeling of the warm sun on his face once more, the visit with his sister, and the positive outcome of Dave's suggestion regarding Allie's baby. It had been a good day all around.

But even that morning, as Dave had turned onto the interstate highway headed for Livingston and then on to Bozeman, Pen had felt a lingering reluctance to leave Maura's house. He went over all the good points of the day and was puzzled as to why he felt so pulled in two directions. He wanted to see his sister, but he didn't want to leave Billings. What was the hold for him here? It certainly wasn't the school, even though he was actually looking forward to going back again. Since his recovery and decision to once again face life, everything had changed, it seemed. But no, it wasn't the school.

It certainly wasn't Allie. He liked her but he didn't care one way or the other if he saw her or not. He cared about her and her baby, and he was thankful for all her help, even if she did enable his addiction to a huge extent, but no, Allie wasn't the pull he felt.

It certainly wasn't the city of Billings. For a man who had grown up in the untamed country of an Indian Reserve in Canada, cities held no pleasure. Being outside of Bozeman was close enough for him, and at times it had actually been a little too close.

He didn't want to admit the obvious to himself but it was Maura, soft-spoken, kind, Maura. Maura had become the one light in his persistent, gray world. It was Maura who made him want to get up in the morning. It was Maura who, unbeknown to her, made him want to become all that he could be in his new challenged condition. He wanted to . . . what did he want? He wanted to be a whole, normal man again. He wanted to be worthy, he wanted . . . Maura.

There it was in its entirety. He was in love with Maura. He wanted to be a man she could love in return. But being blind, he was going to have to become totally self-sufficient in every area of his life. Oh, he would never be able to drive, of course, but they had made it abundantly clear at the school that there were few other limitations for him. There was no reason he couldn't learn to cook, clean, wash, and go pretty much anyplace he wanted to go. And there was the option of a seeing-eye dog too.

All of these things he could see himself accomplishing, but one thing remained. He was going to have to find some way of supporting himself financially. There was no way he would ever ask a woman to marry him and expect her to support him. No way! He was going to need one more miracle.

As his thoughts continued to run riot, and his emotions varied from enthusiasm to despair, he began to pray. For over two hours he talked with his Lord, as despair, worry, anger, hope, and finally complete trust were alternately spoken out loud, in whispers, and silently. He finally realized that only with God's help would he be able to accomplish what he hoped to do. So be it. God had never left him, even when he couldn't feel His presence, and He was with him now.

The tears he had shed unnoticed in his agony of reasoning dried on his cheeks, and he slept.

Chapter 24

After Pen went to his room, Maura and Dave visited for a few minutes longer, and then Dave excused himself to call Allie. They agreed to meet at the same café the next afternoon when Dave would fill her in on the decisions that had been made.

The thought of seeing Allie again put Dave into turmoil. She filled his thoughts as no woman had ever done, and he found himself sweating at the anticipation of seeing her again. It was well after midnight before he was able to fall asleep.

Maura made arrangements for Pen to go back to school during her break time the next day, and also lined up transportation for him. He would start on Monday.

Pen spent the day thinking, planning, and making a more concerted effort at finding his way around Maura's house with special attention to the kitchen and bathroom. He would have to prove to himself and to Maura that he could be trusted as much as a sighted person, but it soon became apparent that it was going to be much easier said than done. So be it. He was not going to quit.

Dave arrived at the café earlier than the first time; anxious, scared, and thrilled at the opportunity to see Allie again. He didn't have to make up excuses to see her, at least not for now. He didn't know how he was going to handle things when he went back to Bozeman, but for the next couple of days, he could probably see her every day, if she was willing.

Allie entered the café with a sparkle in her eyes and a broad smile on her face.

"I'm assuming you have good news for me, don't you?" she said breathlessly as she slid onto the chair opposite Dave. "At first when you called I was really worried, but your voice sounded so upbeat I convinced myself that everything went well yesterday. I'm right, aren't I?" Hope echoed in her voice.

"Yup, everything went really well, Allie. Raven and Gus were thrilled with the idea of adopting your baby, just thrilled. I know there are lots of details to work out, but they were agreeable to letting you at least know how the baby is doing. I don't think it's wise for you to see him, but I'm sure they will send you pictures and updates whenever you want. Does that sound OK to you?"

Allie reached across the table and grabbed Dave's hand in both of hers, her excitement obvious in her beautiful, animated face.

"Dave, I can't thank you enough. I think I'm going to be able to pull this whole thing off after all, even without Pen. Oh, I would have preferred to keep my baby, but reality says I can't. This is perfect, as far as I can tell."

He smiled at her. "I think it's a pretty good solution too. I'm glad you're agreeable. But Allie, it's going to be hard for you, you do know that don't you?"

"Oh, I know. I'm expecting that."

"I mean when you actually have to give that baby up, well, it's a whole lot easier to talk about it than to actually do it. I hope you fully understand that." His eyes were anxious, but he did not withdraw his hand from her grasp.

Her face clouded at his words. "I know. I guess I'll eventually have to decide whether I want to even see my baby after the birth or give it away without ever seeing it. I just don't know what to do." She shook her head in her distress.

Dave gave her hands a squeeze. "I'll be there for you, if you want, Allie. When the time comes." He swallowed hard. "I'll be here for you from now on, if that would be of help to you." He held his breath, waiting for her answer. What if she didn't want him around? Didn't want to ever see him again, now that she had her "problem" figured out?

Her head shot up. "Would you? Would you mind too much helping me through this?"

"I would love to help you in any way that I can. Just let me know what you need." His brain had just kicked into overdrive at her acceptance of his help. Maybe, just maybe . . .

She withdrew her hands as the momentary excitement passed and reality seemed to settle in. "Dave, I don't know quite how to say this to you, but there's something about you that is, I don't know, almost restful. Definitely calming. If you don't mind too much, I think I'm probably going to want to talk to you often as my due date gets closer. I'm starting to feel like walls are closing in on me, and I have to admit I'm scared. Are you sure that's OK with you? I know you have lots of other people you have to take care of, being a pastor and all, but . . ."

"No problem, Allie. I want to, if you must know." He lowered his eyes, hoping she wouldn't see the longing that must surely be evident there.

"Thanks, Dave. I mean it. Thank you. I don't know what I would do without you."

"Allie, I just had an idea."

"What? What more could you be thinking?"

"Well, you have no family here, do you?"

"No, no family anywhere around here, thank goodness."

"How about friends? Anyone you're really close to?"

"Not really. Just a few acquaintances at work, but nobody I'm really close to. Why do you ask?"

"I'm just thinking, wondering; would you consider transferring to Bozeman? I'm sure you could get a job at one of the medical centers there, and you'd be close to, well, close to Raven and Gus when the time comes." *And to me.*

"I don't know right offhand. Let me think about it a bit. I can see the logic of moving. I won't have to deal with the looks and speculation that's bound to go around at work when my co-workers figure out that I'm pregnant. No one knows me in Bozeman, except you of course. And I would be close to you, if I need you, wouldn't I?"

"That's right. I can be your support through this whole thing, and I do think you're going to need someone, that's for sure. So? Need more time to think?"

Allie laughed, the smile back on her face. "No, I guess not. One CNA job is pretty much like another, and it's not like they're hard to find. OK, I'll do it!"

"Great! I'll get you the names, addresses, and phone numbers of the institutions in Bozeman and you can pick where you think you want to work. I'll also find you a place to stay so you can move whenever you're ready. How does that sound?"

"I'm scared, I admit, but if you're going to be there, I guess it will all work out OK, won't it?"

"When you're ready to move, just let me know and I'll take care of it. Do you have a lot of things?"

"Not really, but I'll find a mover."

"No, you leave all of that to me. I'll take care of everything."

"Dave, I'm starting to actually get somewhat excited. Crazy, huh?"

"Babies are always exciting, even in your situation. Good girl."

They stayed for another hour, making plans, enjoying each other's company. Dave was thrilled. Allie would be moving to Bozeman where he would be able to see her regularly. It was still true that she wasn't right for him, but he couldn't think any farther than the promise of being able to spend more time with her in the next few months. That was enough for now. Later, if this infatuation for her didn't pass, he didn't want to think about the trouble ahead. God would always come first in his life, but now there was Allie, too. *Lord, I know I'm in trouble already. I'm going to need a lot of help; I can see it coming. But I can't seem to help myself right now, so help me, Lord. Please.*

The next day Dave packed up the few things he had brought with him to Billings and after saying his good-byes, he left for Bozeman.

It was now just Maura and Pen. Maura had said that arrangement was fine with her. She had no concerns now that Pen had sobered up completely. He was a perfect gentleman and she was careful to keep her distance.

On Monday Pen went back to school, determined to make the most of the opportunity. A cab had picked him up in the morning, and since he had practiced with Dave and Maura before, he had no difficulty making his way from the house to the cab, and from the cab to the school entrance, where a staff member welcomed him.

His day was long and full. He was welcomed back warmly, and found he was actually pleased to "see" some of his old classmates. A few were still there but many had graduated and left. He had a lot to learn, and he was determined to learn as much as he could as fast as he could. Somehow he had to get on with his life, to make a real life for himself, if that was possible.

Maura had supper ready for him, warming in the oven, when he arrived home from school. It smelled wonderful and he was hungry, as always nowadays.

"Maura? I'm back, and whatever you made smells awfully good!"

There was no answer.

"Maura?" He listened closely but heard nothing. Wondering, slightly concerned at the quiet, he left his cane in the living room and counted his steps down the hall toward Maura's room. Where was she? As he got closer he heard her; soft sobbing sounds were coming from behind the closed door to her room.

He knocked lightly on the door. "Maura? Are you all right? What's wrong?"

Sniffling. Then, "I'm OK. Go away."

He couldn't stand it; he had never heard her cry before. Something was definitely very wrong.

"I'm coming in so you'd better be decent." He opened the door without waiting for an answer, smiling as he entered. "Like it makes any difference to me whether you're decent or not. I can't see you anyway."

She sobbed louder at that for some reason, and he couldn't stand the sound. He walked over to the bed and feeling the edge, he sat next to her, his arms out in invitation.

"What's wrong, Maura. Please don't cry. Just tell me what's the matter."

She sat up and melted into his waiting arms.

"Did I do something to upset you? Did I make a mess that I don't know about?"

"No. It's not you. It's something at work. I'm sorry, but I just can't stop crying."

He held her close and began stroking her hair, rocking her slightly. "Can you tell me about it? I'm a good listener. Can't do much else but I can still listen."

She sniffled once more and he felt for the Kleenex box with one hand, then handed her several he pulled out. "Here.

Blow your nose, and then tell me what's going on that has you so upset like this."

She blew, sobbed once more, then began.

"Oh Pen, I love being a nurse but sometimes, sometimes it's just so sad."

"Go on. What happened?"

One of my patients was only twelve years old. Only twelve! He had a brain tumor, and they did surgery on him, and . . ."

"And?"

"They were pretty sure they got it all, and his chances looked good. But today—today he threw a clot and died. He was doing so well! He was planning to go home in a couple of days, and now he's just gone!"

He hugged her tighter, trying to ease her pain.

"There was nothing we could do, it happened so fast. We were all so attached to him; he was such a sweet kid, and brave."

"I'm sorry, Maura. I wish there was something I could do for you. If there is, tell me and I'll do it, if I can."

"You know, I've lost patients over the years. It happens all the time. But twelve? He was special, you know? If I'm this upset, imagine how his parents must be feeling." She paused, and then said softly, "I hate this."

He continued to hold her as her sobs lessened. He felt awful for her, and yet he was so grateful for the chance to be this close to her. He rested his chin on the top of her head, inhaling the scent of her hair. What color was her hair? He didn't know; it didn't matter.

"Maura, I know this isn't the right time to be saying this, but I have to tell you something. I hope you won't be offended, but . . ."

She pulled away at this, apprehension on her face.

"But what?"

"I care about you, my nurse friend, and I might as well admit it, I'm afraid it's a little more than friendship."

"Well Cowboy, that's one way to get my mind off my patient!" She hesitated and then continued. "But Pen, I'm aware of how you think you feel about me and have been for quite some time."

"Not how I THINK I feel about you, but how I really feel."

"Pen, you aren't the first patient of mine who thought they were in love with me. It actually happens quite often. Gratitude gets mixed up with all sorts of emotions, but trust me, this will pass."

"No, it's not going to pass. I'm not a child, Maura. I may be blind but I'm a grown man and I know what I feel!"

"Look, I thank you, I really do, for caring about me. But it's not real, Pen. Lots of men fall in love with their nurses, and we've been around each other for so long now in close quarters that it's only natural." She reached over and patted his hand in reassurance. Seeing the look on his face, she said comfortingly, "It's OK. You'll get over me in due time." She seemed to forget for a moment that he couldn't see her smile.

Pen was angry, and pulling abruptly away from her, he got to his feet and headed for the door. "I told you, I'm not a child. I'm not some sixteen-year-old kid, and I know what I feel. You don't need to patronize me. I'm sorry I said anything to you." He slammed the door behind him as he left the room.

Maura heard the front door bang shut only seconds later.

Pen was seething. He grabbed his jacket and his cane and headed outside. He had no idea where he was going, but he knew he had to get out of the house and away from Maura. He couldn't stand it if she patronized him one more time. He was blind; he wasn't stupid! Being sightless didn't mean he couldn't love someone just like any other man. Obviously she wasn't interested. He should have known; he should have kept his mouth shut.

Tapping his way none too cautiously he just started walking, following the sidewalk, paying no attention to his direction, speed, or numbers of steps.

How long he walked, he had no idea. The air was brisk, clear, and cold. It was March and there were patches of ice here and there. Finally he stepped on one of those patches, his feet went out from under him, and in a split second he found himself on the concrete. He hit hard, and his hip screamed with the pain. His cane went flying. He cursed, fluently.

He sat there for a bit, then determination set in. He couldn't just sit there forever. He had to find his cane, first of all. Getting to his knees he started making a small circle, sweeping one arm in front of him searching for it. Stupid cane! He made his circle wider before he finally found it. For an instant he thought about smashing it on the ground, but then reason asserted itself; he was helpless without it.

Getting up, he started his tapping again, heading for . . . where? He had no idea where he was. In his anger and recklessness, he had paid little attention to his direction, and after falling he now realized he was totally lost. It was dark, it was cold, and he had no idea where he was. How far away was Maura's house? One block? Two? Four? And what direction was it from where he now stood? He heard the occasional car pass on the street, but they gave him no clues. He wanted to cry, but he resolved that was something he was not going to do again. He wished he had a few Valium; they would help more than anything right now. He swore loudly once more as he recognized his weakness.

He began walking slowly, tapping his way carefully. It was only a few steps before he felt a tree next to the sidewalk. Sighing heavily, he moved to the side and leaned his back up against the trunk. He stood there until his legs began to get tired, then he slowly slid down the trunk to sit on the cold ground, and found he was on another patch of ice. His head in his hands, he waited.

Maura had stopped crying. When she heard that front door slam she knew Pen had left the house, and from the noise he made as he left he was pretty angry. Well, she couldn't help it; she had been through this before with other patients and she was sure she was right. Pen wasn't in love with her, he was just grateful. Oh, she could wish it was true, but reason told her it was not.

Well, he would be back soon and he would be hungry, since he hadn't eaten. She went to the kitchen to check on the casserole warming in the oven, and then sat down to wait for his return.

But half an hour later he still wasn't back. She glanced at the kitchen clock, starting to get worried. He was right; he wasn't a little kid. He had had enough training at the school that he should be able to find his way around the block. There was no need to sit here and worry about him. He would be back when he cooled off.

Two hours later she couldn't stand it any longer. He should have returned at least an hour ago. It was cold outside, and he had to be tired after his first day back at school. She reached for her purse and car keys and then left the house to look for him.

Proceeding slowly, she started by driving around the block. She lived in a subdivision where the blocks were extra-long and curving, with no real pattern to the streets. He could have gone anywhere; but where?

Fifteen minutes later there was still no sign of him. Her heart began to pound in her worry. Keeping her headlights on high beam, she drove slower and slower, searching the darkness for any sign of a lone man walking.

Half an hour had passed before her headlights highlighted a speck of white well off to the side of the road; moonlight reflected the white of his cane. She backed up, pulled over to the curb, and killed the engine. She saw him then, sitting under the tree, his knees to his chest with his head cradled in his hands.

She walked up to him slowly, carefully.

"Pen, I'm here. Let's go home."

"Why don't you just go away and leave me here. I'm fine."

"Don't be a lunkhead! You're not fine and we both know it. Do you need help getting up?" She reached out to take one of his hands but he shook her off angrily.

"Don't touch me! I can get myself up."

"OK, OK, I got it." She backed away and waited for him to get to his feet.

"The car's over here. Want to take my arm?"

"No, I do not want you to touch me, thank you very much. I'll follow your footsteps with my cane."

She walked slowly as he followed, noticing he was limping and walking hesitantly. She said nothing until they drove up in front of her house.

"What happened? You're limping."

"I fell if you must know. Slipped on some ice. It isn't easy being a cripple, for your information.

"Oh, cut it out! You're not a cripple so don't be saying stupid stuff like that. OK, so you can't see. So what? Besides, anyone can slip on the ice. Happens to people all the time and you know it."

"Sure."

"Look, Pen, I'm sorry if I hurt your feelings. I really am. But this isn't ever going to go anyplace and there's no use leading you on in any way, shape, or form. It wouldn't be right. Once you're on your feet and have regained your independence, you'll look back on this and realize just how mixed up your emotions are right now. And I know you'll find a really good woman who will love you and suit you much better than I ever could." *But oh, how I wish your feelings were true, as true as mine are for you.*

"What's it going to take, Maura? What's it going to take to make you believe that what I feel for you is real? I was only going to hint that I really liked you, but the truth is, I'm in love with you. I'm not going to stop loving you, not today and not next week."

"Pen, I . . ."

"Look, I know I'm not good enough for you. I know that. What woman like you would give a man like me a second look? But I will promise you this: I will not give up, but I will not approach you again until I am totally independent and able to provide for you on my own. I will not be a burden to anybody. It's going to take some time, but I will do it. And then I'll be back for you."

"You—"

"I'm cold. I'm going to go in and take a shower, and then I'm going to bed." He opened the car door, grabbed his cane and stepped out.

"I have supper in the oven. Will you eat first?"

"I told you what I'm going to do. Eat it yourself." Slamming the car door shut, he tapped his way to the front door, let himself in, and disappeared down the hall to his room.

Chapter 25

Pen was angry, and that was putting it mildly. He went to take a hot shower and found himself swearing the whole time. In his frustration he lost his focus and began knocking things over, which resulted in more intense, loud cursing. The more upset he was the more accident-prone he became. Maura could hear the swearing clear back in the kitchen.

He finally managed to get the bathroom picked up and neat again, or at least he hoped he had done so. Kind of hard to know what's where when you can't see, and he cursed his blindness.

In his bed, warm and alone at last, he reflected on the disastrous evening. As he calmed down and thought about things honestly, he realized he had definitely overreacted about everything.

Maura hadn't intended to be cruel or treat him as less than an equal, but he had taken it that way. She was the first woman he had ever loved, and she had thrown it back in his face. But then, why wouldn't she? What did he have to offer a woman like her? Nothing; absolutely nothing. His fist pounded the bed at his side.

So, he pondered, was it really anger he was feeling or was it frustration? Was it both, just compounded? And where did he go from here? How was he going to face her in the morning? He threw embarrassment and shame into the mix as well. And oh, what he wouldn't give right now for a few of his favorite pills!

Calm down, Pen, calm down. Your swearing, ranting, and raving hasn't changed a single thing, has it? So think, man, just exactly what are you going to do now? You'd better come up with a plan, don't you think? Yes, he needed a plan. He needed to set some of those goals like his sister had told him he was good at, and then he had to plan how to reach them. What did he actually, really want?

He wanted to be independent. He wanted to be able to support himself. He wanted Maura. OK, goals set. Now, how to reach them.

He went over what they were teaching him at the school, understanding that all skills were beneficial for his independence, but some were more so than others. Focus on them. What skills did he need the most if he was going to be able to earn a living of some sort? It came to him: he needed first of all to be able to read braille. Reading was crucial. Typing? Should he learn to type? Could he ever use that in the real world? Well, why not? Dictation jobs. Medical transcriptionist. Ideas began to flood his mind and he saw real possibilities ahead of him.

He wondered just when it was that he had decided to live again, and found he couldn't really pinpoint a time. It had just sort of evolved. Allie's baby had a part in it, as did Dave and Maura. Detoxing whether he really wanted to or not, as he got clean he began to think more clearly, and the man who had lost himself for so long began to reappear. Pen was back in more ways than one.

They avoided each other as much as possible over the next few days, but on Friday Pen went to sit in the kitchen when he came home from school. Maura was always home before he was due to her schedule, but she was spending more and more time in her room in an effort not to upset him any further.

"Maura, can you come in here for a moment? I have something I'd like to discuss with you if you don't mind."

She came softly down the hall to the kitchen and took a seat opposite him.

"Yes, what did you want to talk about? Did I do something else you didn't like recently?"

He heard the sarcasm in her voice, but he couldn't blame her. "First of all, can we start over? Can we be friends again? I promise not to ever mention my feelings for you."

She looked at him warily. "OK. Let's do that. We won't talk about 'us.' Is that it? Anything else?"

"I guess I need to clarify that last statement for you, though." He raised his hand as if warding her off. "I told you I was coming back for you when I am independent again, and I fully intend to do just that. I told you I loved you, and whether you believe me or not doesn't really matter. I won't mention loving you until that time. But Maura, I WILL be back. I can only hope that you will still be here, and single, when I do. I don't know how long it will take me, but it will happen."

"Pen, I told you . . ."

"Be honest with me, will you, Maura? Can you in all honesty say you feel nothing for me beyond the normal nurse-patient relationship? Nothing for me at all beyond friendship? Give me honesty here, please. I know I'm not much of a catch, but is there any hope at all for me with you? Or do you really feel absolutely nothing for me? The truth, Maura, the absolute truth."

"The truth?"

"Yes, honesty at all costs."

She sucked in a deep breath, then let it out slowly.

"The truth. OK. I won't tell you I feel nothing for you. But that's as much as I'm willing to say at the moment. You get your life together and come back, and then we'll talk. How's that?"

"Fair enough. But Maura, if you think for one minute that it's never going to happen then you don't know me very well. I don't have any idea how long this is all going to take, but we will definitely have this discussion at a later date. I don't give up easily."

"OK, Cowboy. I'll take you at your word. Is that it? Was there anything else you wanted to talk about?"

"Yes. I've decided I want to go home just as soon as I've learned everything I can at that school. I'll get out of your hair as quickly as I can. In the meantime, do you think you could look into a gym membership for me, and maybe set up cab transportation so I can go after school several times a week and work out? Oh, I guess I should ask if we can afford it, well if whoever is paying for me can afford it. We all know I don't have a dime to my name."

"Well, of course I can do that, but are you sure you want to be going to a gym? Haven't you got enough on your plate at the moment?"

"I want to get back into shape, and just sitting around here and at the school isn't doing anything for this body. I need to get all my strength back as soon as possible. Will you help me?"

"I'll try to get it set up tomorrow. Soon enough? And don't worry about the money. Let's just say you have a benefactor who is happy to pay a lot of your bills for the time being."

"Can I ask who that might be? And tomorrow would be great."

"Nope. My lips are sealed on that one, sorry."

"Well, OK then. Thanks." He smiled at her, a wide, friendly smile. "And we can be friends again?"

"Yes, we can be friends, as long as we don't talk at all about that 'other'."

"You got it. Now, are you going to feed me tonight? I am pretty hungry!"

Maura didn't know what to say. He was leaving as soon as he could? She was convinced that he didn't really know his own mind, that he wasn't in love with her but only grateful, but she wished so much that she was wrong. And now he wanted to leave? This house would be so empty without Aspen Windchase in it. How would she survive without him? *Lord, it's going to break my heart when he leaves, but there's nothing I can do to make him stay. If I tell him how I feel he'll never be free to be all that he can potentially be. It would be tying him to me, and that would be so very unfair! I can't do that Lord, I just can't. But how will I live without him? Stay with me Lord. I need you.*

She set up the gym membership and cab connections the next day, and Pen began going three times a week, working out on the treadmill, lifting weights, and swimming laps. At the end of the month he presented a striking figure of a man, well-muscled, tall, and straight. He had finally started wearing sunglasses as many blind people do, and while they annoyed him, his good looks nearly took Maura's breath away when she watched him. He was an unbelievably handsome man, the male equivalent of his twin sister, Raven.

He became a model student at the school, where he did indeed learn to read and type, as well as cook, clean, and navigate most daily activities. His concentration was not easily broken, and he applied himself to the best of his ability in all areas of learning. His goal of returning to Bozeman and somehow becoming totally independent never dimmed, and he worked diligently to attain it.

The only negative aspect of these weeks was the knowledge that he would indeed be leaving Maura. He was sick at heart at the thought, but his resolve never faltered. He loved her, and he would be back for her one day.

Maura watched him as he worked to attain his goals, and depression settled over her like a mantle. How was she going to live without him? She couldn't help noticing his achievements and knew the day was drawing close for his departure. Finally he announced he was ready to go to Bozeman for the weekend, to see how he would manage there. She was devastated.

He called Raven one morning while Maura was at work and gave her the news.

"Hi, Raven?"

"Yes—Pen, is that you?"

"Hi, sis."

"Oh Pen, it's so good to hear your voice! Thank you so much for calling." As usual Raven took over the conversation.

"Raven, if you can be quiet for just a moment, I have a favor to ask." He was smiling in spite of himself.

"Oh, OK, sorry, I know I get to talking a bit, don't I?"

"Yes, you do tend to do that, but that's OK. I'm used to it."

"Yes, well, what's the favor?"

"I think I'd like to come spend the weekend with you and Gus if you don't mind. What do you say?"

"What day and what time? Oh my gosh, you're really, finally coming home?"

"Not to stay yet, just for a weekend to see how it goes. I'm assuming you won't mind if I infringe on your privacy with Gus?" He laughed into the phone, already knowing the answer.

"Like I said, give me a date and a time and we'll be there."

"How about this Friday any time after nine in the morning?"

Raven's joy could be heard in her voice. "How long will you stay, Pen? A week? Two? I don't know if I can wait until Friday!"

"You'll have to wait that long, girl. I'll see you Friday morning then. I'll be packed and ready whenever you get here."

"I love you, Pen, and I'll be there Friday morning."

He let the school know he was going home for the weekend and would be back on Monday morning. His teachers were excited for him to finally be branching out from his "safe spots" and thinking about rejoining the world at large.

Friday morning Raven showed up alone around ten o'clock. She explained that Gus had stayed at home to work with the horses, as they were booked full at the moment.

He asked Raven to write a note for him to leave for Maura, who was at work.

She tilted her head and flashed her brother a quizzical look. "Pen, did you tell Maura you were going home for the weekend?"

"No, that's why I want you to write a note for me. It doesn't make any difference one way or the other if I'm here or not."

"Why didn't you tell her?"

"Because I didn't want to. How's that for an answer? And it's really none of your business." He sounded harsh but he was smiling at her.

"What's going on, Pen? Something's off, I think."

"Didn't I just say it was none of your business?"

"Understood. Well, what should I write?"

"Just say you came to take me home with you for the weekend and you'll bring me back sometime Sunday afternoon or evening. I'm sure she'll be happy I got out of here for a while." His face took on a more grim expression at that remark.

Raven did as he asked and left the note on the kitchen table; then, taking her brother's arm in hers, she escorted him out to the waiting pickup. She never stopped talking until they pulled into the stable yard over two hours later.

Maura was tired. She had been working four twelve-hour shifts in a row and was looking forward to the next three days off. She had been thinking about some things that Pen might like to do, if she could interest him. Maybe a movie? She knew he couldn't see, but if the movie was a drama he should be able to get most of it. Action movies were obviously out of the question, but a drama should be OK. Just getting him out of the house away from the school might do wonders. She thought perhaps she shouldn't spend any extra time with him, but even though she doubted his feelings, she did not doubt her own, and looked forward to being with him. He had mostly avoided her since their argument and she missed him.

She sat on the sofa and, putting her feet up, it wasn't long before she was napping. When she awoke over an hour later, she was somewhat confused at first. The house was dark, which was not unusual. Pen usually forgot to turn the lights on for her. But the house was deathly quiet. Pen always made at least a little noise when he came home. Where was he? Why wasn't he home? Surely he didn't decide to take another walk on his own!

She walked back to his room, just in case she had simply slept through his arrival, but his room was empty, as was the bathroom. She began to worry as she walked through the house, turning on every light as she went.

Finally, she saw the note on the kitchen counter, informing her that he had gone home with Raven for the weekend. So, it was happening at last. He was leaving; this was the first step. She sat down hard on a chair, desolation washing over her. Why hadn't he told her he was leaving? Was he still that angry with her?

She poured herself a glass of red wine, and then took it into the living room to sip as she readied herself for the impending pity party she was going to have.

Lord, I know he'll never be mine, and I know that his leaving is totally for the best on everyone's part, but God, I miss that man!

Chapter 26

Aspen's heart constricted as he walked arm in arm with his sister into the stable. His emotions nearly overwhelmed him as he heard the familiar stable sounds and the scent of horses filled his nostrils. Gus was working a colt in the arena, and the squeak of well-oiled saddle leather along with the soft thuds of hooves sinking into the sand were welcome sounds.

It was good to be back, even if only for a couple of days, but oh, he missed Maura! He had purposely planned to leave while she was at work, knowing it would be harder for him if she were there. He didn't want to ever leave her, and yet he knew that a long separation was in store for him in the future. He said he was going to find a way to be totally independent, and he meant both physically and financially, but how on earth he was going to accomplish that goal . . . well, he had absolutely no idea. But he knew if he was ever going to be able to convince the woman he loved to believe in him, he was going to have to do it. He could never ask her to stay with him, and yes, to marry him, if he didn't. *But how, Lord, how? Show me Lord, show me the way, because I'm still very, very lost.*

Conversation flowed nonstop until Pen pled exhaustion and a desire to go to bed. Raven offered to escort him but he insisted on following her while using his cane. He had to learn his way around, and the sooner the better.

After Raven left, he explored the entirety of his room and his bathroom, then stretched out on top of his bed to rest a bit and think, but he was unable to organize his thoughts. Perhaps he was too tired. He got up and went to the bathroom, took a long, hot shower, and then returned to bed; his own bed, again, at last! It did feel wonderful, he had to admit. He was asleep in seconds.

Saturday morning was spent finding his way around the stable with all its nooks, corners, and rooms. He tapped his way carefully, with the only major obstacle being Brandi, who somehow managed to get under his feet quite often. Her presence taught him to be even more vigilant in his excursions. But he loved dogs, and was thrilled to have her for company.

Raven and Gus both were hesitant about letting him get around on his own, but at his insistence they let him have his own way. His sister was so happy to have him with her it was all she could do to walk away from him, but somehow she managed. There was a lot of work to be done; that was true.

By that afternoon Pen was tired of roaming around doing nothing. He wanted to feel useful in some way, but had no idea what he could possibly do to be helpful. He certainly couldn't help with training the horses in any way, and he didn't want to just sit around listening to his sister and brother-in-law working the colts. He was restless, and starting to feel a little irritable.

"Raven, can't you think of anything I can do around here? I'm going to go nuts just sitting around. There must be something?"

"No, we don't want you to work, so just sit and relax."

"Relax? I've done nothing but sit around for nearly a year! When I wasn't in a coma I was happily in my favorite fog, so I think I'm pretty well rested. I need to feel useful, Raven."

Gus was listening, and, being a man, he understood full well what Pen was talking about. A man didn't feel like much of a man if he couldn't work at something, no matter how minor, to make himself feel that he had at least some value. He knew Pen pretty well from church before the accident, and he had never been a lazy person. He was going to have to think of something, and quickly.

Suddenly, he had an idea. He was pretty sure Raven was going to have a fit, but Pen's pride was more important at the moment.

"Pen, look, if you think you're up to it, how do you feel about grooming a horse or two for us?"

Two faces turned in unison toward Gus at this question.

Raven was beside herself. "Groom a horse? Gus, have you lost your mind? He's, well, remember he . . ."

"Yes, I haven't forgotten that he can't see. But there's nothing wrong with his hands and his feet. He can certainly feel, and when you're grooming a horse you usually have one hand on the animal while you brush with the other. I really don't see any reason why he can't, unless he doesn't want to. What about it, Pen? Want to take a stab at it? Or, wait, I'm sorry. I wasn't thinking there for a minute."

"What, Gus? I think I can do that. Why not?"

"Well, it just occurred to me that it was being kicked by a horse that got you into this condition, and maybe you don't want to be that close to one. What do you think?"

Raven grabbed her brother's arm and spoke up loudly. "Of course he doesn't want to be that close to a horse! What are you thinking?" She gave his arm a light squeeze and cajoled, "Pen, you don't have to do anything you don't want to do. Let's think of something else. Are you sure you don't want to just go have another cup of coffee or something? Please? For me, so I don't worry?"

Pen shook her arm off angrily. Why was everyone trying to make him out to be helpless? He was blind; he wasn't totally helpless for heaven's sake, and being around horses again sounded good. He certainly wasn't afraid.

"Gus, I think I'd like to do that. I'm sure not afraid of them. You have to remember that even though I got kicked, and obviously pretty hard, it was a freak accident. That colt wasn't mean or anything, he was just trying to get a fly that was biting him. And to tell you the truth, I don't remember anything at all about the whole event. I remember working with him in the running W rope, and I remember starting to take it off, and that's it. So no, I'm not afraid to get around them again. I'm not sure I want to tackle a fresh colt just yet, but if you have some with decent stable manners, sure, I'd like to give it a try."

Raven looked like she was going to cry. "Pen, please."

"Leave it, Raven. Gus, let's go."

"Follow me, Cowboy. Let's get you back in the groove. It's about time you started earning your keep around here." Gus was all smiles.

They walked away, leaving Raven standing alone, shaken and worried. Men were crazy, just plain crazy.

Gus took him to a stall and asked him to wait while he got the comb and brush, but Pen insisted on tapping his way to the tack room behind Gus.

"I want to be able to get my own gear and navigate around here on my own. There's no reason after I get a little practice that I can't get my supplies and return them when I'm done. And if you give me stall numbers I should be able to handle things on my own. What do you think?"

"Sounds good, Pen. Follow me."

Pen counted steps and noted doors, alleyways, and obstacles as he followed Gus to the tack room, gathered what he needed, and then followed him until he stopped in front of a stall.

"Pen, this is Leta's stall. I thought you might want to start with her since she's old and gentle. Should be pretty easy for you, but there is a heads-up with her."

"Oh, what's that? I remember Raven's mare; she's a sweetheart. But I'm hearing something odd; what am I hearing?"

Gus laughed. "Leta has a colt in here with her. He's just a couple of months old, but gentle as a lamb, so I don't think you'll have any trouble. And Leta doesn't mind anyone fooling with her baby."

"A colt you say? How did that happen? You don't have any studs around here, do you?" Pen's brow furrowed in puzzlement.

"No, we don't, but do you remember Osage, that leopard Appaloosa stud Raven broke for Tom Martin last year?"

"Sure, I remember him. Beautiful horse, one of the finest I've ever seen as I recall. Raven was really crazy about him; she really loved that horse. She probably loved the horse as much as she loved his owner! So?"

"I don't know how much your sister told you about her breakup with Tom. You do remember they were about to get married, right before her accident, right?"

"Yes, she only told me they had broken up after the accident, but she never went into any details. It didn't sound like it was a friendly parting though, at least on her part. So what happened?

"Did she tell you she has a colostomy, Pen?"

"Well, yes, I think she did mention something about having one, but she didn't go into detail and I really don't know what a colostomy is. A scar? Something internal? Is that why she can't have children?"

"They had to resect her colon. She's left with what's called a stoma, and she has to wear a bag that attaches somewhat like a Tupperware lid that collects the stool. It's permanent and irreversible. The fact of the matter is, Tom couldn't handle it." He did not mention Tom's infidelity.

"Oh." He didn't really know what to say to this revelation. He had thought about himself to the exclusion of his sister all this time. It never occurred to him that other than possible scarring she might have been left with other concerns. As the reality of her situation sank in, tears welled in his eyes.

"I had no idea, Gus. She pretty well glossed it over and I just . . . I had no idea. Poor Raven! She was always so obsessed with her looks and perfection. She must have been devastated!"

"She was. She had a very hard time facing the reality of it."

"But you say Tom couldn't handle it? He didn't love her enough to stay with her?"

"No, he just couldn't do it."

"The jerk! Why . . ."

"No Pen, don't judge him too harshly. He's certainly not the only man that would have trouble with that condition. I know he loved her, but this is something totally different than, say, an amputation. I'd show you a picture but obviously that won't work for you. But being a man, you understand that we guys are pretty visual creatures. He just, well, he could not be a husband to her after the accident, if you know what I'm trying to say."

"But you married her? What about you?"

"For some reason, it just doesn't matter to me. I love Raven so much I don't even notice it. But that's me, and I know I'm a little different from most men."

"Will you describe it for me? I'd like to try to understand what you're talking about."

"How about we get this mare and her colt taken care of first, and we'll talk about it later. Sound OK to you?"

211

"Sure, but back to my question: How did Leta end up with a foal?"

"Well, she came into heat about the time they broke up, and Osage was still here, so I called Tom and asked permission to put the two together. He felt so badly about breaking up with Raven that he was all for it. Your sister was totally shocked to see her mare getting a bigger and bigger belly as the months went on, and then this beautiful little baby showed up. He's a cutie, that's for sure."

"What's he look like, Gus? Does he have color? I know a lot of Apps are essentially solid, but Osage was loud. How about this colt?"

"Pen, this colt is the spitting image of his dad. He's one of the prettiest black leopard Appaloosa colts I've ever seen. He's going to be easily as good as his daddy. Raven hit the jackpot with him, let me tell you. Of course, it's been like having a human baby or a new puppy around. This baby is spoiled rotten and totally fearless. But there isn't a mean bone in his body, and I'm positive he won't accidentally hurt you. Raven has worked hard on his manners already, so I feel confident you'll be fine in here with the two of them."

"Well, let's get on with this, then. I want to meet this new addition!"

"I'll come in with you till you feel comfortable, how's that?" Gus offered.

"No need, Gus. You just go on about your business and I'll be fine. I'll put the grooming stuff away when I'm done and meet you back either in the kitchen or the arena later. Sound OK?"

"You're sure?"

"I'm sure. See you later." He opened the stall door and, speaking softly to the mare, entered slowly, one hand outstretched in greeting.

Gus stayed only long enough to be sure Pen would be all right, but it soon became obvious that if you didn't know Pen was blind, a person observing the grooming process would never guess that the groomer had no vision. Smiling to himself, he left Pen to his new work and went back to the arena.

Pen was lost in his task. He loved being around a horse again. While he had never had the latent talent that his sister had, he was good with horses and loved them fiercely; just the smell of them was soothing. Leta was gentle, and seemed to remember him from before. She was quiet, and knowing her colt was safe with her, she cocked a hip and was soon nearly asleep as Pen brushed and combed rhythmically. He crooned to her softly as he worked, soothing both the mare and himself. He couldn't ever remember being more content in his life than he was right now. It was blissful.

The colt was curious about this new human, and kept sniffing him all over, but made no effort to bite or kick in any way. Keeping one hand always on the mare, he worked the brush and comb with the other. When Pen finished with Leta he turned to the colt and groomed him thoroughly as well. He even cleaned out their feet, finding that the colt had obviously had his feet picked up and handled before.

"What's your name, kid?" Pen asked. "Gus never told me your name. Let's see, what can I call you until I find out what Raven named you? How about Hank? Fred? Kiddo? Wilber? I think I kind of like Fred. How does that sound?" He chuckled to himself. "Like you care. I know, I know, all you care about right now is a good warm meal and a soft spot to sleep. I feel the same way, kid. Us men got to stick together!"

When he was finished he gathered his kit and, placing it next to him, he sat carefully in a corner of the stall on some fresh straw. It was good to be back. The smells, the sounds, it was all good, and he loved it. There was only one problem with the whole thing; he would never be able to support himself, let alone a wife, grooming horses. But he was still glad he had come home.

He had no idea how long he sat comfortably in the corner of the stall, listening to the soothing, ordinary sounds of horses munching on their hay, stomping the occasional hoof, nickering to each other, but he was content. Fred came over to check him out and snuffle his head every now and then, but finally, bored with his new toy, Pen heard him lie down at his mother's feet.

Pen sighed, then rose to his feet, and gathering his grooming tools, he let himself out of the stall and tapped his way back to the tack room to return them. From there he found his way to the kitchen, located the always-on coffee pot, carefully poured a cup for himself, and sat at the table to wait for whomever would be the first to come and quiz him. He was pretty sure he wouldn't have long to wait; Raven had probably been checking on him every ten minutes. Well, she could fuss all she wanted, but he had gotten along just fine.

Sure enough, only a few minutes passed before Raven walked quickly into the kitchen, looking for her brother.

"There you are! I've been looking all over for you. Are you OK? Did you hurt yourself?"

Pen heard the concern in her voice. "I'm just fine, and don't be telling stories; I'm pretty sure you had your eye on me most of the time, knowing you."

She blushed at the accuracy. The twins knew each other very well. "Well, I just don't want anything else to happen to you. You're the only family I've got, remember? Well, besides Gus, that is. Oh, you know what I mean." She sat next to him, cradling his arm in hers.

"To answer the questions I know you are bursting to ask, I got along just fine, and really enjoyed doing something useful for a change. And it's something I'm used to doing. It felt good, sis. Thanks."

Gus showed up just then with all the same questions that his wife had. Then, apparently satisfied that Pen had accomplished his task with no difficulty, suggested more chores for him.

"Since that seems to have tickled your fancy a little, want more work? You know full well there's never a shortage of chores around a stable, and there's no reason you can't take charge of some of them, if you want to, that is. What do you say? Are you up for it?"

Pen beamed his pleasure. "Gus, I am more than up for anything. It feels so darn good to be useful again. Got more horses to groom, or what did you have in mind?"

"Well, there's always horses to groom, you know that. Most of them should be no problem for you. But I was thinking, there's also a lot of tack that could sure use some soaping and oiling. You know yourself that seldom gets done. Pick your poison, unless you're tired and want to rest a bit."

"How about I soap a couple of saddles for you?"

"That would be great! I know you're half owner of this place, but I still feel like we should be paying you or something." Gus seemed thrilled to have a volunteer willing to clean tack.

Pen laughed. He finished his coffee, then asked Gus to accompany him to the tack room where he could get him started with oil, rags, water, and saddle soap.

By suppertime he was actually pretty tired. He had been using muscles he hadn't used in nearly a year, and was thankful he had been working out at the gym for the past month or he would be really sore. As it was, a good hot meal, a warm shower, and he was ready for bed. It had been a good day. He had proved to himself and two others that he was capable of actual productive work and didn't need to be coddled and fussed over at every turn. He slept well.

Chapter 27

Sunday morning came all too soon. Gus cooked a big breakfast for all of them, explaining that while Raven wasn't a bad cook by any means, he kind of liked spoiling his wife one morning a week. Pancakes, eggs, sausage, juice, and coffee made a real feast.

"Are you coming to church with us, Pen? We'd both like to have you, you know that, and Pastor Dave would be thrilled to see you. What do you say?"

Pen was tempted, but declined. Going to the school every day with others like himself was one thing, but being out in public? Maybe not quite yet.

"No, I don't think so, Gus. I don't think I'm quite ready for that yet. Maybe next time I come."

Raven gasped. "You're not coming? Pen, do you remember at all how often you tried to get me to come to church with you? And now you're going to stay home?"

Pen smiled. "Yes, I sure do remember. I'm assuming Gus knows your history, so I won't be saying anything I shouldn't here, but if I remember correctly most of my invitations came the morning after a pretty rough night for you, didn't they? What a difference a year makes! Now it's a role reversal."

Gus and Raven both laughed at this, but it was true.

"Are you sure? I'll make sure you get around OK, you know. And Gus will help. Please?"

"Nope. I'm staying here. You two go have a good morning. You can tell Dave that I'll be expecting a really top-notch sermon when I get moved back here permanently. He'll know what I mean."

"If you're sure." Raven's voice was low.

"I'm sure. See you both when you get back." He excused himself from the table and counted his steps back to his room.

An hour later after they had left for church, Pen debated what he should do while they were gone. Groom another horse or two? Work on some more tack? Sit around and rest?

He went to Raven's room and let Brandi out to have some company. There was nothing like a good dog to warm a man's heart, and Brandi was a pretty good dog. He took her to the tack room and, passing his hands lightly over the workbench, found the radio that had always been there. Turning it on, he turned the dial until he found a Christian station, then pulled up a chair, put his feet up on the bench, and slouched back, listening to familiar Southern Gospel music. This was church. Brandi lay on the floor next to him and Pen fondled her ears while the music washed over them both. It really was good to be home again. That's where Gus and Raven found him when they got back from church.

After lunch, Pen was ready to do some more work before heading back to Billings.

"Gus, have you got a few more horses I could groom this afternoon? I sure enjoyed working with Leta yesterday."

"You know, I've been thinking, you used to love riding, I know. How about riding with me in the arena for a while? You know that old saying: 'There's nothing so good for the inside of a man than the outside of a horse.' What do you say? Want to give it a try?"

Raven looked like she was ready to blow a gasket. "Gus! What do you think you're doing! He can't ride . . . he's . . ."

Pen interrupted her. "Yes, I know. I certainly haven't forgotten—I'm blind. As long as the horse isn't blind too it shouldn't be a problem, right?" He laughed at his own joke, trying to cover up the annoyance he felt every time his sister tried to coddle him these days. "I'm blind, Raven, I'm not crippled. There's a difference. I am also not feeble-minded. Please remember that."

"But Gus! You can't . . . he can't . . ."

Gus was grinning from ear to ear. "Come on, Cowboy, let's get you mounted. Glad to hear you're up for it. See you later, Raven, and I don't want to see you anywhere around that arena while we're riding. Go brush a horse down or something. We're going to be fine, and we're gonna be having some 'man talk.' We'll see you later, woman."

Pen was a little anxious about all of this, but he wasn't about to let it show. If Gus thought he could do it, then he would give it his best shot. He trusted Gus completely; if he said it was OK to ride, then it was OK to ride.

"Lead the way and I'll follow. See you later, sis."

Gus had a six-year-old gelding that was nearly ready to go home. The owners had purchased the horse for their daughter who was ten, and they had wanted to be sure he was trail ready and dead broke before they let the girl ride on her own. The horse would be the perfect mount for Pen to start out on. Gus brought him out of his stall and cross-tied him in the alleyway.

"How much do you want to try to do on your own, Pen? Want me to tack him up or do you want to try? He's plumb gentle, just about like Leta, so you should be fine, but whatever you're comfortable with. I don't intend to baby you any, but I don't want to push you farther than you're comfortable with either. Something tells me you don't want any of that, am I right?"

"If you start treating me like a cripple too I'll, well, I don't know what I'll do but I bet I come up with something you won't like. If you bring the gear out here, I'll see how I manage, as long as you think he'll stand for my clumsiness."

"This horse is pretty much bomb-proof. I don't think you can do anything to rattle him, so go for it, as much or as little as you'd like. I'll bring his saddle out and let you have at it while I get my own horse ready."

"Sounds good. Let's go for it. And Gus?"

"Yeah?"

"Thanks."

"Enough said. Let's not get mushy; let's just get mounted."

Gus brought his own horse back to the alley, and then went to get Pen's gear. He helped Pen feel where everything was, and then left him to saddle and bridle his horse, all the while keeping a sharp eye on him to be sure there were no problems.

Pen hadn't wanted to say anything in front of Raven, but Gus's suggestion had taken him completely by surprise. Ride again? By himself, and not double with either Raven or Gus? Could he? He wasn't really prepared mentally for this challenge, but all it had taken was for his sister to suggest that riding was something he couldn't do because he was blind, and, well, the game was on. He was not going to be treated like a sub-human; he simply was not. If Gus thought he would be OK, then he would go for it.

Working slowly, one hand always on the horse beside him, he brushed the gelding down quickly, then carefully placed the saddle blanket, smoothing out any wrinkles he could feel. It took him a few seconds to figure out a way to be sure it was centered, but when he was finished, he was confident it was in the right spot. Then it was time for the saddle.

Since he couldn't keep a hand on the horse, he kept contact with him with his left knee and leg. Since the touch was light, the horse did not move away. Picking up the saddle, he deftly swung it over the horse's back, just as he had done hundreds of times in the past. Even that little task made him smile. This was what he loved.

He carefully felt for the girth and then cinched the horse up lightly; he would tighten it after Gus checked his work.

Moving to the horse's head, he picked up the bridle, and, working slowly and carefully, he soon had the gelding bridled and ready to go.

"Gus, want to come over here when you're ready and check this all out? I want to be sure I got everything right. Not only can I not see anything, but it has been a while, after all. I think it's OK, but I think the teacher had better grade my work for me before I try to mount up."

Gus finished saddling his horse, then came over to inspect Pen's work. He found nothing out of place, and his face showed his pleasure; he hadn't been wrong about Pen's abilities.

"Looks just about perfect to me, Pen. You haven't lost your touch. Good job; just don't forget to tighten that cinch before you mount up."

"That I will surely do. Now what's the plan?"

"I'll bring my horse over here and steady yours while you mount up. I'll lead my horse over to the arena and let us both in. You can follow me and then we'll work it all out once we get in there. OK?"

"Fine with me." He took a deep breath when he heard Gus walk away to get his horse.

When he returned, Gus held the gelding's bridle while Pen mounted, then handed Pen the reins.

"He's all yours, Pen. Here we go. He'll want to naturally follow my horse, so you can pretty well just let him have his head for now."

Gus was right. Pen's horse followed nose to tail as they entered the arena, where Gus closed the gate behind them. He had brought a stick about four feet long with him, and once he was horseback, he reined up next to Pen and handed him one end of the stick.

"If you keep your hand on your end and I hold onto the other end, you'll know where you're at with me and my horse. That should help you gauge the distance between us until you get used to everything by sound. I don't think it will take long for you to be able to pretty well assess the distance between us and we can ditch the stick. I figure we'll just walk side by side around the arena for a while, do some talking, and just kind of relax. No work today for man or beast, only a good time. Ready?"

"Ready. Let's go." He was terrified, but there was no way he was going to let it show. Not being able to see what was in front of him, he wanted so badly to stretch his arm out, or maybe even his cane. But he didn't have his cane, and he knew he had to find a way to conquer his fear. He could do it. He would do it. One step at a time, just one step at a time.

They started out at a slow walk and Gus kept that pace for the entire ride. They walked side by side, around and around the arena, and as the horses plodded calmly along, Pen began to visibly relax; it wasn't long before he was really enjoying himself.

As they rode, they talked. Pen started by asking Gus questions. He wanted to know more about Raven's colostomy, and asked Gus to describe it in more detail. He had a lot of questions that he wanted answered, and now, while they were alone, was the perfect time.

Gus answered all of Pen's questions to the best of his ability, hiding nothing and glossing nothing over. Eventually the conversation turned to Pen's parents, and all that Gus had found out the previous summer about their journey to Canada. He had told Pen everything, but his friend had been in a coma. Gus had no idea if Pen had heard the story, and if he had, did he remember any of it? Pen said he remembered some conversations, but nothing about his parents.

So Gus related everything he had found out; how his mother had been posing as a gay cowhand as she hid from her abusive ex-husband, Todd. How her ex had found her and beaten her senseless, and when Todd had been found dead, the twin's father, Jesse had been accused of murdering him. He told as much as he knew about Francine and Jesse fleeing horseback through the Bob Marshall Wilderness in a desperate attempt to escape to Canada, and how they had simply seemed to disappear from the face of the earth. No one knew what had happened to them until that lawyer found Aspen in Canada to notify the twins of their inheritance.

Pen listened spellbound. It sounded totally unreal, like something out of a movie. How could that possibly be? He knew he was going to have to find out more; he wanted to learn the whole story and the whole truth. Was his father really a murderer? The man he remembered, while tough, couldn't possibly have killed anyone—or could he?

"Gus, when you get time, would you help me find out what really happened? I want to know everything, but obviously I can't drive and I can't read. I'm getting pretty good at braille, but I don't think their story is in that format at the moment. What do you say? Will you help me?"

"You know I will. I wanted to follow up after I found out the little I did but just haven't gotten back to it. I've been busy, I guess. But sure, let's get the whole story. I'm with you. When do you want to start?"

"In a week or two, when I get back. Maybe I'll stay a few more days at a time. I'll just have to see. Thanks again, Gus. I know it's more work for you, but I want to know everything."

Gus smiled warmly. "I'm just glad you want to come back. There's nothing your sister wants more than for you to come home permanently. You know that, don't you?"

"Yeah, I know that. I wasn't sure before, but it's been so good to be back this weekend that I think it will be a new goal for me. I don't really want to leave Billings, I . . ." his voice trailed off. How could he tell Gus that Maura was there, and the thought of leaving her was nearly crippling for him.

Gus caught the hesitation. "What is it, Pen? What's the hold that Billings has on you? The school? Allie? But Allie's moving to Bozeman any day now, so . . ." His face held a startled look.

"It's Maura, isn't it? You don't want to leave Maura! I'm right, aren't I?"

Pen's face showed his every emotion, and it was easily read now. "I guess you figured it out, Gus. Yes, it's Nurse Maura."

Gus laughed out loud. "Pen, don't tell me, you finally tumbled! Aspen Windchase is in love!"

"Zip it, Gus. You don't have to broadcast it all over creation. Raven doesn't need to know about it. I wish you hadn't figured it out either."

"Why not? What's wrong with somebody knowing you finally, finally, have fallen in love? I think it's wonderful. Good for you; it's about time. You're not getting any younger, you know. And Maura's a good woman. You could do a whole lot worse."

"I don't think I could do any better, that's for sure. In fact, I know I couldn't. But it's no use, me being in love with her."

"Why not? Does she know how you feel or are you too much of a coward to tell her?"

"She knows."

"And?"

"And she turned me down."

"What? Turned you down? Did she give you a good reason? Or are you just not her type?"

"She says I'm just mixed up, confusing gratitude with real emotional feelings of love. Says what I feel is definitely not real, and that as time passes, I'll figure out that it isn't love at all."

"I'm assuming you don't agree?"

"Nope. I'm a grown man, and I'm certain that she's the only woman I'm ever going to love. But I haven't a clue how I'm going to convince her. I'm not sure that there's any way I can. Besides, let's get real here. Why on earth would a woman like her give a man like me a second glance?"

"Why wouldn't she? What's wrong with you?" Gus sounded genuinely puzzled.

"Gus! Get real, would you? I'm blind, remember? What normal woman wants to hook up with a blind man? Besides, I'm an addict too, remember?"

"OK, you're blind. So?" He didn't mention the addiction aspect.

"So I've made up my mind that if I'm ever going to have any chance at all, I have to somehow find a way to be totally independent, both financially and physically. I will not have my woman supporting me; I'll stay single for the rest of my life before I'll let that happen. But I'm having a terrible time trying to figure out what I could possibly do to earn a living."

"Well, lots of blind folks are totally independent, so we're just going to have to come up with something, aren't we?"

Pen's jaw was set as he rode. "I think you're a little more optimistic than I am. But one minute I feel like it's all hopeless and the next I'm wanting to be with her so badly that all I can think about is finding something I can do with my life, some way to make it all right."

"Well, Pen, I think you have to remember that as you keep reminding us, you're not a cripple. You just can't see. As far as I know, all the other parts of your body are working just fine. You're a good man, Pen. And trust me on this, you're still what women call a 'hunk.' Heads still turn when you walk into a room, cane or not."

Pen snorted at his friend.

"Pen, when Maura said you were all confused about love and all, did you ask her how she felt about you?"

"I asked her if she could honestly say she had no feelings for me, and she said she couldn't say that. I told her that I was going to leave, but I would be back when I could provide for her. She said we could talk more when I came back, but Gus, she doesn't believe for a second that after I leave I will ever return."

Gus laughed out loud at that.

"What's so funny? I don't see anything funny at all in any of this." Pen was irritated at his friend. How could he laugh at his heartache?

"Pen, it's funny because Maura sure doesn't know you very well, does she! I've known you for a very long time now, and one thing I've learned is that if you say you're going to do something, heaven help the rest of the world, because you won't quit until you accomplish what you set out to do." He laughed again. "I have no idea how this is all going to play out, but I'm pretty confident that in the end, I'll be attending your wedding. You may have missed mine, but I guarantee you I won't miss yours!"

"You won't tell my sister, will you? She's liable to run to Maura right away and twist her arm or something. I don't want her getting in the middle of any of this, understood?"

"Got it. I won't say a thing to her, but would you like me to talk to Maura? I could let her know that you generally mean exactly what you say, and to be prepared."

"Nope. You stay out of it too. One thing at a time. I'll be doing a lot of praying in the future, and if you think you want to help me out, you could pray for me too."

"You know I will."

"Thanks. Now, it's getting a little late and someone still has to take me back to Billings tonight. I've got school in the morning, remember?"

Gus rode over to the arena gate and dismounted. Leading his horse through it, Pen's mount followed closely once more. It didn't take long to put the horses up and go find Raven, who was waiting for them.

In less than an hour the three of them were headed back to Billings. They ordered pizza before they left, and dinner was pizza and soda as they drove. Raven, as usual, talked non-stop all the way.

Chapter 28

Pen waved good-bye to Raven and Gus as they drove off, then unlocked the front door and walked in. Maura's unique scent, ever present in her house, greeted him.

"Maura, are you here?"

"I'm sitting here in the living room. You're back." It was a statement of fact.

"I am indeed back."

"How did it go? Were you . . . ?"

"I was fine. I had a good time, but I have to admit I'm pretty worn out. May I sit with you for a while?" He wasn't sure about his reception.

"Sure, come sit with me and tell me all about your visit. What did you do while you were there? How was Raven besides tripping over herself trying to help you with everything?"

"Got her figured out, do you?"

"Pretty much, I think. She just can't help it; she loves you too much."

"Is it OK if I sit next to you on the couch? That's where it sounds like you are."

She hesitated only a moment. "Sure, come on over."

He didn't want to irritate her, but there was nothing he wanted more than to sit next to this woman, if she would allow it. He tapped his way over to the couch and sat gingerly next to her.

"Do you want a recap or do you want to talk first? Your choice, you pick. But I think you realize we have a couple of things to sort out whenever you're ready."

"You're right, we do." She took a deep breath. "Let's start with you telling me why you didn't let me know you were leaving on Friday? That was a little mean, don't you think?"

He sighed and reached over for her hand. "Can I hold your hand or are you going to get mad about it?"

She took his outstretched hand in her own and clasped it warmly. "Why didn't you tell me, Pen?"

"Actually, I can't tell you why I did that. Guess I was still a little angry with you. It was petty and childish, I know, and I'm sorry. In all honesty it never occurred to me that you might be upset about it. You pretty well shut me down the other day, so I figured it didn't matter. But I guess even if you didn't care, it would have been the polite thing to do. Sorry." He gave her hand a light squeeze. She squeezed back.

"I'll agree; it was childish. Please don't ever do that again. I'm just glad I saw the note or I would have been frantic."

He kept his face pointed straight ahead. Then, softly, hesitantly, "Did you miss me?" He didn't realize he was holding his breath after his question.

"As a matter of fact, I did. It was pretty quiet around here."

"You sound like you don't want to admit it. Am I right?"

"You're right. I don't want to admit it, but I did, in fact, miss you."

Pen beamed. She did feel something for him. All was not totally lost. "So, we are in fact friends again?"

"Yes, friends. OK, so now, what did you do all weekend?"

He proceeded to fill her in on his activities, about grooming a horse and cleaning some tack. He finally got around to telling her about his afternoon riding activity, and heard her audible gasp.

"You rode? A horse? By yourself?"

He leaned back comfortably then, relaxed as he remembered the day's events, but not releasing her hand. He told her about Gus insisting that he could do it, about riding with him in the arena, and he even related the story Gus had told him about his parents and how they got to Canada.

"There's a lot more to the story than Gus was able to find out. He's agreed to help me unravel the tale when I go back in the next week or two. I'm having a hard time wrapping my head around it all, but I can't for one minute believe my dad was a murderer. If there's any way to prove his innocence, I want to clear his name."

"But how . . . ?

"I don't know just yet, but Gus and I are going to work on it. For now, I have to get back to school; I've still got a lot to learn."

They sat in a comfortable silence for a few minutes, before Pen began talking once again.

"Maura, I know we agreed to be friends, and you want to table any talk about anything more than that between us, but I don't know if I can do that. I just care way too much, I guess."

"Pen, I . . ."

"Look, I don't want to make you uncomfortable, but I haven't changed my mind even a little bit. Being away from you for just two days was hard for me, and I don't anticipate it getting any easier. But I told you I will be leaving, and that hasn't changed. I will, in fact, be moving out in a few weeks. I also said I was coming back for you, and I will. If you tell me that you absolutely do not want me around on a permanent basis, that you have no feelings for me at all other than as a patient or a friend, then no, I won't come back. I won't hang around where I'm not wanted." Silence again.

"Maura, do you remember when I kissed you?"

"Uh, how could I forget? What about it?" She sounded cautious.

"Can you honestly say you didn't feel anything? I sure did!"

"I don't know. What am I supposed to say here?"

"Say you'll let me kiss you just one more time to see if you remember correctly, how's that?"

"I don't know if that's wise . . ."

His hand came up to her cheek. "Why not? I promise, nothing more than a quick kiss. Maybe I don't remember it right. Maybe you don't either. Let's try it one more time, OK?"

He heard her draw a deep breath.

"Maura?"

"OK. Just once. Just to see, but . . ."

"Hush. Let me see you again." His hand began to lightly stroke her cheek, then her forehead, her nose, and her closed eyelids. His fingers were whisper soft against her skin as he traced her image once more. Slowly, ever so gently, he stroked her upper lip, then her lower lip. Clasping her head with his hands, he began feathering kisses very slowly all over her face. The places he had traced with his fingers he now blessed with his lips—her forehead, her cheeks, her eyebrows, her lids, the corners of her mouth—before finally claiming her mouth fully with his own.

He kissed her. Slowly, gently, not wanting to frighten her, afraid she might draw back, he took his time branding her as his own. His other hand went to her neck, holding her steady and close.

He felt her arms come up and around him, clasping him close in return. It was Maura that increased the pressure of the kiss. It was Maura that leaned closer to him. It was Maura who sighed when the contact was broken at last and the kiss ended.

He didn't let her go, but began stroking her hair as she rested her face against his shoulder.

They sat like that for some time, not talking, just breathing, close. Pen was afraid to move, afraid Maura might pull away from him. He spoke softly into her hair.

"I think it may be safe to say that at the very least you don't hate me, am I correct?"

"Don't make fun of me, Pen. Please don't."

"Maura, the last thing on my mind is making fun of you or teasing you in any way. But at least I'm sure now that you definitely are not indifferent to me. Thank you for that."

She started to pull away, but he didn't let her go. "No, stay for a while. Let me just hold you, please. You're comfortable, aren't you?"

"Yes."

"Then stay."

"Pen, are you still going to leave?

"Yes, I am. I have to. I told you that I love you, and if there's any chance for me at all with you, I have to leave. But if you'll let me, I will come back, I promise. And I always keep my promises."

Maura lay in bed, eyes wide open in the darkened room. What on earth had she done? Why had she kissed Aspen again? All she had done was reinforce her feelings for him while ensuring more heartache when he left in a few weeks.

He had made it very plain that he was, in fact, leaving. Of course he was also telling her that he loved her and would come back for her, but she wasn't that stupid. Once he was finally moved out of her house and back in his own world, he would forget her soon enough. She had been down this road before, and she knew she was right. He wasn't the first male patient of hers that thought he was in love with her. Twice before she had dared to hope, to believe, and twice she had crashed hard back into reality. It had been gratitude they had felt, not love. While she had really liked both men, she had never felt about either of them the way she did about Pen. He was special, and she loved him, for all the good it did her; he would leave, never return, and break her heart.

She understood all too well that if he had his sight he would never give her a second look; men never did. She was plain, and she wasn't getting any younger. She was thirty-seven years old, still a virgin, still single, and likely to remain that way for the rest of her life. But she wanted to fall in love, get married, and have children and a family like other people did.

Oh, she wanted to believe Pen; she wanted so badly to believe him, but once she was no longer needed, it would be the end. Besides, he hadn't considered the fact that she was seven years older than he was. Most men would never look at a woman that much older than themselves. She was sure Pen was no different.

But oh, it had felt so very good to rest there in his arms! He was so warm and comforting; he made her feel loved and safe and wanted. It had been nice to not feel so alone, for just that little while. She should have refused him when he asked to kiss her again, but he had been right about making sure. She too needed to know if she had imagined her response to that first kiss.

Well, she didn't have to wonder anymore. Her eyes glistened in the dark with her unshed tears as she remembered her response to him. She hadn't just let him kiss her, she had kissed him back with more ardor than he displayed. She was such a fool!

Oh, the whole thing was such a mess. It would only be worse now when he left. What could she do? How could she protect herself?

Finally she came back once more to the fact that Aspen did not really love her; she was the only one in this scenario that was going to suffer. Better to back off again and hold fast. Be polite but remote, and for sure, never kiss that man again. But it was going to be hard to keep away. Her heart seemed to skip a beat whenever he walked into the room. When she heard his cane tapping in front of him it seemed that her blood warmed in her veins. Thank goodness he couldn't see the expressions on her face since she probably wasn't hiding her feelings very well. She sighed deeply. Her life was a mess.

Lord, it's me again. I don't know why you brought Aspen Windchase into my life like this. I'm not sure it was a kind thing to do. But You did bring him, and I fell in love with him. I know I'm going to have to get over him somehow, but Lord, without Your help it's going to be nearly impossible for me, if I can do it at all. Stay with me, Lord. Be my strength and my guide. Help me to find a way out. Thank You, Lord. Amen.

Pen had a very hard time falling asleep. Kissing Maura may have been a mistake for him. He probably should have just left well enough alone. What had he done? He was sincere when he told her he loved her, but nothing had changed yet. He could not support a wife. He still had no business even thinking about a permanent relationship with anyone, least of all her. She was a professional, smart, and honest. She didn't need a man like him in her life.

Oh, she had definitely responded to his kiss. It had surprised him, actually, how much she had responded. He hadn't expected that, but it was a wonderful surprise. There was no way she could try to tell him she wasn't interested in him as a man, not after that kiss.

But he was still going to have to leave her, and it was going to kill him. *Lord God, why? Why has my life turned out like this? Things had been going so well for me and my sister, and then, it all crashed around us both. Raven lost her fiancé and her dog, and I lost, well, I guess you could safely say I lost everything in an instant. Why, Lord? I just don't understand.*

It came to him then, that voice in his head. *You haven't lost everything, Pen. You have your mind and your limbs. You have your sister, Raven, your good friend Gus, and you have Maura. And you have Me. Stay close to Me. It will all be well. I know the plans I have for you, remember? Trust ME!*

Trust You? It was a lot easier to trust You, Lord, when I had a normal life; when I could see. It wasn't so hard then, but now? I know we're supposed to give You thanks in all things, but I'm finding that a little difficult right now. But I'll do my best, Father. Thank You.

He wished there was some way he could look into the future, some way to determine that it all would, in fact, be OK. But he couldn't look ahead. All he had was right here, right now. Back to his goals. One step at a time. Right, left. Forward. Don't look back.

He returned to school the next morning, more determined than ever.

Chapter 29

He studied harder than he ever studied in his life. He learned braille, and found himself reading fluently in record time. There were computers with braille keyboards, and he learned to type proficiently. A braille printer enabled him to check for any errors, and while it was all new and difficult for him at first, his determination paid off, and his new skills were his rewards.

Maura kept her work schedule and her reserve. They never spoke again about either kiss, and both acted as if it had never happened. They each suffered alone, locked up in their separate worlds, afraid to reach out to the other.

Raven picked him up every Friday afternoon and he stayed at the stable each weekend, learning new tasks. He rode every weekend, also, with Gus, his mentor and advisor.

Finally it was time for him to leave Billings for good. He had learned everything they could teach him at the school, and it was time to get on with his life, to find something he could do, some way to support a wife, because he fully intended to marry Maura at some future date, if she would have him. There had been talk about getting a guide dog, but they were extremely expensive, and that idea was tabled for the present. Perhaps one day in the future.

On a Thursday evening after supper he asked Maura to come into the living room with him. He wanted to talk to her. Her face betrayed her fear of what was to come, but of course Pen had no idea.

"Sit with me on the couch, Maura?" He sat slowly, leaving room for her at his side.

"I'm not sure that's such a good idea. Remember what happened last time we did that?"

"How could I forget? It wasn't so bad, though, was it? You didn't seem to mind if I remember correctly." He smiled warmly at her.

"No, it wasn't, but I don't think we should go there again." She sat in one of the easy chairs across from him.

He began, hesitantly. "Maura, I . . ."

"I know, you're going to tell me you're leaving, aren't you." It was a statement, not a question. "Pen, you don't have to go. You can stay here as long as you like, I've already told you that."

"I know. But you and I both know I can't do that. I have to move on. I'm sorry, but that's the way it is."

"You're sure?"

"I'm sure."

"When?"

"Raven is coming to get me tomorrow morning. I'll be gone when you get home from work." He waited for her to say something, but she remained silent at this news.

After nearly a minute she got up from the chair and walked away from him down the hall toward her room.

He heard her go. "Maura? Can we talk about this?"

Silence.

"Maura?" His voice was louder, calling out to her. He heard her door shut softly. "But I'll be back," he said quietly into the empty room.

Raven showed up at his door around eight-thirty the next morning. She was so excited to have her brother moving home with her, he almost worried about her driving ability on the highway.

He didn't have much to pack, just some clothes and a couple of books in braille. Raven helped him so he didn't miss anything, and they were ready to leave in minutes.

"Before we go, can you help me with something, Raven?"

"Sure, what do you want me to help with?"

"I want to leave the bedroom vacuumed and clean sheets on the bed so Maura doesn't have extra work to do. OK with you? I can dust and vacuum while you change the sheets if you don't mind?"

"Sure, but can you really do that?" Her skepticism could be heard in her voice.

"I keep telling you, I'm blind, not helpless. What do you think I've been learning at that school, anyway? How to sit on my hands or something? I can cook, too, for your information."

"I'll believe it when I see it. You weren't so good at any of that before the accident so you're going to have to forgive me if it's a little hard for me to believe now."

He found the clean sheets and the vacuum cleaner in the closet with Raven's help, and he did in fact dust and vacuum while she changed the sheets.

Smiling at a job well done, Pen left his house key on the kitchen table. Raven turned the knob and the door locked behind them as they left the house. In minutes they were on I-90 headed for Bozeman, and home.

Raven, as usual, talked nonstop, barely pausing long enough to draw a breath.

Pen sat quietly, aching inside as they traveled farther and farther from Billings. *I'll be back, Maura. I will come back for you. I don't know when, but I always keep my promises.*

Maura arrived home to her empty house later that afternoon. She knew he was gone, but she was still not prepared for the onslaught of emotions that assailed her. He was gone. He was really gone. Now what? How was she going to keep breathing?

The walls seemed to echo with the silence. She found the key on the kitchen table and sank hard onto a chair, the key clutched in her hand so tightly it left an imprint on her palm.

That key somehow made it final. She had been right, too; if he had really planned to come back he would have kept his key, wouldn't he? No, he wasn't going to return, no matter what he said. Maybe he already realized he didn't really love her.

But she did love him. She loved him so much there was physical pain with his absence. Desolation. Isolation. Grief. Indecision. He had taken a vital part of herself with him.

She rose and walked down the hall. Maybe some part of him, his scent, remained there for her to console herself with. Opening the door to his room, she nearly gasped at the sight that greeted her.

The room was spotless. They had obviously cleaned it before they left. She noticed the clean sheets and pillow cases on the bed, perfectly arranged. Nothing remained of Pen. She pulled the door closed softly behind her.

Walking down the hall, she made her way to the bathroom. He had tried so hard not to leave the bathroom messy or dirty for her while he was living there, but he was after all a man, and even if he could see she supposed it would never have been as neat as it could have been.

It looked as it always did; towels hung crookedly on the towel bars, a comb on the counter, his water glass out of place.

Then she saw it—he had forgotten his toothbrush. *Thank you, Lord, for his toothbrush.* She chided herself for being so stupid and foolish, but she clasped his toothbrush to her chest, cradling it as if it were a treasure. To her, it was in fact a treasure. It was all she had left of him.

She took it to her room, and taking a box from the top shelf in her closet, she carefully placed the worn toothbrush in the box with some other mementos. She patted the box, and then replaced it on the top shelf.

The next day she began looking for another job in another city. Pen was never coming back; the key he had left was proof of that. There was no way she could stay in her home, alone, any longer.

For two weeks she continued to hold out some hope that he might contact her, if nothing else just to say "hi." But there was no word. She secured another nursing position for herself in Great Falls and listed her house for sale. The pay was lower but she didn't care. She just needed to get away from Billings.

It took nearly two months to sell the house, pack everything, and move. She kept nothing that Pen had used: not his bed or any furniture. She sold everything but her own bed, including the kitchen items. She wanted nothing around her to remind her of the man she loved so much, the man who had, in fact, broken her heart, just as she had known he would.

When everything was settled she drove out of Billings, heading north; she did not look back. She had not shed a single tear, not even one, from the moment she had come home from work and found him gone. She had gotten exactly what she felt she had deserved. She should have known better.

Pen had been very busy from the moment he arrived at the stable. He worked hard, intentionally trying to stay occupied so he wouldn't think about Maura too much. He cleaned tack, groomed horses, rode whenever Gus made time to ride with him, learned to clean stalls, and measured grain to help with feeding the horses. His work kept him busy from early in the morning until nearly nine o'clock at night. He knew Maura left around five in the morning, and would have been in bed and asleep by the time he had a minute to call her. So the days flew by, and he didn't call.

Finally, after a couple of months had passed, he made time on a Sunday afternoon to place his call to Billings. He needed to hear her voice, even if just for a few moments. He was stunned when he heard the canned message, "The number you have dialed is no longer in service." No longer in service? What had happened? Where was she?

He managed to find the number for the rehab center where she worked, and placed a call to that number. They would know where she was.

He was sure they did in fact know, but they refused to give out any information other than the standard "I'm sorry, she no longer works at our facility. No, we can't give you any forwarding information. Privacy rules, you understand."

He slammed the receiver down. How could she? How could she leave without telling him? Didn't she understand how much he loved her? Hadn't she heard him promise he was coming back for her? Ah, but she had never really believed him, had she. He pounded his fist on the table in frustration. There was nothing he could do about it now, however. It might take a private detective to track her down, and they cost a lot of money, money none of them had. Finding her would have to wait for now. *Lord, I know You have a plan, but I sure wish You'd give me a hint. Help me, please, to find a way. I pray for wisdom, Lord. Show me what I'm supposed to do, please!"*

The next morning he took Gus aside and told him about Maura leaving. Gus could hardly believe it.

"Are you sure, Pen? Are you sure you called the right number? You are, well, I hate to remind you of the fact but you are . . ."

"What? Blind?" Pen snorted in disgust. "I can hardly forget that fact, but I did learn a few things at that school. I had the right number. I guess you can try it yourself if you don't believe me. Go ahead; try calling her number."

He did, and shook his head in disbelief when he heard the not in service message.

"What the . . . ?"

"I don't know, Gus. I have no idea. The center where she worked wouldn't give me any information as to where she went. What am I going to do? How on earth am I going to find her? Gus, I don't know if I can live without her, you know?"

Gus wrapped an arm around his friend's shoulder. "I know all too well exactly how you feel. I've been there, with your sister. When she was engaged to Tom I thought I might die with longing, I loved her so much. But God worked it all out, and He'll take care of this for you too. We just have to have faith."

"I don't know, Gus. I just don't know."

"If it's OK with you, I'm going to give Pastor Dave a call and fill him in. The more people praying the better, right? Maybe we can just pray her back!"

"Go ahead, do whatever you want. Guess I'll just have to get back to work and keep my hours filled." He sighed deeply, pain etched in his handsome face.

"OK. Prayer chain starting up for you again today. I won't give any details, just ask people to pray for you. God knows what you need; we don't need to tell Him."

"Thanks for your support, Gus. I don't have anyone else I can confide in."

"You're more than welcome. It's the least I can do for you."

Two days later Pen asked Gus about possibly giving him a ride to the MSU campus library.

"I think I want to find everything that's out there pertaining to my folks. I've been thinking about all that you told me, and I want to get it all, as much as I can, and maybe write it down. Something tells me there might be a lot more to it. Sound OK to you?"

"I think it's a great idea, Pen, but how do you intend to do your research? I doubt everything's in braille, you know?"

"That's what librarians are for! I bet I can find everything I need. They taught me a lot at that school in Billings, believe me. I never dreamed I would ever be able to do as much as I'm able to now."

They talked some more and made plans for the next day. Raven was included and was excited not only about finding out more about her parents, but was also thrilled that Pen had a new interest to occupy his time.

"Pen, why don't we see if we can get you a braille computer, or a braille keyboard, or whatever? You said they have them. Wouldn't it be a lot easier to write everything down as you do your research? Maybe we can order one for you while we're in town tomorrow."

Gus beamed at his wife. "Brilliant idea, my love. How does that sound to you, Pen?"

"Sounds expensive, but I can't say I don't like the idea. I would love to have a computer that I can actually use. You know, besides my research, I can keep records for the stable, do billing—I think there's actually quite a little I can do to help out around here with one of those. Thanks! But what about the expense? I know neither of you are that flush. I remember it wasn't easy to pay the bills every month."

Raven spoke up. "Ah, but what you don't know is how good a horseman your brother-in-law is."

"Well, I know he's good with horses and he can ride."

"Not only can Gus ride, brother dear, but he's nearly as good a horse trainer as me, and we all know how good I am!"

Gus blushed at the praise. "Now Raven, don't . . ."

"Gus, you know full well I'm not saying anything that isn't the truth. Pen, he really is good, and since he started training with me this stable stays full to capacity, and we're doing OK. Maybe not getting rich, but I think we can afford a computer for you. So tomorrow, we'll see about getting one."

The next day Pen went to the library to begin his research, taking a small voice recorder he had gotten at the school along with him. Gus and Raven did their own research, and before they went home they had ordered a new laptop for him.

Pen searched the library for any information he could find on Jesse Windchase and Francine Larson. He recorded his notes, and after the computer arrived, he played his them back in the evening and typed them into the computer. Raven sometimes just sat and listened as Pen worked, wonder evident on her beautiful face.

He dug up prison records from his father's imprisonment after a murder conviction for killing his first wife. He found birth records, death records, newspaper and magazine articles; there was, in fact, a lot of information available as one lead led to another. They found a reference to a man by the name of Ben Richardson, and set a date to interview him. He turned out to be a wealth of information, since he had been Jesse's best friend and Francine's employer for five years.

The story began to take shape and form an ordered reality. Pen and Raven were thrilled to be able to learn so much about their parents, and were shocked when they realized all they had gone through to reach Canada, and safety; their flight, on horseback, which lasted for months as they desperately tried to stay ahead of law enforcement, was a story in itself.

They were even able to find the names of the lawman who had chased them and the Indian tracker who trailed them, and were sad when they heard how the lawman died from a bear attack. With a lot of effort they were able to find the tracker, interview him, and learn what had actually happened up in the Bob Marshall Wilderness as the fugitives' flight came to an end.

Finally, they came to the end of the trail. They themselves knew the rest of the story. They had grown up on the Indian Reserve in Canada, and remembered how their parents had been washed away in a flood when they were just children.

The story of Francine and Jesse was out in the open at last, and Pen had committed it all to paper and a file in his laptop.

One evening as they ate supper together, Gus put his fork down, a look of wonder on his face.

"Pen, Raven, I've got an idea. Tell me what you think of this." Excitement rang in his voice.

"What is it, Gus? Tell us!"

"Well Pen, you've got a computer and a printer, and you've got a whale of a story about your parents; why don't you write it all down coherently, like a book, instead of leaving it as just notes? You have it all and you can type, and well, why not?"

Pen looked somewhat confused. "Just what do you mean, Gus?"

Raven got it in that instant. "Pen, you can write a book! Write their story as a novel! You can do it, and well, who knows? I know I'd like to read the story in a more orderly fashion. You've got the time; why don't you?"

"I don't know. I guess . . . well, do you really think I can?"

"I know you can! Do it, Pen." Raven was positively glowing.

"Well, you're right about me having the time, I guess. And it would sure make good use of that computer you were so good to buy for me. OK, I'll do it. Well, at least I'll give it a try. I'll start on it tomorrow. You'll have to do a lot of proofreading for me, braille or not. I have no idea how this is going to work out. Are you up for it? This is going to have to be a joint project, you know." He was catching the excitement.

"We're in." Raven spoke for both of them. "I'm so excited I don't know if I can wait until it's done! What a great idea, Gus! You are so smart; I knew there was a reason I married you."

"And here I thought it was my good looks you were after." Gus smiled at her.

Pen laughed out loud. He remembered very well what his friend looked like!

The next morning Pen went to the office to begin work on his new project. He was excited about it and started in with a lot of enthusiasm, but it soon became apparent it was going to be a lot of work, and it was going to take a lot of time. *Well, I guess I do have plenty of that, don't I?*

Chapter 30

Allie had indeed moved to Bozeman, and Dave found her a private-duty personal care job taking care of an elderly gentleman, Joe Bankston, in his own home with room and board provided. It was a perfect situation for a young woman expecting a baby; the pay wasn't bad and the work was easy. Allie grew to love her patient, and they spent many companionable hours together, just talking and reminiscing. Dave took her out to dinner at least once a week, telling her she needed to get away for some free time and breathe a little fresh air, but in reality using any excuse he could find to be with her. He was only too happy to provide the breaks for her, but his obsession only grew as they spent more time together.

Finally her due date was right around the corner. Expectation permeated the air for all involved. Raven was so excited she was nearly bouncing off the walls. Gus was also looking forward to the new arrival, but spent a lot of time just smiling at his adorable wife. Dave was more concerned that Allie might decide to keep her baby after all, and that would present a whole new set of problems.

She went into labor on a Friday morning and immediately called Dave. Joe's family had been prepared for this event and another caregiver arrived within a couple of hours. Dave took Allie to the hospital, and the waiting began.

Her labor lasted nearly fifteen hours, but finally around two o'clock in the morning, she gave birth to a beautiful baby girl. Dave had called Raven when he took Allie in to the hospital, and he called again soon after the baby was delivered. Allie had not changed her mind but it had been a difficult decision for her. She had decided to hold her baby until the new parents arrived to take her home with them. She was unable to stop her tears when Raven and Gus left with their new child, and the nurses had to sedate her. But to her credit, she never wavered. Dave's heart broke for her in her sorrow, and he stayed with her through it all.

Two days later, she was discharged; she decided not to move back to Billings, but would stay in Bozeman to be near Dave. She went back to work with a new maturity about her, and while she was sad, she was also grateful. She had a very good friend in Pastor Dave Benson, she had a good job, her parents would never know about their grandchild, and her baby had a new home with wonderful parents. They had agreed to send updates yearly to Allie, along with photos, but Allie had promised not to make any physical contact. The adoption was finalized and Raven finally had the baby she so desperately wanted. She had blonde hair and blue eyes; she looked nothing at all like Aspen. They named her Catherine.

A new baby at Chase the Wind Stables resulted in major upheaval for everyone. Raven loathed leaving her new daughter for any length of time, but if she and Gus weren't training horses there was no income. She couldn't take care of a newborn full time and work horses too. Pen would have gladly become the full-time nanny, but that was one task he conceded as being hopeless for him; he simply wasn't comfortable taking care of a baby. In the end Raven and Gus hired a girl to help them out during the day so they could continue training horses. Pen went back to working on his manuscript.

It was an agonizingly slow process, but he never gave up. Days turned into weeks, weeks turned into months, and soon nearly a year had passed. There had not been a single day that Pen hadn't yearned for Maura, and he still planned to hire a private detective to find her just as soon as he had the funds. About once a week he tried calling her old phone number, just in case, but it remained disconnected. Sometimes he thought he might strangle the girl for leaving without letting him know. But he had promised he would go back for her, and he fully intended to keep his promise.

And then one day, it was finished. He printed it out on his braille printer, and then sent the PDF file to the stable's office computer. His sister and Gus could print it out later.

He gathered the collated pages of his book, clipped them together, and went to find Raven and Gus.

He found them in the tack room, organizing equipment. "Hey guys, I've got a little present for you!"

"What . . . ?"

Pen held the book out to his sister. "Here, I finally finished it."

Raven took the manuscript carefully into her hands, so full of pride for her brother she felt like she would literally burst with it. "Oh . . . but . . ."

Pen laughed. "I know you can't read it, but I can! That's OK, I sent a PDF file to the stable computer, so you can print it out whenever you want and read it at your own pace. Just don't wait too long; I want an honest opinion about it. I need to know what you really think, so don't sugar-coat your evaluation, promise?"

"I promise. Oh, I can't wait!"

"And I also would greatly appreciate it if you would individually make any necessary corrections as you read."

"We'd be happy to, wouldn't we Gus?"

"You bet," Gus replied.

The book was over 350 pages in length; they made another trip to town where they purchased a black and white laser printer and lots of paper. After they finally had the novel printed out, they vanished for hours at a time as they read his work. He waited, nervous, wondering what their opinion would be.

It was unanimous: Raven and Gus both loved it.

"Pen, do you have a title picked out yet? I have to tell you, this is a great story. We need to find an editor and an agent for you, because I think this will sell." Practical Gus could probably be believed, as he was not one to exaggerate.

"Do you really think so, Gus? You're not just trying to make me feel good?"

"Oh, I really think so, yes. Of course, I'm no professional and you're going to have to get a professional opinion, but yes, I think it's pretty darn good, especially for a first try. I need to read it again and look more closely for errors, and then make some corrections, but it's a great read. Have you picked out a title yet?"

"Well, I had thought, since Dad was half Crow, that I'd title it *Flight of the Crow,* and rather than using my own name, I thought I'd write it under the name of Paul Brandt. What do you think?"

Raven was delighted. "That's a great title, and appropriate too. I even like the name you chose, but why not just use your own?"

"I don't know. Guess I just don't want the recognition. Neighbors might laugh at me or something. This way it almost feels like I'm hiding, you know? Safer, at least for now."

"Well, whatever the reason, I think this calls for a celebration, don't you?"

That evening the whole family went out for dinner; Gus, Raven, Pen, and baby Catherine. It was a celebration for many reasons: Raven and Gus were happily married, Pen was finally home again, Catherine was an answer to prayer, Pen's manuscript was completed, and most importantly they were together as a family. After all they had been through over the past couple of years, this was the greatest blessing and cause for celebration of all.

Finding an agent to represent Pen's writing took another four months. Getting it accepted for publication was three more. The whole process was new and exciting for them all, and when the book was a success in the marketplace, no one was more surprised than Pen. When the first royalty check arrived in the mail, he was amazed not only with the realization that his work had value, but at the size of that first check.

He had done it. He had found a way to support himself, and Maura, if he could find her and she would accept him. After all he had been through—the coma, the addiction and recovery, learning to cope with his blindness, and becoming independent—it was all overwhelming. He never forgot to give God the praise and glory for all He had done in his life, and he recognized fully that without His help, he would still be in his drug-induced fog somewhere, if he were even still alive. But God had sent the right people into his life to help and guide him, and He had never left his side.

Now, all that was left was to find the woman he loved. He had finally accepted the fact that he would never see again, but he had also learned that being blind was not the end of the world. He could, in fact, do nearly everything he had done before the accident, and by necessity had even learned another vocation.

He began writing his second book. After hearing, in detail, his sister's story, he asked her permission to put it on paper. She agreed, and he spent hours every day working on his second manuscript. Royalty checks continued to arrive monthly, each one larger than the last. Pen, who had been desperate to find a way to simply put food on the table, was now a very wealthy man. It was time to find Maura.

With his friend Dave Benson's help, he hired the best private detective they could find. He lived in Oregon, but agreed to come to Montana for this case. He was expensive, but now it didn't matter. He would find Maura, and soon.

Maura Anderson had found a good job in the ICU at Benefis Health System in Great Falls, Montana. working twelve-hour shifts as she had done in Billings. She isolated herself, going out only to church and to work. She had made a couple of friends at the hospital, but while friendly, she volunteered nothing about herself and made no overtures. Keeping to herself, she became an automaton: work, sleep, work, sleep. Not wanting free time, she volunteered to work overtime and took no vacation days. When she did have free time, she thought, and Aspen Windchase occupied those thoughts almost exclusively.

She tried her best to move him completely out of her head, but it was hopeless. He was the one man in her life she had unreservedly loved with all of her being, and he had left her. He was never coming back, she knew that, but for some reason she thought of little else. Why, in heaven's name, of all the men she had met over the years in church, at work . . . why did it have to be Aspen Windchase, a blind drug addict? She had held out at least a little hope until the day he had left for good. Finding the key he had used while staying at her house was all she needed to understand: if he had planned to return he would have kept his house key. She had been right all along; his declared love for her was based on gratitude, not real love, and obviously what little feelings he had for her had passed when it was time to leave Billings.

Her appetite left with Pen's departure. When she had met him, while she had never been a woman to turn heads, her figure had been at least average. Over the past year she had lost over thirty pounds, and now her clothes and uniforms hung on her bony frame. She was not aware of her weight loss.

She had quit wearing any makeup; there was no point in it. She no longer styled her hair. She was clean and neat, a solid, dependable employee, an excellent nurse, but only a shell of a woman.

Pen had been gone nearly two years, but her heart was still as raw as if it had been just yesterday. Would she ever get over him? *Lord, why? Why Aspen Windchase? Why a man that would only leave me and break my heart so totally? If You were going to send a man into my life, why not a good man who would truly love me and stay with me?*

The detective found Maura in less than a week. He had a home address, a home phone number, a work address and a work schedule for Pen. At Pen's request, he read the file aloud while Pen typed it into his computer, and then printed it out on the braille printer, so he would be able to read it later. His work completed, the detective collected his check and caught the next plane back to Oregon.

He had an address, at last. He knew now where Maura was, where she worked, her work schedule, and her phone number. Her phone number! What should he do next? How should he contact her? Should he phone her? Yes? No? Should he just make the trip up to Great Falls and show up on her doorstep? How should he go about this reunion in a way that wouldn't scare her to death and possibly make her disappear again? He couldn't risk that. No, a phone call would not be the best way since she might leave before he could be there with her physically. He would somehow make the trip up to Great Falls and figure out the next step when he got there.

Chapter 31

He called his best friend, Pastor Dave Benson, and told him he needed to see him whenever it was convenient. Dave drove out the next day, picked Pen up, and drove the two of them into Bozeman to the Baxter Hotel where they had lunch together, while Pen filled Dave in on his success in finding Maura.

Dave and Gus were the only people who knew that Pen was in love with Maura. Neither of them had ever mentioned it to Raven. Pen was essentially a very private person, and felt that his love life was no one else's business. Dave agreed with him on this. Besides, Raven had enough on her mind with the stable, a new baby, and Pen himself living with them.

"Dave," Pen began, "I found her, Dave. I found Maura."

"How? Did you manage to reach her with her old phone number somehow? Where is she?"

"I finally made enough money with royalty checks from that book I wrote to hire a private detective, and he found her in just a few days. She's working in Great Falls. He gave me her phone number, address, work address and even her work schedule."

"Good for you, Pen. So, what are your plans now that you're found her? Are you going to call her, or are you thinking of going up to Great Falls and surprise her? And how can I help?" Dave was smiling with happiness for his good friend who had been through so much over the past two years.

"I've been trying to decide on the best plan, and I'm not sure."

"I'll be happy to drive you up there, whenever you want to go, just let me know."

"No, that was my first thought, but I think not."

"Well, why not? What are friends for, anyway?"

"I just feel like this is something I have to do all on my own. Besides, you're pretty busy and it would be an all-day trip if you took me up and came back on the same day. I'm not planning on leaving her, you know. I'll be staying in Great Falls for as long as it takes to convince her to have me."

"I really don't mind, Pen. Just tell me when and I'll make time."

"No, but thanks anyway."

"So what are you going to do, and what are you going to tell your sister? I don't think you can just take off for parts unknown without telling her something, you know."

"I'll tell her, but only right before I leave. No sense getting her all excited ahead of time. But I'm thinking I'll catch a regional jet from Bozeman to Great Falls, and a taxi from there, maybe to the hospital. I could catch her after she gets off work." Pen was still working the details out in his head.

"Well, if that's what you want to do—but do you think you can handle it on your own? You haven't really done much like that by yourself. By the way, have you ever even been on a plane before?" Dave voiced his concern for his friend.

"No, this will be my first time on a plane, but Dave, I've learned I can do just about anything on my own now, except drive, of course. It's actually pretty amazing how helpful people are when they see that white cane! Oh, and I'm not too good with babies, either. But then I'm not so sure how good I'd be with a baby even if I could see, but it's hopeless when I can't." He smiled to himself.

"If you're sure . . ."

"I'm sure. I'll let you know when I have it all figured out. I'll let you drive me to the airport, though, if you don't mind?"

"Be happy to, friend."

"Now, Dave, I have a feeling you might want to talk to me a little about your own love life. I'm assuming you're still seeing Allie, am I right?" Pen knew his friend all too well.

Dave sighed heavily. "Yes, I am seeing her, Pen. I know it's not right; she's not the right woman for me, not even close, but I can't seem to help myself. I just want to be around her, you know?"

"Oh Dave, you know how well I do understand. I'm sorry for you, my friend. I know what it's like, those feelings that just won't leave no matter how hard you try or you pray. I'm assuming you've been talking to God a lot about this?"

"Of course I have, but I never get a firm answer on what to do aside from never seeing her again. But I can't seem to do that. I know the Bible says God never gives us more than we can handle, and that in times of great temptation he always provides a way of escape, but right now I just don't feel strong enough. The flesh remains awfully weak, unfortunately." He smiled ruefully. "You know, Pen, pastors are still human, and I seem to be a pretty weak one at that. I don't know what I'm going to do but I just can't leave that woman, even knowing all that I do about her. She's, well . . ."

"I totally understand, Dave. Say no more. But I'll be praying for you. God will work this all out somehow. I'm just really sorry you have to go through this. Ah, affairs of the heart!" He shook his head in sympathy. "There's no rhyme or reason to them, and they hold us captive in the most binding ways. But when it's right, there's nothing else on this earth like it."

That evening Pen told Raven about Maura; that he loved her but she had rejected him, and that when he had tried to contact her she had vanished. He related that Dave had helped him to hire a private detective, and Maura had been found working at Benefis Health System in Great Falls. He informed both Gus and Raven of his plans to fly to Great Falls, find Maura, and attempt to convince her that his feelings for her were real.

They said very little, but both were very supportive. They smiled at each other occasionally as Pen told them how he felt about Maura; how could they possibly want anything less for Pen than what they, themselves, had together? Raven's only concern was how he was planning to get to Great Falls.

"Are you sure one or both of us can't drive you up there, Pen? We don't mind, do we Gus? We'd be more than happy to do that for you."

"We wouldn't mind at all. In fact it would give us a nice day out and about; we could see some new country, and get away for a day."

"Dave already offered and I turned him down, too. This is something I have to do on my own."

"But Pen, you're, well, you're blind, remember?"

"Like I could ever forget! Thanks, sister dear. But that's all the more reason why I need to do this myself. I need to prove to myself and to her that I really am a capable, independent man, and that she can depend on me. That I'm not some cripple. If she feels sorry for me it will never work. I'm thirty-two years old now, a grown man. I vowed to become independent, and that's exactly what I will be. I'm even thinking about a guide dog next year now that can afford one."

"If you're sure . . ."

"I'm sure. I'll make flight reservations tomorrow and let you know what day I'm leaving. I'm buying a one-way ticket; with any luck I won't be coming home for some time."

Raven had tears in her eyes. "Pen, don't say that! You will be back, won't you?"

"At some point, of course; I just don't know when yet. Don't worry, I'll keep you informed."

Two days later Dave drove him to the Bozeman airport where he caught a flight that left at 10:16 that morning. It was a Friday. There were no direct flights to Great Falls so he had to fly from Bozeman to Denver where he had a two-and-a-half-hour layover before landing in Great Falls at 4:25 pm. He would take a taxi to the hospital where he would wait for Maura until she got off work at 6:00 pm. He had planned it all out; he only wished he would be able to see her face when she saw him. To say she was going to be surprised would be an understatement.

The flight arrived in Great Falls on time, which was a great relief. He wanted to be at the hospital when she got off work, and if the plane was late he might have missed her. As it was, he had brought only one carry-on so he didn't have to wait for any luggage, and with the help of an airport assistant, he was able to hail a taxi and arrived in good time at the hospital.

He walked through the front door, and again, the white cane brought all sorts of assistance in short order. He explained that he was there to see a nurse, Maura Anderson, and asked where he could wait for her until her shift was over. He was escorted to the main waiting area and told Maura would be given the message that a gentleman was waiting to see her. Asked if he wanted to leave his name, he declined. He didn't want to give her an opportunity to avoid him if she knew who he was ahead of time.

Maura was given the message on a folded piece of paper. She read it and shook her head in the negative, then crumpled the note and threw it into the wastebasket. It was probably a patient from sometime in her past, and she had no desire to make small talk with anyone. She had cared for so many patients over the years that the odds were she wouldn't remember the man anyway. He would leave when visiting hours were over, and hopefully have better things to do tomorrow and not return. She clocked out and left through an employee entrance without ever checking to see who might be waiting for her.

Pen was more than tired from the day's traveling. It was his first time on a plane in his entire life, which was stressful enough. The anticipation of seeing the woman he loved at last, coupled with the added hardship of being blind and his anxiety had left him exhausted. He had less than an hour to wait until Maura was off work, but he was asleep in minutes. He did not awaken until after midnight, when he found someone had covered him with a blanket and propped a pillow under his head.

Maura hadn't come. If she had, certainly she would have seen and recognized him. Or had she come, seen him, and, not wanting to talk to him, simply left? He didn't know. All he knew was he was still tired, his muscles ached from sleeping in an awkward position, and it was the middle of the night. He certainly couldn't show up on her doorstep at this hour, even if he could find a taxi. He repositioned himself, adjusted his pillow and blanket, and went back to sleep. He would try to catch her in the morning.

The staff gave her another note when she came in the next day, but again, she didn't trouble herself to see who was there. She wasn't interested. If it wasn't Pen, it didn't matter, and there was no way it would be him, so she didn't even bother to look. She worked her shift and went home again that evening.

Pen woke early that morning, well before Maura was scheduled to come to work. He folded the blanket and gave it to housekeeping along with the pillow, then sat back to wait for her to come. He got up once and went to the desk to be sure she had received the note he had sent. He was informed that she had indeed received it. No, they had no idea why she hadn't come to see him. They were sorry. Was there anything they could do for him?

He asked them to call a cab for him, which they did, and he gave the driver Maura's address. He would wait for her there; she had to come home sometime.

Twelve-hour shifts made for a long day. He sat on her front steps the entire day, waiting. It was cold, and he shivered off and on, but he was not leaving. He had to see her just one more time. If she didn't want him after that, well, there was nothing more he could do, but he was not leaving until he had his chance.

He was still tired; he had had nothing to eat or drink since he left home the morning before. There wasn't a force on this earth strong enough to move him from Maura's front steps until he was able to talk to her, and so he waited.

Maura had the next three days off, so she decided to stop on her way home to pick up some groceries. It was after dark when she arrived and, turning into her driveway, she pulled into her garage and proceeded to carry her several bags of groceries into the house through the back door. She never saw the man sitting on her front steps, waiting quietly in the dark.

After her groceries were put away, she poured herself a small glass of wine, set it on the coffee table in the living room, and then opened the front door to go out to get her mail. She did not bother to turn the porch light on, since there was enough moonlight to see her way to the curb where the box was.

She screamed as she tripped over the object on her front porch.

Pen, being tired, cold, and stiff, still somehow managed to move fast enough to catch her before she tumbled onto the sidewalk. They fell together in a heap at the bottom of the few steps, Maura flailing her arms and screaming in terror.

"Maura, it's OK, it's me, Aspen!" He clasped her solidly to himself, rolling to keep her body on top of him and off the cement.

She stilled and her body stiffened in shock. They remained together like that for what seemed like minutes but was actually only seconds before what he had said finally registered with her.

"Pen? Aspen Windchase?"

He smiled in the darkness, "Yup, in the flesh. Kind of tired and cold flesh at the moment, but you're doing a fine job of warming me up."

Extricating herself from his embrace, she scrambled abruptly to her feet, smoothing her hair and her shirt, forgetting for the moment that Pen couldn't see her. "Is this a joke?"

"What do you mean, a joke? It's no joke, Maura. I told you I'd be back for you, and, well, here I am. I know it took me a while, but better late than never, right? Isn't that what they say?"

"Why are you here? How did you find me, anyway? And just what is it you want?"

This was not exactly the reception he had been hoping for, to put it mildly. He ran his fingers through his hair, and then asked, "Look, I'm kind of cold and a little tired. Do you think you could ask me in and we can talk inside? I'm sure you remember me well enough to know I'm not exactly a threat or anything."

"Oh, OK. Yeah, you can come in. I suppose we need to talk, right?"

"You could say that." He wasn't smiling now. He sensed the resistance in her voice and it saddened him; he had hoped for so much more. It was not going at all as it had when he had daydreamed about this reunion, not even close. He lowered his head as he prayed silently. *Lord, I think I'm going to need some help here. This is definitely not going like I thought it would! Help her to hear me, Lord, to really hear me. Be with us both. Amen.*

"Follow me," she said as she turned to go back into the house.

"Excuse me, but do you think you could find my cane? I lost it when you stumbled over me."

"Sure. Just a minute while I look around." It took only seconds before she picked it up and handed it to him.

"Can I take your hand?"

"No. If I remember correctly, you're the one who wanted to prove his independence, so use your cane and follow me."

He followed her voice as she led him into the living room.

"Would you like a cup of coffee while we get this over with?"

"Sure, that would be great. I really did get chilled waiting for you out there. Thanks for the offer."

She came back shortly with a steaming mug, gave it to him carefully, and picking up the glass of wine she had poured for herself, sat in a chair opposite him.

"OK, start. What are you doing here after nearly two years?"

"What do you think? And by the way, let's start at the beginning. Why did you leave Billings without letting me know?"

"You left your key on the kitchen table, and that pretty well told me you didn't plan to come back. You lied to me about that." Her voice was cold.

"Maura, my leaving the key had nothing to do with whether I planned to come back or not. I didn't think it was a good idea for a blind man to keep a single woman's house key like that. I might have lost it or, well, it just didn't seem right to keep it. Believe it or not, I was trying to be thoughtful."

"Well, I took it that you had no intention of ever seeing me again."

"Obviously you were dead wrong about that, now, weren't you, since here I am," he replied wryly. Somehow he was going to have to get through to her.

"I was at the hospital yesterday; I left a note and a message for you. Didn't you get it?"

"I got it."

"Then why didn't you come?"

"You didn't give your name, and I assumed it was a former patient of mine that wanted to thank me or something.

Or another one that thought he was in love with me, but like the others, in time he would figure out it was just gratitude."

"Like me, huh?"

"Yeah, just like you."

"If I had left my name would you have come?"

"No, probably not."

"Maura, do you really think I searched for you until I found you out of gratitude? I told you two years ago that I loved you, and would come back when I was physically and financially independent. Well, now I am, or at least as much as I think I ever will be. What do I have to do to prove that to you?"

She changed the subject. "How did you find me, anyway?"

"I had to hire a private detective. And by the way, he wasn't cheap, either. Just so you know."

"Am I supposed to feel bad about that?"

"Absolutely not. You're worth every penny!" He leaned forward, toward her voice. "Maura, I love you. I loved you when I left you in Billings and I love you now. Everything I've done and worked at for the past two years has been done with you in mind; it was all for you, to be a man worthy of you." He sighed deeply. "I know I was nothing when I left Billings, but Maura, I've worked really hard, and I think perhaps now I'm able to be the right man for you. Can you just give me a chance?" Tears glistened in his eyes, hidden behind the dark glasses he had finally consented to wear at all times. He couldn't lose her now, not now after all this time.

"Come over here and sit with me for a moment, please? I did come a very long way to find you after all. Just for a few minutes?"

Putting her wine glass down, she rose hesitantly, and then wordlessly joined him on the couch.

Pen held his hand out, palm up, waiting for her to put her hand in his. She finally did, and then he pulled her slowly, carefully to himself.

"Maura, why can't you let yourself believe me? I told you before and I'm reminding you now that I'm not kidding, and I'm not a cripple. I know what I feel, I know what I want, and what I want is you."

"Pen, I . . ."

"Hush. Let me remember your face again, and give me just one more kiss. Please? I won't push you, I promise."

How could she possibly refuse? "OK." She closed her eyes and waited.

Once again Pen's exploration began, refreshing his memory. He cupped his palm against her cheek, and then began tracing her face with his fingers. Whisper soft, tentative, relearning and remembering every feature. Her cheeks seemed somehow less full than he remembered, her eyes deeper set. But when he traced her mouth and lowered his head to kiss her, he found her lips exactly as he remembered them: intoxicating, addictive.

Maura, still, quiet, and rigid at first, slowly began to melt as her heart thawed under his touch. Her cheeks became flushed, her arm came up around his neck, and she kissed him back with all the love she had been holding back for so long. She remained afraid to believe, but for right now, for this moment in time, she couldn't help herself. He was back, and he had told her that he loved her. Could it really be possible? Could a man like him actually love her? Did she dare to hope?

The kiss ended and he pulled her tightly to himself, resting his head against her hair. He began stroking her arm and then her back, when his hand suddenly froze. Something was wrong. This was not how he remembered her.

"Maura, have you been sick?"

"No, why? What's wrong? Why would you ask me that?"

"You're thinner than I remember, a lot thinner. What's going on?"

She tried to laugh it off. "Oh, your memory just isn't quite as good as you think it is. I'm fine."

"No, my memory is one thing that works really well. You are definitely thinner, so tell me what's going on with you. What happened?"

"True confession?"

"It had better be because I don't think I'm going anywhere until I get the truth from you."

"I guess the truth is that I missed you, in spite of my best intentions."

"You missed me? Are you serious?"

"Yes."

"Then why?"

"I know you're blind so obviously you haven't seen yourself in the mirror for a while. Do you remember how handsome you are, by any chance?"

"Me? Handsome? This is no time to joke, Maura. Get serious here, please."

"Oh, I'm very serious. You, Aspen Windchase, are a very handsome man."

"So? What's that got to do with anything, assuming it's true."

"You've never seen me, so you have no idea what I look like."

"I have in fact seen you, and you're beautiful. So what else?"

"No, I'm not. I am a very plain, mousy-looking woman. Men have never in my life given me a second glance. I have very plain brown hair and tons of freckles." She turned her head away from him. "And I'm a lot older than you are."

"Again, what's any of that got to do with anything? To me you are a very beautiful woman, and who cares if you're older than me? I sure don't, and I think I'm the one that should be concerned, right?"

"Oh Pen, you just don't understand."

"About what? What else are you worried about?"

"I guess for one thing," she paused to take another deep breath. "I'm afraid you will leave again, and I don't think my heart can take it. There, happy now?"

"I am very happy! Kiss me again, will you?"

She did; they drew very slowly apart afterward.

"Maura, I came here to ask you to marry me. I have no intention of ever leaving you again, unless you decide to kick me out. I even thought about bringing a ring with me, but since I can't see and have no idea what you like, I figured that if I could convince you to keep me, we could go to a jewelry store together and you can pick out whatever you want. So, will you?"

"Will I what, exactly?"

"Will you marry me, dummy?"

She didn't have to think very long. "Yes, I will marry you, Pen."

He hugged her so tightly she could barely breathe.

"Pen, you're squashing me! Stop!"

He released his grip only slightly, not willing to let her get even inches away from him this time.

"Better?"

"Better. But I don't need a ring, Pen. You don't need to spend money on me like that. I know things must be tight for you, so a ring really doesn't matter. If I have you that's all I need, so save your money, OK?"

He laughed out loud at this. He really was a very wealthy man now, and she obviously had no idea.

"Maura, do you read much?"

"Not really, but once in a while someone recommends a good book to me, and I read it. Why do you ask?"

"Has anyone recommended ***Flight of the Crow*** to you?"

"Oh, yes, someone at the hospital told me about it and I did read that one. I loved it. Actually, I was wishing there was a sequel, but who knows. So far I haven't heard about one."

"Well, I'm the author. And for the record, there's going to be a sequel about Raven and her journey. Apparently you weren't the only one who liked the book since it has made me a very wealthy man. You can have any ring you want, my love, and I won't bat an eye at the price." He laughed at her, imagining her look of shock at his success.

"You? But the author was a Paul something or other?"

"Paul Brandt, my pen name. If it turned out worthless I didn't want my real name affiliated with it."

"Oh my goodness! God has really blessed you these past two years, hasn't He? Unbelievable! You're an author now!"

"God has blessed me unbelievably with you, that's for sure. It's all been for you, as I already told you."

They sat together for another hour, talking softly, catching up, interrupting the conversation now and then with a quick kiss.

Finally Maura thought about the time, how late it was getting. She supposed since he had been sitting on her porch it had been a while since he had eaten anything.

"Pen, you must be hungry; why don't I fix us both something to eat? I bought some steaks before I came home. I was going to freeze them to eat later, but I can broil a couple quickly, with a potato? Sound OK to you?"

"Sounds wonderful. You're right, it's been a while since I ate."

"What exactly is a while?"

"Well, I ate breakfast Friday morning before Dave took me to the airport." He had to think hard to remember the sequence of events; low blood sugar was making his brain a little fuzzy. "I went straight to the hospital after the plane got in, intending to meet you after you got off work, but you didn't come. I slept in the waiting room, hoping to catch you the next morning, but again, you didn't come. Then I had someone help me get a taxi to your house, where I sat on the front steps and waited some more. I figured you had to come home some time, and you weren't going to be able to avoid me any longer. Guess I was right about that, at least. Anyway, here I am."

"So, when was the last time you had anything to eat? Didn't you get something at the hospital while you were waiting?"

"No, somehow food wasn't high on my list of important things while I was waiting for you. So I guess the last time I ate or drank anything was early yesterday morning. I have to admit, I'm really thirsty, and to say I'm hungry doesn't describe how I really am." He was smiling again. "Who cares? I got you back!"

She went to the kitchen and returned with a tall glass of water. "Here, start with this. You must be dehydrated after all this time."

"Thanks." He drained the glass in seconds. "Can I have another, please?"

"Be right back. I'm going to put the steaks under the broiler first. Just stay put. I won't be long."

It seemed like only seconds before he heard a muffled cry from the other room. His instant reaction was to run to her; he jumped to his feet, not thinking about his cane or the fact that he had never been in this house before and had no idea how to get to her. He just took off running.

His dehydration and low blood sugar rendered him extremely weak, and combined with rising from the couch so suddenly he was instantly light-headed and faint. He managed only three steps before he passed out, hitting his head against a wall.

In the other room Maura heard him fall. She had accidentally touched the oven rack and burned her finger slightly, which was why she cried out.

Racing back to the living room, she found Pen out cold on the floor. She didn't wait, but ran for the phone and called for an ambulance, which arrived in seconds. She had no idea how badly he had injured himself when he fell, but she was taking no chances.

Following the ambulance in her car, she gave the admitting doctor all the information that she knew about Pen; his time spent in a coma, his addiction problem, his loss of sight from an accident. He had come around in the ambulance and insisted he was fine, just a little weak, but they weren't going to let him leave before he was thoroughly checked out.

When they were finished, the doctor and nurse left to write up his discharge papers.

Maura was alone with Pen for a few minutes, where he chided her for her overreaction.

"Maura, I heard you cry out and I just got up too fast. Nothing's wrong with me that a good meal won't cure, so quit worrying, OK? I'm fine, really."

"But you scared me so badly when I heard you go down! Why didn't you just stay on the couch and wait for me?"

"Why did you scream? What happened?"

"I just burned my finger a little on the oven rack when I went to put the steaks in. It's nothing, really, a little tiny burn. It's not even going to blister. I just wasn't being careful. It's all your fault, you know!"

"How is it my fault?"

"You show up on my doorstep after two years and tell me you love me. You kind of upset my regimented little life!"

"Are you sorry about that? You don't want me to leave, do you?" He knew she was playing with him.

"This time, if you leave there's no way you're going without me. No more separations, right?"

"Right. And we'll go find a ring on Monday?"

"No ring. Let's just skip that part. How about we get a marriage license instead? And you can give your friend Pastor Dave a heads-up about a wedding he'll be performing as soon as we can arrange it?"

"Come here, Maura. Kiss me again, please. I do love you!"

"I love you too, Cowboy. You have no idea."

Holding hands, they prayed silently to the God they both loved, thanking Him for their reunion and the life they planned together in the future. Perhaps they would even have children, a family. They would go back to Bozeman just as soon as Maura could get her affairs in order.

The doctor and the nurse came back into the room to discharge the patient. Pen sat up at the side of the gurney, ready to leave and get that steak Maura had promised. He was still hungry!

Dr. Briles handed the discharge instruction sheet to Maura, patted Pen on the shoulder, and wished them both well.

"I do have one question, however."

"What's that?" they asked in unison.

"Well, you told me this young man was blind and had been since his accident a few years ago. But as I examined him, his right pupil reacted strongly to the light when I checked his eyes. I think someone has misdiagnosed him somewhere along the way. Either that, or things have changed recently. If his pupils are reacting, it won't be long before he'll be losing that cane of his. I'm confident he's going to see again, and soon. Well, good luck to you both." He shook their hands and left the room.

"Pen, did you hear what the doctor just said? Did you hear him? You have a reactive pupil! He really thinks you're going to see again!"

Tears welled in Pen's eyes, uncontrollable in his joy at this news. *Thank You, Lord. You really didn't ever leave me, even when I was sure that You had.*

The wedding took place one month later, almost to the day. Maura planned to take a few months off, and then work at Deaconess Hospital in Bozeman. Pen continued working on his sister's story, the sequel his publisher had requested. When he wasn't writing he was grooming horses, and riding when Gus had time to spend with him.

They stayed with Raven and Gus for a few months, but it was obvious everyone would need their own space, so a home for the newlyweds was carefully planned and soon built on a corner of the land the twins had inherited. In less than two years, Maura was pregnant with their first child. Pen was realizing the dream he had believed would be denied to him.

One year after his wedding, the gray film that had permeated Pen's world lifted from his right eye, and he began to see shadows. Full sight returned in that eye later that same year. The next year, full vision was restored to both eyes, and he was able to look his wife and his new son full in their eyes, seeing them clearly. He knew he had never seen a more beautiful woman than his wife, and he told her so regularly. Maura eventually learned to believe him.

With the grace of God, prayer, love, and time, Aspen had ascended from the depths of darkness and despair to a height that could never be fully appreciated by anyone other than himself, or perhaps another lost soul who had walked in his shoes.

God is so very good!

Terms

Ostomy: an operation (as a colostomy, ileostomy, or urostomy) to create an artificial passage for bodily elimination.

Colostomy: surgical formation of an artificial anus by connecting the colon to an opening in the abdominal wall

Texas Catheter: an external urinary collection device that fits over the penis like a condom; used in the management of urinary incontinence.

Percocet: painkiller used for a preparation of acetaminophen and the hydrochloride of oxycodone

Running W: the Running W is essentially an upside down surcingle and hobbles on both front feet. A rope runs from the right side to the right hobble, back to the surcingle, to the left hobble, back to the surcingle, and to the trainer. Used only with horses that simply refuse to learn "whoa"; the trainer can force the horse to stop by pulling the horse's feet out from under him. The most recalcitrant horse usually gets the message quickly.

About the Author

    Catherine Boyd holds a BS degree in Agricultural Production, Animal Science as well as an Associate degree in Nursing. She spent thirty-five years living and ranching in Montana in the general area where this novel is set. She was married to a rancher for twelve years, and after her divorce she worked in the area as a general ranch hand and then as a sheepherder near Bridger, MT. After becoming a Registered Nurse, she returned to Montana and worked in small rural hospitals and nursing homes.
    She has written and published the first two books in this series, "Flight of the Crow" and "Raven's Redemption" as well as two pamphlets, "Choosing a Nursing Home and Living With Your Choice", and "Are You Sure? Are You Really Going to Heaven?" now in its eighth printing.

Made in the USA
Middletown, DE
10 January 2020